In the Tennessee Country

Peter Taylor

IN THE
TENNESSEE
COUNTRY

Picador USA ✿ New York

Picador® is a U.S. registered trademark and is used by St. Martin's Press
under license from Pan Books Limited.

A portion of this novel appeared in slightly different form as the story
"Cousin Aubrey" in *The Oracle at Stoneleigh Court*,
published by Alfred A. Knopf, Inc., in 1993.

Library of Congress Cataloging-in-Publication Data

Taylor, Peter Hillsman, 1917–1994
In the Tennessee country / Peter Taylor.
p.   cm.
ISBN 0-312-13521-1
1. Missing persons—Tennessee—Fiction.   2. Family—Tennessee—Fiction.
3. Tennessee—Fiction.   I. Title.
PS3539.A9633I513   1995
813'.54—dc20   95-22810   CIP

First published in the United States by Alfred A. Knopf, Inc.

First Picador USA Edition: September 1995
10   9   8   7   6   5   4   3   2   1

For Judith Jones and Mark Trainer
without whose patience and persistence and encouragement
this book of mine could never, ever
have got itself written.

In the Tennessee Country

Part One

IN THE TENNESSEE country of my forebears it was not uncommon for a man of good character suddenly to disappear. He might be a young man or a middle-aged man or even sometimes a very old man. Whatever the case, few questions were ever asked. Rather, it was generally assumed that such a man had very likely felt the urging of some inner compulsion and so could not do otherwise than gather up his chattels and move on to resettle himself elsewhere.

Such removals were especially common in our early history, long before the Territory had achieved the dignity of statehood even. They were known and reported first by settlers in the tiny, northeast corner of the state, which was sometimes referred to by erstwhile historians (such as they be) as the Lost State—or the Lost State of Franklin. Later on, such disappearances are mentioned by settlers in what is referred to as the Miro District, an area of Middle Tennessee, and so called allegedly under the hegemony of the Spanish. And there are even similar references to vanished men in the westernmost part of the state, which is often—if perhaps incorrectly—referred to as the Purchase. These disappearances from our midst would continue to be common all through the nineteenth century and into the twentieth. Even in my own lifetime there have been several such vanished men. Their names were well known to all in my generation. We were indeed brought up on the stories of these mysterious men. And in some measure the life of one such man has cast a shadow over my own life's story, though the contrast between the course of his life and that of my own could not have been more marked.

The man I refer to was named Aubrey Tucker Bradshaw. He was the natural son of one of my maternal great-uncles, and somehow or other he had very early come under the protection of my maternal grandfather. I first made Aubrey Bradshaw's acquaintance when, as a small boy, I was his fellow passenger aboard the special funeral train bearing the body of that same very distinguished grandfather of mine. With my mother and father, along with numerous other relatives and with certain government dignitaries, I was en route from Washington, D.C., to this grandfather's designated burial site—his originally assigned site, that is—a grassy cemetery plot just outside the city of Knoxville.

I say "originally assigned" because at a later time and under peculiar circumstances, this grandfather's remains would be exhumed and removed to another location. This seems especially worth mentioning here and now because as a young adult and in a highly emotional state I was destined to be present at the old gentleman's second interment also. While alive, the grandfather to whom I refer had, like so many of my forebears, distinguished himself in the political arena. He had up until the hour of his death actually been senior United States Senator from Tennessee, and our "cousin" Aubrey

Tucker Bradshaw had served in some vague capacity on the Senator's office staff.

When I was originally aware of his presence aboard the funeral train I did not know even so much as that about Aubrey Bradshaw. My first awareness of him came at the moment when he stepped into the dining car where I was having an early supper with my parents. It happened that I was the only child aboard the entire train—for the good reason that of all the grandchildren in the family I was the only one below school age. For the older children it was deemed that the long trip from Tennessee to Washington—and back again—would entail too much absence from the classroom. At any rate, I was the lone child in the dining car, and as that tall, stooped figure of a man made his appearance there my eyes were on the plate glass of the heavy dining car door. As he entered I took note at once of the wide black armband he wore. I could not, of course, have identified it as being ostentatious of him to be seen wearing such a band or to have known at all what the band represented except that momentarily my father had nudged my mother, saying in a lowered voice: "A mourning band, no less—mind you!" There was a condescension in Father's voice which communicated itself to me, as might well be the case with even a very young child sensitive to its parents' slightest feeling—and the more so perhaps in moments of distress and uncertainty. What increased the uneasiness of that moment for me somehow was the fact that my parents sat with their backs to the entry door to the dining car, which I saw ahead of me, and that they yet managed to recognize the stooped figure beyond the glass door panel. They could recognize him in a mirror arranged for some strategic purpose at the opposite end of the car. It struck me as odd that they should know this man so well as to recognize him thus instantly. I assumed at once that he had more than a passing acquaintance with them. But it was not till a good many years afterward that I would learn how intimately all the various members of my mother's family had been acquainted with this cousin of theirs.

"TIME IS NOTHING," said the Chinese philosopher and painter Fu Min, "character and experience and precious memory is all." And remembering this quotation from my studies as an art student I am compelled to interrupt my narrative here to report an event from my mother's earlier life. When she was a girl of fourteen her widowed papa occupied the Governor's chair, at Nashville. As the youngest child of the family she was generally known as little Trudie, and as such was the darling of the Governor's staff. Since in those days there was no official Governor's mansion in the state, Trudie's papa occupied what was designated as the Governor's suite in the old Maxwell House Hotel. Trudie and her two sisters were then boarding students at Belmont School, but they spent most weekends with their papa at the Maxwell House. More than fifty years later, well after the Second World War, I myself once had occasion to spend the night in the old hotel. It was then in a fairly dilapidated state. At my request, I was taken upstairs by the hotel manager to view the rooms which the Governor and his retinue had occupied in former years. By then there was an identifying plaque on the door to the suite. It was easy to imagine little Trudie and her sisters arriving there from Belmont to spend the weekend, to visualize the many happy hours, as well as certain unhappy hours, they had passed in that suite and in the adjoining rooms that were reserved for the girls on any weekend. When I was shown upstairs to the suite, so many years later, it was still furnished with the great, dark, heavy Victorian pieces that would have been there in my mother's time. That furniture with its marble tops and swinging mirrors enabled me more than anything else to picture the boring hours as well as the painful events that my mother in later years described to me. For, you will understand, it was not by my aunts, on my visits from Mr. Webb's school, that I was told about the very significant episodes in that chapter of my mother's life. It was Mother herself who would tell me those things during her very last years after she had come to live with me and my wife. She was quite an old woman when she died, and it seemed that a certain strong censorship in her nature had broken down. And it was then, so long after the event, that she told me about the days at the Maxwell House.

On my grandfather's staff—or in his retinue—was his nephew Aubrey Bradshaw. Aubrey was usually referred to as the Governor's courier, which meant that he ran all kinds of errands and performed all manner of tasks, both personal and official. One of his duties was to hire a carriage and fetch the Governor's daughters from Belmont to the Maxwell House on whatever weekend they were free to come. He also squired them about on their shopping expeditions to the Arcade or to other downtown stores. He might even be requested sometimes to take a hand at cards.

I have already explained that Aubrey Bradshaw was in effect the Governor's ward, the illegitimate son of my grandfather's dead brother. During summers he had lived always with his mother in what was no more than a mountain shack, but in winters he had, like myself in later years, been kept at Mr. Webb's school in Bellbuckle. At the time I speak of he was several years out of school, and though he had not attended college he was intent upon educating himself and was often to be found seated outside the door of the Governor's suite, reading something profound and arcane. I suppose it was inevitable that this preoccupation would have great appeal to the scholarly little Trudie—my mother, that is, at the age of fourteen.

It seemed to my mother that Aubrey was so engrossed in his studies that he took no notice of her admiring glances or even of sympathetic inquiry. She did not realize that he was very much on guard against any personal feelings that might develop between the two of them. Perhaps she ought to have understood even better than she did, because she knew quite well that, only a few years before, there had been periods when first Bertie and then Felicia had felt herself the object— or, they would have said, the victim—of Aubrey's romantic attentions.

For her older sisters Aubrey had long since become a laughingstock. Trudie had laughed with them until that time when he began to reveal the previously unknown studious side to his nature. He was a tall, rather stooped young man with a head of heavy dark hair which extended into a peak in the center of his rather low forehead. His nose was what truly could have been called aquiline, but his mouth was small and almost feminine. And his chin, his weakest feature, was receding to a degree that escaped no one's notice—least of all the attention of my mocking aunts.

SOMETIMES AUBREY was required to escort the three sisters about town on a streetcar. If he talked to them then, they were conscious of his being overheard by the other passengers. He had a loud, boyish voice, and his East Tennessee speech was full of soft *i*'s and harsh *r*'s. But most embarrassing of all was the naïve, "country" kind of things he said to them for all the streetcar to hear. One day he suddenly blurted out, "I happen to have been eating onions. I wonder if you young ladies have noticed it?" At such utterances Bertie and Felicia might burst into giggles, but they would say afterward that they had been "humiliated." Even Trudie would say she had been "mortified."

But this was before Aubrey began studying so assiduously to improve his mind—or at least before Trudie began to take notice of his worthwhile endeavors. From that time it seemed to her that he left off his gauche and naïve utterances. Almost at one moment she began to take notice of everything that was best about her cousin. First of all, she found herself looking over his shoulder to see what he was reading. It was mostly philosophy—Kant, Hegel, Schopenhauer. During the week back at Belmont, she would go to the encyclopedia to look up the significance of their names. Even though she did not fully grasp what the encyclopedia had to tell her, she was sufficiently impressed by the profound nature of Aubrey's reading. At last she was emboldened to ask him questions about it.

Aubrey was astonished at how familiar she seemed with the names of his authors and with the subject matter. They moved from philosophy to art to literature. Neither of them expressed any interest in the sciences. In fact their interests coincided so perfectly that it seemed almost incredible to them. I suppose such coincidences seem so to all lovers! Aubrey was, of course, the teacher in most matters, and Trudie was the student. But above all, by unspoken agreement, the intensity of their newfound friendship was kept secret from all others.

They met in the Governor's reception room when her father was at the capitol or when he was closeted with his aides in his rooms and at any time when Bertie and Felicia were in their own rooms. Sometimes the two of them got together on the mezzanine, overlooking the main lobby of the hotel, slumped beside each other in one of the big upholstered settees that were concealed by the high balustrade around the mezzanine—concealed from the eyes of anyone who might have looked up from the lobby below. Aubrey talked to her about all he was reading, and she recited the reams of verse which she already had begun setting to memory. Back in the Governor's suite Aubrey coached her openly in her school-work. Neither her sisters nor her papa suspected there was any attachment developing between them. After all, she was a miss of fourteen with breasts only beginning to show themselves, and he was a man of twenty-one with a little trace of mustache that he was growing on his upper lip. Yet the comfort and the consolation they were to each other would soon be regarded by them above any and all other considerations.

One Sunday night when the three sisters were scheduled to return to Belmont, Trudie announced she was suffering from a headache and from an unaccountable ringing in her ears. Her papa insisted that she be put to bed and that a doctor be sent for. Her sisters were hustled off to Belmont, escorted, of course, by Aubrey, but the doctor ordered that Trudie remain home from school in the hotel for a week of rest.

During that week Aubrey was in almost constant attendance upon her and was actually instructed by her papa to see that she was not left alone and unattended at any time. Aubrey often took his meals with her in her room during that week. And in the afternoons he coached her in her studies. From Belmont the two headmistresses, Miss Hood and Miss Herron, had sent in all her books and assignments for the week ahead. Aubrey had ample opportunity to observe just how great was Trudie's aptitude for study. She could grasp what the algebraic problem was, and almost as quickly she would have the solution. Her Latin and Greek exercises were no more than little games that stimulated her mind and delighted her ear. But her memory for lines of English verse was the most phenomenal. Her capacity for learning lines from memory seemed limitless. And it would be only a year later that her elocution teacher at Belmont would teach her to recite "Lasca."

It snowed that week that she remained away from school. The snow piled up upon the windowsills, making the interior of the hotel room seem more intimate. Trudie delighted Aubrey by reciting "Snowbound," and afterward "Locksley Hall." Tennyson's lines were thrilling to both of them.

> For I dipt into the future, far as human eye could see,
> Saw the Vision of the world, and all the wonder that
>   would be; . . .
> Heard the heavens fill with shouting, and there rain'd
>   a ghastly dew . . .

Aubrey, who attended all stage productions at the Ryman Auditorium, only three blocks from the Maxwell House, and where he sometimes stopped at the opera, predicted that Trudie's remarkable memory might allow her to become a great actress. During that week that she stayed out of school he learned to admire what he termed her genius, and he came to love her passionately. To him she called herself Trilby and she called him her Svengali. When she returned to school, his loneliness was more than he could bear.

The next week he sent a note to her at Belmont asking her to meet him under a certain elm tree on the lawn and near the great portico of the old mansion which constituted the principal school building. She met him there at ten o'clock of a cold Wednesday evening after the other girls as well as Miss Hood and Miss Herron were in their beds and sleeping soundly. She led him to the pavilion near the old brick water tower and there for the first time he took her in his arms. Perhaps he kissed her.

WHEN AUBREY returned to Belmont the following Friday afternoon, to fetch her and her sisters, she was waiting for him in the columned atrium that constituted the school's visitors' parlor. She was standing at the bottom of the great staircase there when he came in from the carriage entrance. She ran to him and threw herself into his arms. He pushed her away at once in deference to the sound of her sisters' first steps atop the stairs. In the carriage on the way to the hotel she remained silent but barely took her eyes off Aubrey's pale countenance. It seemed to her that in that hour life was taking on new meaning. In her satchel and in her small piece of luggage were not her books and papers, or the ordinary needs for the weekend, but important items for a long trip, items intended to last through the first days of setting up housekeeping somewhere with Aubrey.

On that late Friday afternoon, Trudie's papa wasn't present in the Governor's suite nor was any member of the Governor's staff excepting Aubrey. The Governor was out of town for the day and would return before his daughters' bedtime that night. Bertie and Felicia immediately upon their arrival retired to their own rooms to write the week's letters which they were required to send various female relatives of their dead mother. Both Aubrey and Trudie were aware they might have uninterrupted use of the suite's reception rooms. Trudie had gone there at once without making any pretense even of dropping off her satchel and bag in the rooms reserved for the girls' weekend occupancy. In the pavilion on the previous Wednesday night Aubrey had whispered in her ear,

"Trudie, I love you and I must find a way to make you my own."

"When? . . . When?" was all she could reply.

"At the earliest possible moment," he said.

And for Trudie the earliest possible moment could mean only the following Friday afternoon. She had by that time given her whole heart to the grown-up-looking cousin. She was prepared, quite literally as well as psychologically, to elope with Aubrey and, abandoning all others, to board a Friday night train from Nashville to some unknown region, to a place where she and he could throw themselves into a new life—a life devoted to love, to art, to the mind. She could not have stated it more finitely than that, and she felt she had no need of doing so. Though she could not have said when it began, she knew she had for a long time wished to overthrow the absolute authority of Miss Hood and Miss Herron, as well as the oppressive compliance demanded by her sisters. But only now did she understand that she needed a strong companion, someone stronger than she, a man to instruct her and lead her in what she accepted as her destiny.

Yet from the moment she entered the hired carriage from the Belmont mounting block she sensed a coldness about Aubrey's behavior that frightened her. Most of the way into town Aubrey stared out the window, only turning now and then to respond to some fatuous remark made by Bertie or Felicia. But each time he did turn from the window he saw Trudie direct her passionate gaze at him. At first almost a pathetic smile would form on his lips, and then he would turn away again.

She was waiting for him in the suite of course when he came from delivering her sisters to their rooms.

"We must go at once," she said, though she had not meant to begin that way.

"My dear little Trudie," he began, "my dear little Trudie, you seem beside yourself. You know we cannot go anywhere tonight. Nobody would ever forgive me if I broke the Governor's trust like this, if I broke everybody's trust."

"Oh, Aubrey," she burst out. "You'll break my heart!"

"I've been awake for three nights thinking about what to do," he said. "I must not take you away. I'm thinking of *you*."

"You're thinking of *me!*" she screamed. "You are thinking only of yourself! Oh, I'll go throw myself out that window!" And she now ran across the room and began struggling with the big heavy window sash. He followed her and made an effort to restrain her, seizing her by her upper arms and drawing her to him. But her wish to end her life was so genuine and intense that her strength was almost greater than his. He held her in his arms so tightly that momentarily she gave way. For a time she let her head rest on his shirtfront while she sobbed, and presently she began to wail in high, deafening peals which he must have feared someone in the corridor might hear. Or perhaps even her sisters in their rooms! At last he led her to the settee and managed to quiet her for a time. Then her sobbing began again. Her long brown hair had now fallen about her shoulders and over her face. He held her away from him in order to talk with her, to reason with her. She sprang up again and ran instantly to the window. This time she was able to raise the sash a little way before he got to her. But again he took her in his arms. She closed her eyes momentarily and as he held her there she could think only of how much stronger he was than she. "Trudie, what does this mean?" he asked her, almost shouting his words. "What does this mean?"

Suddenly she crumpled and fell to the carpet at his feet. "I don't want to live," she wailed, "I don't want to grow old in this life."

As he looked down at her she must have seemed a small child, a spoiled child not having its way. Perhaps it occurred to him that this was really only the first onset of adolescence in her. Perhaps in that moment he felt the difference in their ages. However this might be, as Trudie looked up from his feet, she knew she had been suffering a very long time from her suppressed feelings and strongest drives. At last she allowed him to take her to the settee again and to go through the motions of comforting her. She did not afterward remember what he had said in the hour that followed. She was never again to listen seriously to anything he said to her. She seemed afterward to hear him only through the ears of her sisters and to see him only through their eyes. Her papa returned at nine that night, and neither he nor Bertie nor Felicia was ever aware that the scene in the Governor's suite had taken place.

WHEN I WAS given my mother's account of those events in her life, she was very nearly ninety years old but she was able to speak of it as if it only happened yesterday. I at first found it difficult to understand this early infatuation of hers, so lately revealed to me, in contrast with her later experience with my father and her almost nonexperience with her fatherless son. But the shock she underwent as a motherless girl was very great. Perhaps she never allowed herself to face anything again. Or perhaps from the mere embers that remained of her feeling there were occasional sparks of emotion that showed themselves in her recitations, occasional little flames that leapt up momentarily, then died away again. Her yearnings after an intellectual, artistic life must have been powerful when she was fourteen. All that she repressed at that tender age must have come to life again when she accepted my father and when she saw my own first efforts at painting. And she concealed her deeper feelings so successfully that I did not comprehend the disappointment she would someday most assuredly feel in my own artistic career.

THAT DAY in the diner Aubrey Bradshaw was a man of about thirty-five years. When he had advanced to where my parents and I were seated I may have stared up at him with what seemed unpardonable rudeness on my part. In any case, he made no allowance for my being a small boy who had seldom before been aboard a train. I interpreted his glance at me as no less than malevolence, which indeed it may have been. In retrospect, I do think I was correct in my assessment. I would learn all too soon that here was a man who felt an aversion to children. It was something no doubt that went back to the singular circumstances of his own early childhood and upbringing. Perhaps his feeling was in part that no one should have brought any child on such a solemn journey as this. But I felt sure at that time that the aversion he felt was an aversion to me in particular, to me as an individual child. And this was not merely an uncomprehending childhood impression! It was one I would receive again on each of the rare occasions when our paths crossed in years ahead—as an adolescent and even as a young adult.

What I scarcely noticed at the time, since I was not then at all aware of how well acquainted this Aubrey was with my mother—and to a much lesser extent with my father, too—was that this stranger in the dining car himself barely acknowledged the presence of my two parents and that he proceeded to permit himself to be seated by the black waiter at another table at the far end of the car.

During the long train ride to Tennessee I would see him again any number of times and have his identity made clearer to me by other members of the family. But nothing would equal the lasting impression received in retrospect when it was afterward and so often pointed out by my mother and by my aunts that Cousin Aubrey, at the end of the long journey from Washington, had seemed to disappear forever into the green hills surrounding Knoxville and into that general verdure of Upper East Tennessee. This was, in fact, the part of the state which was Aubrey's very own. It was that part of the state which had once back in the eighteenth century formed itself into the state of Franklin and separated itself from the old colonial states on the seaboard. In their isolation the early settlers had gathered on the Long Island of the Holston River and elected a Governor and a legislature and had even fought a little war with the mother state of North Carolina in a vain effort to establish their independence. This very Aubrey Bradshaw's ancestors, on both sides—in his legitimate and illegitimate lines—had played some part in the battle, those forebears of his from the little cove where his mother's people had always lived and those from the wide, fertile valley of East Tennessee, into which most of the settlers had come down from Virginia. After the Senator's funeral Aubrey Bradshaw seemed to have gone to let himself be swallowed up and lost there. And, so far as it was noticed at all, it was with a certain sense of relief that other members of the funeral party acknowledged his disappearance from our midst.

ABOARD THAT FUNERAL train, the memory of which has so often haunted me, Senator Nathan Tucker's widow occupied the drawing room in the first of the two Pullman cars. I remember such details not merely because I was present but because I would afterward hear accounts of this train ride repeated endlessly by other members of the family, for whom without exception it would seem the most important journey of their lives. I particularly remember that in the drawing room of the second Pullman car there were the late Senator's three daughters by an earlier marriage, one of them being my mother. Young matrons they must be called in the language of that day, though despite each being married and the mother of one or more children they were scarcely more than girls, really.

In the lower berths nearest to the private compartment would sleep their young husbands, each taking his turn during the long journey to Tennessee at sitting with the dead Senator's corpse up in the baggage car. Among these, also taking his turn, was my father. The Senator's nephew, the aforementioned Aubrey Tucker Bradshaw, would from time to time offer to relieve one or another of the three sons-in-law at his watch. But the sons-in-law regarded their vigil by the Senator's coffin as their exclusive prerogative. And the fact was that the very presence on this train of this odd-looking and eccentric kinsman of the Senator was resented by all members of the immediate family. The three sons-in-law agreed among themselves that even the wide black armband on the sleeve of Aubrey's dark suit was a presumption and an affront. More than anyone else, perhaps, they bore in mind the irregularity of Aubrey's very kinship to the family—that is, that he had been born out of wedlock, being the child of the Senator's deceased elder brother and a "mountain woman" of obscure background. In the eyes of the family there was something infinitely lugubrious, if not sinister, in the young man's very bearing. The eldest of the three sisters was moved to remark (while I, her little nephew, was sitting on her lap in the drawing room) that only by the black mourning band on his sleeve could this cousin Aubrey be distinguished from the long-faced undertakers who had abounded on the scene at the railway platform as they were setting out on their journey.

That special train would leave the Union Station in Washington at 2:40 on the afternoon of September 18. The year was 1916. Although the funeral procession from the Willard Hotel to the station had been led by a horse-drawn hearse bedecked with a mountain of floral wreaths, the rest of the official procession consisted of four elegant black limousines and eleven other black motorcars. In the uncovered driver's seat of each of the high-set limousines rode not only a chauffeur uniformed in black but a black-uniformed footman as well. I remember my father's commenting that these funeral vehicles and their funeral attendants were supplied not by the federal government, as one might have supposed, but by the Washington undertaker who would be in charge of all procedure and all protocol until that moment when the Senator's coffin would be lifted onto the baggage car.

It must be mentioned that alongside the highly polished limousines rode a number of government-provided plainclothesmen—outriders on horseback, as it were. And it cannot go without mention that these men were present because inside the limousines, among other notables, were two very great personages indeed. Though the American manners of the day forbade that the bereaved family openly acknowledge the presence of any such person on this solemn occasion, I think it all right, so long afterward as in this latter day, so to speak, for me to make known the rank of those great personages. They were none other than a former President of the United States and the present incumbent himself! Their presence is, however, scarcely a significant part of my story. The important point is that the mounted presidential guard with automatic pistols showing on their belts underneath their jackets seemed impressive to me at the age of four, and actually frightening to my mother and her two sisters. It gave those young-lady daughters of the dead Senator the uneasy and altogether absurd feeling that the funeral procession might be attacked as it moved along Pennsylvania Avenue.

One of these three sisters who had this irrational response to the armed guards was my mother. This youngest daughter of the Senator was of relatively apprehensive and nervous temperament. Already, at earlier events of the funeral, she had kept glancing almost suspiciously in the direction of her eccentric cousin, as if to see if he were experiencing an anxiety similar to her own. (I do think I observed this for myself at the time and was not merely told of it by my mother long afterward.) It was always at Aubrey she glanced during the funeral service and not at her handsome and youthful husband. The sight of Aubrey Bradshaw was somehow reassuring to her during the early period of the funeral, as his presence had often been to her as a child and particularly just after the death of her own mother. At one time or another this same Aubrey had made declarations of undying love to each of the three sisters. (All three of the sisters would in later life give me hints of these outbursts of Aubrey's.) Anyhow, my mother certainly was aware of Aubrey's sensitive, serious nature, and though she had since her marriage—and probably through the influence of her husband—come to think of Aubrey as a ridiculous, unmanly sort of creature, she wondered if he were not today imagining, like herself, that outrageous and terrifying things were going to happen to the funeral party. As a matter of fact, I think that without being conscious of it, my mother sensed that this occasion marked the end of an era in the life they had all known.

The two other sisters, my two aunts, who were destined to help bring me up after my father's early death, were persons of a far less apprehensive nature than my mother. And so they were able to speak more openly of the absurd anxiety they felt that day. Even as they rode along the avenue between the Willard Hotel and the Union Station and observed total strangers standing at the curb, with hats removed in the old-fashioned way in the presence of death, my Aunt Bertie and Aunt Felicia spoke to each other openly of their anxiety. But my mother (whose name was Gertrude) was of a more introspective and questioning temperament and was unable to speak out about her fear. Her hesitation was due, in part at least, to the peculiar nature of her anxieties. The fantasy she entertained was not merely that those men on horseback would suddenly turn on the procession and perhaps upset the coffin and the precious corpse inside. (*That* was the "crazy feeling" openly confessed to by my aunts and which, as a matter of fact, they would long afterward laughingly tell me about.) But Trudie imagined those armed men as actually forcing open the coffin and revealing to her that her worst fantasy-fear was come true: that it was not Senator Nathan Tucker's body locked in the casket but that of someone known to her but whom she could not quite recognize, someone whose identity somehow eluded her or, rather, whose identity she could not quite bring herself to acknowledge.

My mother knew in reason, of course, that her father's body *was* present, but during the short funeral service in the hotel ballroom it had occurred to her several times that her father was not really dead at all and locked away in the elaborate, brass-trimmed coffin. She would learn in later years that during the very moments when the three sons-in-law, along with her cousin Aubrey Bradshaw and two other young kinsmen, were bearing the coffin down a center aisle that was arranged between hotel ballroom chairs—she would learn, as I say, that other mourners besides herself had had that same fantasy.

Perhaps it seemed to nearly everyone present that day that whatever else might be inside that coffin it could not be the body of Senator Nathan Tucker of Tennessee. The Senator had always seemed to nearly everybody the liveliest and most alive of men. To all present, moreover, the tragedy of the Senator's death seemed almost beyond belief, if only because of the unlikeliness of the circumstance. They could not accept that this noble, gifted, vigorous, healthy man of sixty who had been more of a gentleman folk hero than a mere politician had been brought down by something as ignoble and trivial-sounding as a gallstone operation.

Of far greater and more lasting significance, though, was the shock to the mourners that this ambitious and talented man would be destroyed at the very peak of his illustrious career in public life. (He had served three terms as Governor and was at the beginning of his second term in the Senate.) No doubt the most difficult fact to be faced—or perhaps *not* to be faced—was that this distinguished son of an old country family, a family that had been distinguishing itself to an ever-greater degree during every generation for more than a hundred years, should now be stricken in the moment of his family's supreme elevation. Perhaps all the kin and connections assembled at the funeral were in fact saying to themselves: "We have invested so much confidence and hope in this man as chief of our tribe! In him who helped lead us back into the divided Union and resolved so many other conflicts within us! If he be dead now, to whom shall we turn to bolster our collective ego, and *where* shall we turn?" These Tennessee people were, in 1916, a people who still identified themselves most often in terms of family ties. To them the Senator's achievement represented generations of hanging together in all things. Perhaps everyone present at the funeral service understood this. Perhaps the notables present as well as the fashionable Washington friends of the three daughters were more observing of the antediluvian family feelings than were family members themselves. There was something altogether archaic about this family, something that made it seem to step out of an earlier, simpler, nobler age. And one could not escape the impression that it was the beloved Senator himself that gave this very impression.

Even while riding in the procession to the Union Station and even when the coffin was being hoisted into the baggage car of the waiting train, Gertrude Tucker Longfort, my mother, continued now and again to entertain her ugly fantasy. Her papa's body *could not* lie inside that coffin! It was not her gentle, witty, silver-maned, silver-tongued, her almost beautiful papa who was dead, but some other Senator, somebody else's head of family and chief of tribe, or just some other, ordinary man of lower degree and less beloved than her papa. Probably this seemed so to a lesser extent for her two sisters also. Because once the three of them were closeted in their drawing room, there in the second Pullman car of the funeral train, with me sitting on the lap of first one of them then another, then each young woman positioned herself in the remotest-seeming corner of the green-upholstered seats, fondling or vaguely trying to entertain me from time to time but totally disregarding her sisters and staring disconsolately into space as if the end of the world had come and she were entirely alone with her grief.

As my mother quietly closed the drawing room door that afternoon the last face she saw out in the aisle of the Pullman car was that of her illegitimate cousin Aubrey Bradshaw. I was standing close by Mother's side, and Aubrey must have observed both of us there. I don't recall what my own impression was. But Trudie noticed, as she would tell me many times afterward, that Aubrey wore a wounded expression on his heavy but weak-chinned face, and as she closed the door he lowered his eyelids submissively as if acknowledging Trudie's right to shut the door in his face. My own impression was, and remained so ever afterward, that his seemingly lowering his eyes actually represented his glancing down at me with a mixture of ire and resentment. My mother, at any rate, would be confronted by her cousin a good many other times before the journey was over, but she retained her impression always that that was the last time they ever looked directly into each other's eyes, that there was never again the exchange of communicative glances there once had been. After the Senator's lying-in-state in Nashville and after the subsequent burial at the cemetery in Knoxville, Trudie would never in effect look upon Aubrey's countenance again. When he did return rather mysteriously to attend my two aunts' funerals, not too many years later, he was unrecognizable to most people, and Mother had no substantive exchanges with him. His reappearances on those occasions seemed afterward more like apparitions, in most respects. And nobody learned anything of the whereabouts of his current residence or of his present mode of life. Not that anybody knew how he learned about the funerals he attended, either. For more than forty years his actual whereabouts would remain unknown to any member of the Tucker clan or to anyone in the entire connection. It was, as my mother and her sisters said, as though that day in the Knoxville cemetery the earth of East Tennessee had simply opened up and swallowed Aubrey Bradshaw whole. From that moment he was no more among them, no more among us. He became another of those men of good character who disappeared without leaving behind any explanation of their going.

MY POINTS OF reference regarding Cousin Aubrey's sev-
erance from the world he knew best would not be complete
without further mention of other vanished men who thus
come to mind. My father had a cousin in West Tennessee
who set fire to his house and went off with a woman from a
neighboring farm. His house was long since heavily insured,
perhaps by design, and so he probably supposed he was not
behaving dishonorably or even inconsiderately with his family. Most of us never knew where it was he had resettled or
whether or not he and the woman from the neighboring farm
had stayed together.

And then there was a banker in Nashville that I would
hear about during my childhood who left his office in the
middle of one afternoon, without so much as taking his derby
hat or his gold-headed cane with his monogram on the crown.
They say he went out through the revolving door, like one of
the ordinary clerks, with a pencil stuck behind his ear just as
though he were only stepping across the street for a few moments. His whereabouts was not known to us for more than
twenty-five years. He did not abscond with any bank funds
when he left, and his affairs were in perfect order. His greatest problem was said to be with demon rum.

IF, WHEN I WAS growing up, I asked one of my fragile
and ever-ailing aunts or my fragile but long-enduring mother
whatever became of Aubrey, she was apt to stare off into
space, genuinely bewildered—so it seemed to me—and mur-
mur something like: "We don't know whatever happened to
poor Aubrey. I am afraid none of us has kept track of him.
Finally he just seemed to have vanished into thin air." They
did not want to think about what might have become of him.
They only wanted to talk of the trying times they had had

with him on the funeral train. If at some other time and in quite another mood I asked whether Aubrey had been like my manly father or like my equally manly uncles as a young man, I would likely be answered with a hoot of laughter. They thought my question utterly ridiculous. If all three of these ladies were present when I asked this question, there would come a chorus of "Oh, heavens, no! Not a bit! Not in the least! Not at all like any one of *them!* They were real men, your father and your uncles!" If at still another time I persisted, trying to arrive at some notion of the man, and suggested that perhaps after all he had been rather like those other men who disappeared, I was apt to be given a very straight look, followed by an emphatic answer: "No *indeed!* Aubrey Tucker Bradshaw was most certainly not like one of them! For Aubrey there was no ugly situation at home that *he* had to run away from!"

The phrase "ugly situation at home" was often used in connection with the hero Sam Houston and with our relative in West Tennessee who burned his own house, as well as with a good many others. Once in later years I happened to use that very phrase in discussing Cousin Aubrey with my son Brax, and when I quoted my mother to him on this subject I was at first shocked by Brax's burst of laughter. The fact was Braxton was quite a young man at the time I speak of, and it only recently had been revealed to him that Aubrey Bradshaw was actually an "outside cousin" of the Tucker family. I think this had not consciously been concealed from Braxton, but it was rather that Aubrey's irregular kinship was seldom referred to by anyone. I don't recall at what age I myself stumbled upon the information that Aubrey was the illegitimate son of one of my maternal great-uncles and that Bradshaw was actually his mother's surname. Upon my use of the all-too-familiar phrase, Brax, laughing out at me and slapping his thigh in the coarse manner he sometimes exhibits, exclaimed to me: "And you, Daddy—you and your mother and your aunts—you didn't call that 'an ugly situation at home'? Poor Cousin Aubrey! I hope you will never find him again!"

What I then felt I must explain to this son of mine was that in my mother's day—if not quite in my own—a natural child like Aubrey was not put out for adoption and was not left to be brought up in disgrace by his unwed mother. Rather, he was drawn into the extended family, which was a reality in those quaint and distant days in Tennessee, and he was given the family's special protection both at home and abroad in the world. I said this was so, at any rate—or that I had been told so by my forebears—in the really best, the "most long-settled and best-regulated families" in our little up-country corner of the world. As soon as I had insisted upon this to Brax, however, I found myself recalling how my mother and aunts had come at last to regard Aubrey with the condescension and even contempt that their husbands had taught them to feel for him, and that the husbands, in their particular, masculine pride of that period, had always felt. My father and my uncles were all three of them sons of Confederate veterans and were so thoroughly versed in Civil War history that aboard the funeral train they delighted in pointing out the sites of great battles and even small skirmishes. More than once I heard them laughing at Aubrey's ignorance of military history. At Culpeper, my father (whose name, incidentally, was Braxton Bragg Longfort, and for whom my own son would be a namesake) announced to all that nearby was the spot where "the Gallant Pelham fell," and it had to be explained to Aubrey who that hero had been. Aboard the train there were many whispered conversations about the eccentric cousin's behavior. One night he was discovered in the area between the two Pullman cars, with his face in the crook of his arm, weeping aloud—ostensibly out of grief for his dead benefactor, the Senator. My two uncles discovered him there and led him into the men's smoking room where they administered large doses of whiskey out of their own flasks. And it was at some time on that long journey that I heard Uncle Hobart repeating what was allegedly my grandfather's own account of how he had gone to the simple mountain cabin where Aubrey was being reared until he was about school age and had "rescued" him from the rough people there, and had placed him in Mr. Webb's school in Bellbuckle, where he was rather harshly disciplined and received a severely supervised classical education. But I think these incidents and stories did not impress me so strongly as did Cousin Aubrey's own contumelious glances at myself. Very early, though, I began to understand the resentment inspired in him by the mere sight of a boy who enjoyed every protection such a life as mine provided and the affection and even adoration of those three particular women who presided over my every activity. And by the time I was an adolescent, I believe I could already conceive that an experience so totally different from mine could have a hardening and corrupting effect upon a being as sensitive to the affection and consideration of others as I believed myself to be.

BUT I MUST TELL you now that in recent years, after I was in fact already well past middle age, I would once again find myself preoccupied with the whereabouts of Cousin Aubrey. And during this period of my life I have inevitably been mindful sometimes of those *other* old stories I heard about those *other* Tennessee men who had vanished. I should make very clear that by the time of my life I now speak of I was already a man with grown-up children of my own. My father had died while I was still a boy, and my aged mother herself had by now been dead for some while. This middle-aged preoccupation of mine would finally develop into what amounted to no less than a somewhat absurd obsession.

At last I would find it existed actually as a resurfacing of a well-buried mania of mine from that long-ago boyhood, which first struck me aboard the train. What seemed particularly impressive so long after was that this Cousin Aubrey had actually managed to vanish not just once but four or five times from our midst before his disappearance seemed complete and permanent. At any rate, I would now in middle age find myself wishing above all things, almost, to know if he was still alive and what on earth might have happened to him and where he might be living out his days. I was far away from Tennessee by now but I could not rest until I knew what had become of the man. More than once—I cannot now say how often it was—I got up at night and walked the floor of my present habitation. It did not occur to me that he had had some great good fortune in life or that he had come to an ignominious and perhaps violent end. The simple knowledge of what his ultimate fate was became an end in itself. In my mind he became more like some ghost of an earlier generation than mine who might yet be living on in another form.

THOUGH I REMEMBERED Aubrey distinctly from childhood and even from very early young manhood, still by the time I would reach middle age there would be for me something positively mythic in his proportions. Yet I would realize in this later period that even as a growing child I had wondered whatever might have become of him. I suppose I had reason enough to wonder about him, because on every occasion of our meeting again he had taken those same particular pains to show his special dislike for me—that is, dislike for the small boy and later for the adolescent and young man —a dislike which seemed totally unwarranted since our meetings were indeed *so* few and *so* brief. But all that aside, my sudden and otherwise unaccountable preoccupation with searching out Cousin Aubrey's present whereabouts would be precisely like some other unnamed and unacknowledged passion of my youth that had been suppressed and was now manifesting itself in a more virulent form.

All the while that I would be making those first few tentative inquiries and investigations concerning this missing man and even later when we found him, I would continue always to think of those other vanished men who had captured my imagination when I was a boy. I think I felt they might offer an explanation of the mysterious Aubrey's disappearances and of my own belated obsession with it. In my mind I knew how little similarity there could have been between those other missing men and himself—as little as there also could ever have been between himself and any one of our family's great achievers, such as my maternal grandfather. But nonetheless, the stories of those other men's disappearances would keep returning to my inflamed and strangely excited mind—even very late in life. My constant reference to him in conversation during this time would very nearly drive my wife, Melissa, as well as my son Braxton to distraction.

My wife and my son Braxton at last came to speak openly of this habit of mine as my "mania." But they would listen sympathetically too—they and all the rest of my little family —as again and again I cataloged the names of vanished Tennesseans and of course ended always with Cousin Aubrey. Apparently I spoke of them always in tones of such a partic-

ular veneration that my son Braxton especially found it both
vexing and wonderfully amusing. He would compare it to the
listing of Homeric heroes! At any rate, by all means the most
famous name in my said catalog was that of our old warrior-
hero, Governor Sam Houston. Everyone, especially that
youngest son of mine, would have heard the story: On the
morning following the night of Governor Sam Houston's marriage to a Nashville belle, he abandoned his bride and abandoned as well his newly won gubernatorial chair. It was
known that Houston went for a time to live among the Indians. And afterward, of course, he went on to found the
independent Republic of Texas. But, for us, the point is that
he never returned to Tennessee. . . . Only somewhat less famous in the annals of the state was a man who had been one
of our Confederate senators and who, after the War, without
seeing his family or his constituents again, went off to live in
Brazil. From there he sent back photographs of himself posed
in opulent surroundings and attired in romantic Portuguese
costumes. But when some relative, later on, made a point of
looking him up, he was found in pathetic rags living in dread-
ful squalor and quite alone in the slums of Rio de Janeiro.
. . . Not all of our vanished men, however, were public men.
They were, some of them, simple landless men who seemed
unable to put down roots anywhere. Sometimes they took
their wives right along with them when they went away, as
well as whatever children they had and perhaps an old grandmother or some other dependent relative or, in the earliest
times, perhaps a little clutch of black slaves and even an in-
dentured servant or two. But even these rootless men, when
they departed, frequently left their former homes under the
cover of night, as if the act of moving in itself were a disgrace.
I'm told that in the first quarter of the last century it was
indeed quite common in Tennessee to see a crudely lettered

sign nailed to a tree trunk in the front yard of an abandoned farmhouse reading simply GONE TO TEXAS. And that was only a manner of speaking, of course. It was merely a statement that another disenchanted man had put forever behind him the long green hinterland that is Tennessee, and that he never intended returning to her salubrious clime.

BUT THERE IS the one incident from my early life with which I most often have entertained my own children—entertained them, that is, or perhaps sometimes put them to sleep while helping my wife nurse one of them through some childhood illness. It is the story of that same train ride which I took as a small boy from Washington, first to Nashville and then on to the city of Knoxville. Admittedly I have always begun with this account because Aubrey Tucker Bradshaw was a fellow passenger aboard that train and because also it would give me opportunity to introduce a number of the persons present who would later play an important role in my upbringing.

During boyhood everything began with the great train ride. For that was how I came to think of the long railway journey from Washington. I really had no earlier memories to speak of, and so it was easy to date everything from that. Since my father died when I was nine and since he was an invalid at home for several years before that, my principal memories of him as an active man are those aboard the funeral train. Much the same must be said of the husbands of my two aunts, both of these men having died as relatively young men and soon after my father. It was because of this, my grandfather's children having been all daughters, that I was destined to grow up in a family dominated by the considerate and kindly natures of three gentlewomen. Perhaps that is why

at some point in adolescence—I cannot say precisely when—
I began to speculate on whether or not my having no father
might have some bearing on my own fascination with the men
in our corner of the world who had made a break with things
and disappeared from the scene. It used to seem so to my
mother, I suggest, when I spoke to her in a strange way about
the missing men in our life. Perhaps even by late boyhood I
vaguely recognized and identified an admiration I felt for any
restlessness in other boys and particularly in older boys who
might be just on the verge of manhood. Not that it ever
seemed possible for *me!* Not for someone as carefully brought
up and relied upon and counted on as I was by my mother
and my aunts.

At any rate, even on my grandfather's funeral train, nothing had stirred my imagination more than a contrast between
the behavior of my cousin Aubrey and that of my two uncles.
I have only to think of that contrast to make various episodes
of that memorable trip come to life again. Even as the funeral
train had moved out of the switching yard in Washington,
still traveling at a very slow speed, the young matrons in their
drawing room noticed a bumping sensation that caused them
to exchange questioning glances. My father, who was then a
young man of twenty-eight, was seated along with one of my
two uncles—it was my uncle Hobart Washburn—in the Pullman section and just outside the drawing room door. Father
told me afterward that his first thought on experiencing the
bumping sensation was that the train had jumped the tracks.
It was in fact while on his honeymoon with Mother, eight
years earlier, when they were passing through the mountains
of West Virginia, that he had heard a similar sound beneath
that train. On their honeymoon trip they were actually riding
in a car that broke loose from the train and overturned. Subsequently the car came very near to rolling down a steep

embankment and into a lake below. This was no doubt what made Father so sensitive now to the momentary unevenness of the train's motion. He sprang to his feet at once, his eye on the drawing room door, but the bumping sensation had ceased almost before he got to his feet. And the train had commenced slowing to a halt with a great cranking and squealing of brakes against the iron wheels. There followed loud hissing exhalations of steam. Sitting down again, Father could see out the window a number of yardmen running toward the train with expressions of alarm on their faces. He could even hear some of them call out excitedly to the train's engineer. Almost immediately before the train had altogether come to a stop, the other men in the Pullman cars were pouring out onto the gravel beside the train. Father and Uncle Hobart, forgetting their young wives in the drawing room—not to mention the Senator's widow and her companion in the car up ahead—followed the crowd out onto the gravel. Only Aubrey Bradshaw did not join them. Aubrey lingered in the car where the three sisters were shut up in their compartment.

A bloody sight confronted the two men who clambered off the train. Somehow or other a cow and her half-grown calf had got loose in the vast switching yard. (Perhaps I should remind you again it was in the year 1916!) Whether the animals had been tethered nearby or had escaped from a cattle car, no one knew. But the calf had been caught between the coal car and the baggage car and had been subsequently run over by the very car in which the Senator's body was resting as well as by the diner and the two sleeping coaches. The terrible sight made most of the weak-stomached men from the Washington bureaus return hastily to their seats on the train. Father and Uncle Hobart were following along with the others when they espied my other uncle, Lawrence Todd. He was coming toward them from the baggage car. Because of

Uncle Lawrence's quite remarkable squeamishness they insisted he not look upon what they had seen. But they detained him long enough to ask if the coffin had been disturbed. He assured them that it had not and that he had himself scarcely detected any roughness in the train's movement. My father and Uncle Hobart stared at each other in astonishment. At the same moment each of them noticed the strong odor of liquor on Uncle Lawrence Todd's breath.

When Father reentered the Pullman car where Mother and her sisters were still shut up in the drawing room he saw the singular figure of Aubrey Bradshaw at the other end of the car, standing there with his back pressed against the drawing room door. It so happened that the crowd outside had gathered and that the gore was most evident on the other side of the train from the drawing room—on the side, that is, where the passageway led to the rear door of the car. As Father approached the adjacent section where he had been sitting earlier, Aubrey must have supposed he intended to enter the drawing room. He pressed himself flatter against the door and asserted, "Braxton, sir, there's nothing to be served by telling the ladies what has happened! They have no need to know!" And it seems to me now that that is how I first remember Aubrey Bradshaw, protecting my mother and her sisters from such realities.

Father and Uncle Hobart took their seats in the first section and, barely restraining a smile I suppose, Father said, "I had no intention of doing so, Aubrey." (Though of course that indeed *had* been his first intention. But he did not tell his wife about it during the first opportunity he had to be alone with her. He waited until a second opportunity some years afterward and Mother would tell me about it many years later.) "And now I suggest," said my father, "that you take your place, Aubrey, wherever it was you were sitting." When telling me about this so many years afterward (my father did not live long enough to tell me such anecdotes) Mother said Father knew Aubrey so slightly that it was only with an effort that he had been able to recall his name at the time. And she said Father had thought Aubrey "a little touched in the head." She said he had thought this without knowing about the two older ladies occupying the drawing room in the first car. For Father didn't know until some hours later that Aubrey had gone twice and knocked on the widow's door to ask if she and her companion were safe and comfortable and if they needed any service that he could render. Upon his knocking there again, the companion, whom we all referred to as Aunt Augusta St. John-Jones, though she was not actually any kin to us, opened the door and gave him a resounding piece of her mind, sending him on his way. Aubrey and Aunt Augusta had never been friends, and at this moment she openly declared the enmity she felt. This Aunt Augusta's dislike and contempt for what she termed "the hordes of Tennessee poor relations and hangers-on in the bureaus" was never more than superficially concealed. And she had often expressed openly to others her special loathing for Aubrey when he had come showering attention on one or another of the Senator's daughters. Her special loathing for Aubrey, so everyone in the family said, was quite as intense as her special high regard for the Senator himself or for anyone else whom she deemed of importance.

After the episode of the calf, the train moved out of the railway yard and out of Washington as planned and without further mishap there. The three sisters as well as the stepmother and her companion must have assumed that although the journey had hardly begun the worst of it must surely now be over.

But this was far from the case. Its duration would last for

the better part of a week. A few miles outside the Virginia town of Culpeper the steam engine developed a "hot box," the sparks of which were thrown into an adjacent field. It was on a very warm afternoon in mid-September and after a long and extremely hot and dry summer. The field contained a burnt-up, lost crop of corn. Where the sparks landed among the dry cornstalks it burst immediately into flames. The train came to an abrupt halt, and, within seconds almost, not only the crew but all the able-bodied men from the Washington bureaus as well as most of the mourners from the immediate family clambered off the train and ran jumping ditches and stumbling over clods of earth to help fight the fire by whatever means they could. Again it was only Aubrey Bradshaw who remained on the train in order to protect and reassure the ladies in the drawing rooms of both coaches, particularly those three sisters whom he clearly regarded as his special charges.

In view from the Pullman windows when the train came to a stop was the distant village of Brandy Station. The features of the place were recognized at once by my father. Long afterward, in his last days, my rediscovered Cousin Aubrey himself would describe to me (it was only a few days after we met in Washington as we were destined to do) those excited spirits in which my father set out to fight the flames. The fact was, it seems that Father, though he was born more than twenty years after the surrender at Appomattox, was an expert on the events of every battle and skirmish fought in Tennessee and Virginia. It was as he rose from his Pullman seat then that he glanced out the window toward Brandy Station and made his proclamation that must have been heard beyond the closed door of the drawing room: "Everyone observe! It was here that the Gallant Pelham fell!" And when Father returned from his fire fighting in the field, with his suit jacket burned beyond repair and one of the trouser legs scorched up to the knee, he had to improvise a change of clothing. In my presence Aubrey Bradshaw would long, long afterward remark, with some show of amusement and condescension, that my mother presently came out of the drawing room and "mirated over the scorched trouser leg as though it were a battle wound," and he would recall that Father reveled in the attention it got for him. The two other sons-in-law came forward, so Aubrey would recall during our meetings in Washington forty years later, offering Father swigs from their flasks as if he needed such to kill the pain in his trouser leg.

The train was delayed an hour at Culpeper for unknown reasons and then proceeded to the towns of Charlottesville and Lynchburg. Since the Senator had attended the University briefly in his youth he had had a certain number of old friends in Charlottesville. A delegation came down to the Southern depot there to meet the train and to make several public speeches outside the door of the crepe-draped baggage car. A number of these friends and admirers crowded into the train in order to pay their respects to the widow, who by that time lay prostrate in the lower berth of her drawing room. Her companion, Aunt Augusta, merely poked her head (perhaps in curlers) out the drawing room door and announced abruptly that the widow was in no condition to receive them.

After that rude rejection, it was deemed incumbent upon the three daughters and their husbands to come down onto the platform and solemnly shake hands with all the delegation from the University. And following this the wide doors to the baggage car were slid open, revealing the coffin with its mountain of flowers around it. Standing beneath the doors on a metal stool provided by the train's conductor, first one and then another of the Charlottesville delegation delivered themselves of brief eulogies of their dead friend. Just as all this was concluded Aunt Augusta St. John-Jones appeared from the first Pullman car fully dressed in her funeral raiment. She presently went about introducing herself as an aunt of the three sisters, implying that she was the Senator's sister, which, of course, she was not, being only the closest friend of the Senator's first wife.

Meanwhile, Aubrey Bradshaw hung about the periphery of those assembled on the platform at the Charlottesville depot. To strangers he seemed to have a guilty look about him, and once or twice was questioned as to his identity—by policemen who had accompanied the delegation from Charlottesville. With his gangling arms and legs and his tight-fitting armbanded black suit his awkward figure must have seemed to those Virginians there to be the very epitome of an up-country cousin from the mountains of Tennessee or Kentucky. (The Tuckers had come to Tennessee from Virginia nearly one hundred and fifty years before in the late eighteenth century, yet the older members of the family still in 1916 spoke of themselves as being a Virginia-Tennessee family, as distinguished from a Carolina-Tennessee family, as were the Bradshaws. Old-timers said one could tell which of the old Colonies a family had migrated from by noticing whether its members referred to a cabinet as a "cupboard" or a "press." And there were other criteria for making the distinction. In the excitement of argument, the older members of the family could for the sake of emphasis or perhaps for authority bring forth a Virginia diphthong that was pure Tidewater.) The three Tucker sisters often accused Aunt Augusta of wishing out of pride to sweep Aubrey Bradshaw under the rug on occasions when the family was on display.

But my aunt Felicia, the middle sister and the most practical of the three, would point out that Aubrey very often proved himself useful at such moments. In the heat of the late-afternoon September sun, standing there beside the baggage car on the wooden platform, Trudie, my mother, suddenly and without any forewarning swooned and fainted away. She might easily have fallen off the platform and been injured except that Aubrey's ever-watchful eye perceived at once the unnatural turn of her head and saw her hand release the black reticule which would presently fall onto the plank floor of the wooden platform. From his position a considerable distance across the platform he dashed to her side and caught her in his arms as her knees buckled beneath her. Her husband, my father, who was at that time on duty with the coffin inside the baggage car, witnessed this rescue through the open doorway. As he saw his wife being carried off in Aubrey's arms to the second Pullman car, my father abandoned his post and ran at top speed through the dining car and through the first of the two Pullmans in order, so he reckoned, to reach the second Pullman car as soon as Trudie was brought aboard. But Braxton found Trudie already inside the drawing room and now under the care of her two sisters when he arrived. To his astonishment, he came face-to-face with Aubrey in the doorway to the compartment. Aubrey regarded him, the husband, with sympathy. But as Aubrey would tell me very frankly so many years later, he was shocked by my father's first words, which did not concern his wife's well-being. Instead of asking after Trudie he seized Aubrey Bradshaw by the hand, pressed it warmly and exclaimed, "The quickness with which you leapt into action, my young kinsman, was no less than heroic! I observed you with keen admiration! I believe you are, after all, a man of action! I believe you will do something worthwhile with your life." It excited my father to have recognized another hero, and he would go through the train telling everyone he met that Aubrey Bradshaw possessed the makings of a hero.

My mother recovered from her fainting spell almost at

once. And it was apparently of no significance. My father must have undoubtedly observed from the baggage car that even before Aubrey started moving toward the sleeping car with Mother in his arms, her sister Felicia had stepped forward and placed her hand firmly on top of Trudie's head. And with her hand so placed Felicia managed to keep pace with Aubrey all the way down the platform, still seeming to feel it was a necessity to hold the head, so to speak, onto the body of her comatose younger sister. As she scampered along at Aubrey's side Felicia explained to him why she felt this necessity. She was, so she explained, holding my mother's elaborate pompadour in place.

Felicia, who would in her life marry two very rich men (after the death of Uncle Hobart), was by all odds the most worldly of all three of the Tucker sisters and was always aware of appearances. She knew, moreover, that someone who still wore her hair in an old-fashioned pompadour, as my mother did, did so for the purpose of concealing a particularly recessed hairline that nature had given her. That is, Trudie wore her hair brushed forward over her forehead into a billowing pompadour, and Felicia had come forth to hold the pompadour in place as the unconscious Trudie was borne alongside the train and up the steps to the Pullman car. It was of course a ridiculous thing for Felicia to have undertaken at that frightening moment. But Aubrey was concerned mainly that Braxton Longfort, her husband, had taken no notice of it.

My aunt Bertie and Aunt Augusta followed afterward, asking what in the world it was that Felicia was doing. Was Trudie injured, in addition to having a fainting fit? Yet by the time Braxton had got inside the drawing room his wife had not only regained consciousness, she was insisting on being allowed to sit in an upright position. In the Pullman car, standing in the aisle, my cousin Aubrey overheard her first words to my father: "Oh, Brax, where were you when I needed you so?" And Aubrey also heard my father's reply: "Why I was where my duty required me to be, at my station beside the body of the deceased!" Even many years later, as a very old man, when I came to be seeing him rather regularly in a Washington hospital, Aubrey could still recall this exchange between my mother and father with perfect accuracy of content and tone. And the old man would tell me then that some delicacy of feeling had at the time made him move farther into the sleeping car and out of the range of the married couple's voices. But he nevertheless heard my mother presently burst into a flood of forgiving tears. And he could all too easily imagine the two young lovers' embrace that must have followed. Even so many years later when at last he and I had met and my own grown-up son Braxton and I were seeing him almost daily, Aubrey could still recall the sound of those exchanges beyond the drawing room door that had shut him out—could recall what he heard and what he imagined. But also he would tell me that his "delicacy of feeling" had soon made him move still farther along into the sleeping car.

WHEN FINALLY we became friends there was nothing my cousin Aubrey would relish more about our acquaintance than to tell me what manner of men my father and my two uncles had "really" been. In the opinion of my mother and two aunts, of course, their husbands were too nobly endowed by nature for any ordinary kind of life. Their three husbands' early deaths would seem to them, in retrospect, almost inevitable. They were men too good for this world! They were men who had, according to their widows, been unwilling to stoop to things required for success in such a materialistic age as the rest of us had lived on into. Each of them was a kind of Gallant Pelham for whom there should exist a present-day Confederacy to memorialize their gallantry! But disillusionment and boredom would make the three of them turn finally to their various dissipations and to death. This was the picture suggested by their widows. But the picture which Cousin Aubrey gave would be different.

Since all three men had died when they were quite young, the Cousin Aubrey I would come at last to know could account for a fair portion of their collective lifetime. He had known each of them, in turn, when they were courting the Senator's three daughters. He had known them as young bachelors. He had been present at their weddings, he had known them as young husbands, and at last, perhaps unbeknownst to the widows, he had been present at the graveside of each man's burial.

This last astonishing fact would have seemed almost inconceivable to my mother and my aunts. But when Aubrey and I would be together at a later time in Georgetown, the then very aged Cousin Aubrey made it very clear to me that though the three sisters had "lost track" of him, *he* had all through the years somehow managed to keep close track of *them*. And so he had, in some almost unrecognizable guise—perhaps merely hiding behind his imperial beard—in order to be present at the funeral of each husband, as he would later manage to be present at the funerals of my two aunts.

At first it occurred to me that Aubrey's talk on this subject would be a tremendous satisfaction to me when fate brought us together. And ultimately it would be so, but my son Braxton warned me not to place too high hopes on this outcome. Brax had often worried me with his assertion that in searching out Cousin Aubrey I was still in search of a "father figure" (*his* jargon). And this son of mine accused me of having an "identity problem" (*more* of his mid-twentieth-century jargon). And blamed it moreover on my having been brought up by three widow ladies and having had in my teens no father and not even any surviving uncles and no grandfathers. My son Brax was fond of pointing out how deeply attached I had ever remained to the art schools I attended and to my older colleagues in the university where I taught nowadays. It was true that I had all along felt a certain dissatisfaction with the idealized image given me by my mother and my aunts of their late husbands, but I am sure it was not to find a father that I sought out my cousin Aubrey. Rather, above all else, I think it was to listen to his version of the events aboard that funeral train.

THE TRAIN FROM Washington departed Charlottesville on the approximate schedule set by the Southern Railroad, and a little more than two hours later it had traveled as far south and west as Lynchburg. It was full dark by then and much switching about of the cars was a necessity at this point. I would by then have been sleeping soundly beside my mother in her lower berth. I doubt that even Mother would have been at all aware of what went on outside the Pullman car. It would be long, long years before I knew. Since the funeral train was being transferred from the Southern Railroad to the Norfolk and Western, the two sleeping cars, the diner, and the baggage car had to be attached to a new engine and coal car. (The same switching about would have to be endured again at Bristol, on the Tennessee border, when the cars would at that juncture be transferred back to the Southern Railroad.) The cars had to wait on a siding for over an hour for the new engine to be brought into the yard and onto the siding. Meanwhile, an evening meal had been sent in to the young ladies and to the two old ladies in the two drawing rooms, and the men in the cars had been allowed to troop up to the dining car a few at a time as vacancies at tables occurred. It was during this interval that Aubrey Bradshaw was discovered by my father and my uncles standing between the two sleeping cars weeping copiously. As I have said already, the two brothers-in-law led Aubrey into the smoker of the second sleeping car and administered to him the drafts from their two flasks. As a matter of fact, Uncle Hobart's silver flask was emptied with Aubrey's first swallow. When my father perceived this he glanced at Hobart in alarm and then gazed at him for several moments afterward to make out what condition his brother-in-law was in. (It might be mentioned here that all three sons-in-law had brought along their flasks at the suggestion of the Washington undertaker in charge.) Presently father opened his own flask which was like a zinc canteen, possibly of army issue, and which was yet still full to the brim. From this he gave Aubrey Bradshaw several more swallows. Those powerful swigs of whiskey acted as a sedative on Aubrey. It was more whiskey than he had ever imbibed in all his life before that time. And for a while he was in no condition to keep a watchful eye on events aboard the train. Had this not been so I think he might have prevented what followed.

To enter Lynchburg, Virginia, the train had crossed over the James River on a high trestle bridge and was now standing on a siding near the bluff there. A full moon had risen and was reflected in the river below. It was bright on that side of the train. The ladies in the two drawing rooms, partaking of the meals sent in to them, may have taken some cheer from their view of the moon's reflection in the water at the foot of the bluff. But the other side of the train was in shadow, and beyond the expansive tracks in the switching yard there were the black warehouses of the town and perhaps a few faint lights from some saloon on a street beyond.

In the shadows immediately beyond the train my uncle Hobart, shortly after his ministrations to my cousin Aubrey Bradshaw, was standing in whispered communication with the train's only porter. He was in fact contracting with him to go into the town and fetch replenishment of his empty flask. Apparently the contract was effected and money had already changed hands when the men from the Washington bureaus, one by one, got word of the transaction and commenced pouring off the train to ask that their money be taken for similar replenishment. At this onrush of business the porter suddenly bethought himself of his duties and experienced a change of heart. He handed back Hobart's money, saying, "I've got my berths to make down," and climbed aboard the train again. At that, Hobart, accompanied by two of the bureaucrats, took off across the tracks in the direction of the warehouses and specifically in the direction of a light which, as the porter had told Hobart, shone from a saloon.

While the three men were still hop-skipping across the tracks Braxton Longfort, my father, appeared on the train steps and was informed of the purpose of Hobart's mission. He called after him to come back, but to no avail. Moments later came the great clanking bumps of the newly arrived engine against the funeral train. Father and the conductor hurried forward to tell the new engineer that the train would have to hold up departure until Uncle Hobart and his companions returned. But the engineer would not agree. Instead, he insisted that the train would either have to go ahead at once in order to clear the tracks for other regularly scheduled trains or would have to wait where it was on the siding for twelve or perhaps twenty-four hours. The train did, of course, go ahead without Hobart and there were dire consequences.

When Braxton Longfort and the Pullman conductor hurried through the baggage car to request that departure be delayed, Father noticed that his brother-in-law Lawrence Todd responded to the news by springing up from the bench on which he had been sitting and by then giving vent to a long, loud moan or wail. When they returned with the news that the engineer had declined to delay departure, Lawrence began cursing the conductor, as well as the engineer up ahead. My father observed that Uncle Lawrence's own flask lay on the bench beside him, unstoppered and obviously drained to the last drop.

When Lawrence continued to rant at the conductor, Braxton Longfort could perceive that his brother-in-law's condition indicated something worse than a mere drunken rage. It must have come to Father's mind that Lawrence was reported by Aunt Augusta to have been unstable as a boy and that because of a nervous ailment he had been for a time under a doctor's "supervision." Presently he heard Lawrence Todd asking rhetorically who was in command of this train. Was it that lowborn engineer up ahead? And now he answered himself saying that he and Braxton were in command now that Hobart had abandoned ship. His increasing rage manifested itself by his shaking his fists above his head and his cursing God and the Devil and all of the Senator's hangers-on who were of the funeral party and even his own wife and her two sisters as well as the widow herself, and especially the widow's companion, Aunt Augusta St. John-Jones. Father and the Pullman conductor were able to quiet him momentarily by asserting that he should not be carrying on so in the presence of the dead, and then they persuaded him to go with them to the smoking compartment in the first of the two

Pullman cars. There he began to shout again and to kick the spittoons all about and to open the water valves in the lavatory. From that point, it was primarily a matter of confining him until he could be put off the train and given medical care.

A wire was sent ahead to Bristol, which was on the Tennessee line near the town of Elizabethton—that being the Tuckers' place of origin. At the depot in Bristol various relatives were waiting with a doctor to receive him and perhaps restrain him. It was past midnight by then, but everyone in the two cars was awake except possibly the ladies in the two drawing rooms. During the four hours since leaving Lynchburg all interest had been focused on the states of drunkenness the men had been in. And they might not have come aboard again at Bristol except that the train jumped a track as it approached and was stalled there for an agonizing period of forty-eight hours before matters could be set right and the train would be on its way again for Nashville. By then my two uncles had been dried out and sufficiently sobered up to allow them to catch up with the train. They had come aboard at different stations and all that each of them could do during the rest of the journey was talk about how beautiful were the fresh wreaths and flowers that had been added at various points along the way, to replace the now-withered flowers and greenery that had decorated the baggage car upon leaving Washington. And so it was that upon reaching Nashville the whole of the original funeral party was aboard again.

BY THE TIME the special train reached Nashville on September 22, 1916, the supplies in the mess had to be replenished twice and a doctor had to be brought aboard to attend the two old ladies in the first drawing room. The train took what would today seem a circuitous route, traveling along the foot of the high Smoky Mountains at Knoxville, though not stopping there since it would return a few days later for the graveside burial service, and then on by way of Chattanooga to Nashville. In recent years a certain old-lady cousin of mine has written to me a description of the train passing her farmhouse door, between Chattanooga and Nashville, and how as a little girl she sat on her back-porch steps and watched the mournful train go by, the baggage car all draped in black crepe and the engine all the while blowing its low, mournful whistle—all this as it passed along the valley between the low-lying hills in that region. Reading about this in her letter, I could not but think of how sad were the circumstances, particularly inside the drawing room of the first Pullman car, where the two old ladies were closeted with their aches and pains and tears and with fond memories of their beloved Senator.

I cannot emphasize too strongly how truly beloved was this Senator Nathan Tucker, my esteemed grandfather. Aside from what he represented as a binding and healing force in the region, which had been badly split by events of the late Civil War, he was a man who by the warmth of his personality had touched the hearts of nearly all men and women. And whatever the failings and shortcomings of his two chief mourners, the two old ladies in the front drawing room, their grief was sincere and profound. Now and again during the journey I would be taken by my mother to visit them in their compartment. It seemed clear to me, as such things are clear to children of an even mildly perceptive nature, that neither of those ladies had any marked fondness for children. Neither had had children of her own, and they were really not women of remarkable imagination. It was not that, like Aubrey, they felt resentment of the mere presence of a child—especially

not some particular child as he did in my case—but for them
there was an indifference to children which some adults man-
ifest and that they cannot disguise from the child no matter
how hard they try. Aunt Augusta St. John-Jones, who as I
have said was actually no kin at all to either side of the family,
was a worldly woman of the most easily recognizable sort.
Though she was well known to everyone as a hanger-on and
a social climber, she was someone to whom my mother and
her two sisters felt they had to show special respect. She had
been their own mother's oldest, closest friend. These two
women had first known each other in Nashville, where their
husbands had been friends during the Senator's first term as
Governor.

The two old ladies had been reunited in Washington when
Aunt Gussie's husband had been elected to the Congress. But
when the new Congressman had died of a heart attack while
making his maiden speech on the floor of the House, Aunt
Gussie became socially dependent on the Senator's first wife,
my grandmother. It was a strange story, which cannot be told
in full here since it has no special bearing on our events, but
it was a familiar story to everyone in their circle of friends,
and so was to that extent relevant. This Aunt Gussie of theirs
possessed certain psychic powers which she had used to cure
my grandmother's headaches when they were all living together under the same roof in the old Maxwell House Hotel
in Nashville. But her powers over my grandmother disturbed
my grandfather to the degree that he forbade any continuation
of the hypnotic sessions. Nevertheless, during her lifetime she
continued to be my grandmother's closest friend and was said
to have been responsible for the selecting of the widowed
Senator's second wife for him. Actually it was only after he
went to the Senate and resided in Washington that he at last
came to feel the need of marrying again—and primarily then

for the sake of acquiring chaperonage for his three young-lady daughters. It was sometimes said by the three daughters that Aunt Gussie would surely have chosen herself for that role except that their papa was suspicious of her psychic powers and he had even on occasion in this connection expressed suspicions concerning the cause of the Congressman's untimely death.

Their papa spoke this in jest no doubt, for Senator Tucker, though an exceedingly kind man, was given to jesting, even sometimes grotesquely when he thought the occasion merited it. At any rate, his second wife (however and by whomever she was selected) was a delicately beautiful spinster lady from Sweetwater, Tennessee. It was said by someone at the time, most probably by Aunt Gussie herself, that there was some advance agreement made about abstinence from certain marital practices between the aged bride and groom. At any rate it was deemed a happy marriage of convenience, if indeed that's what it was. And Cousin Nan's grief—so the old lady was affectionately referred to by her stepdaughters—was no less genuine than that of the ostensible matchmaker.

Lovers of little children the two ladies most certainly were not, as I have indicated. I could see in their eyes the dull reserve and indifference that such ladies feel for any child whose frankness and honesty might strike out at them at any moment. Yet whenever I was in their presence I recognized an effort on their parts to simulate the warmth that I'm sure would have overflowed had my grandfather been alive and present with us aboard that train. So sure am I of the forthright and loving nature of that man that he stands forward in my mind as the very epitome of all that such men as Cousin Aubrey cannot be, as the opposite being of all men who ever vanished away of their own volition from the warm scenes of life which Nathan Tucker enjoyed. It was not until many, many years later that I could articulate the contrast between the two kinds of men and recognize, alas, that there was part of my own nature that had something in common with that *other* sort of man and in some degree always made me feel myself an alien to my grandfather Tucker. Perhaps it represented my greatest and most lasting self-doubt. Somehow the closest I can come to putting this feeling into words is by quoting passages from Grandfather Nathan Tucker's own notebooks that I discovered after I was a grown man. I was such an introvert that as a man I could not identify with this grandfather. He was such a complete and happy extrovert! How amusing he managed to find his own children—whereas I have never been able to find mine so. I took my own children most seriously and tried always to admire them, and was therefore a more satisfactory kind of parent in the usual sense. Grandfather had a much more positive worldview. In his world there was no need or room for disappeared men—no place in his repertory of stories for men like Cousin Aubrey. He knew and remembered well the old slave who had belonged to his own great-grandfather. It was by the respect and affection he expressed in a fragment of one memoir that I came to judge him anew. I found that memoir—that yellowed piece of paper—in the State Library where it had been preserved by a librarian admirer of his. Sitting in the State Library with its profusion of ironwork on the balconies and on the old spiral stairs, I copied it all out in longhand. I have it still, folded away in one of my own academic notebooks. This is how Grandfather Tucker reveals himself through his description of another fellow being:

There was in our family an old Negro, Solomon by name, whom we honored with the sobriquet of Bonaparte because he reminded us of the great Corsican in some of his traits of character, especially in the forcefulness of an indomitable will joined to a remarkably clear intellect, though totally innocent of any written language; also in his executive ability, his bravery and his fighting qualities. He knew nothing of what is meant by the word *fear*. But in his old age he became a most devout Christian, which greatly softened his temper and assuaged his otherwise stormy nature. According to his own account of himself, he was born a prince in the old Congo kingdom in Western Africa; but at the age of twenty-two was captured in one of its frequent civil wars and sold into slavery, and landed from a slaver at Charleston, South Carolina, not long after the Revolution, about 1788, when he was bought by our great-grandfather and brought to live at our place. Proving himself, like Plato, to be no ordinary slave, having learned English with remarkable facility and speed, and exhibiting a judgement and aptitude above the capacity of most white men of the neighborhood, the General—our great-grandfather—made him overseer and manager, and placed all his Negro forces under his absolute command. They obeyed his orders with much greater promptitude than those of the General himself. His agricultural operations from year to year on the estate were remarkably successful and profitable, for in those days good management was supplemented by a virgin soil of great fertility. Thus he served three generations as "boss" for each succeeding master, and virtually boss of the masters themselves and of their families, for he never hesitated to administer to the young sons of the family a sound drubbing when caught in mischief during the absence of the "governor" and his "missus," and by their sanction. The writer and all the rest of us have often felt the cogency of his arguments with the birch when caught depredating upon his dominions on the estate. His *fundamental* reasoning on moral turpitude and the importance of early piety in these tragic interviews were by far more effective than the ablest

efforts of a Kant or a Locke! But for all this, the more he
thrashed us the more we loved the old fellow, for when we
happened to be "good" he was better and kinder to us, if
possible, than our own parents, and immensely more entertaining with his innumerable stories. He would, at times of
leisure, talk to us by the hour, telling us thrilling tales of
African life in the Congo country; about lions, leopards,
elephants, giraffes, baboons, monkeys and snakes, and his
adventures with these and other kinds of wild and ferocious
animals of forests, jungle and veldt; about the black tribes
and their manners and customs; about the great Congo
River, the largest in Africa, the second largest in the world,
and next to the Nile in length; about his battles and exploits
in the Congo civil wars; how he was taken prisoner in battle,
sold to white men, and, bound with chains, placed in the
hold of a slave ship; how he struggled to free himself, and
by his struggles lacerating and bruising his legs and ankles,
and then he would show us their ugly scars. But in his
extreme old age he miraculously escaped from bondage and
disappeared into the frontier wilderness. All the blood-
hounds in East Tennessee could not smell him out. The
frontiersmen sought him in all the thick woods along the
Holston River but never found a trace of him.

On the next shelf but one, there in the State Library in
the capitol, I came on another document among my grandfather's papers, which was of similar and equal interest to me.
I was myself a lad of nineteen by that time and knowing my
first joys of research and discovery among musty old papers
of past days, a pursuit of which I think I may fairly claim I
was destined to become a future master. Perhaps it was my
scholarly instincts which urged me on then as well as a simpler kind of curiosity about my forebears, though the thought
would surely not have occurred to me at the time. I do recognize in myself even then, however, the trait of someone

eager to make significant distinctions concerning the characters of men as they emerge from seemingly dead words in old records. The dry-as-dust art historian which I was someday to become—instead of the living artist I early aspired to be—seemed already to come alive in me that day in the State Library while old Mrs. Moore looked over my shoulder. The document which caught my attention was a memoir my grandfather had written in old age about an adventure he had had at just the age I was then. It gave me such a picture of him as I could not otherwise have imagined except when set as it was against his generous picture of the old Negro slave named Solomon. His own father, my great-grandfather, had served as Secretary of Indian Affairs in the administration of President Andrew Johnson. He, my grandfather, young Nathan Tucker, had at the age of nineteen accompanied his father, the Secretary, as general amanuensis on an expedition for the pacification "of certain wild and hostile Indians" at the Kiowa Medicine Lodge, located in Kansas only a short distance from the Oklahoma line. The task of this commission or council was a most important and difficult one, involving, as it did, the settlement of a war which had been going on for more than three years: the settlement of claims for damages growing out of the massacre of peaceable Indians by General Chivington at Sand Creek, Colorado. Nathan Tucker's father, who in his early days had been a Presbyterian preacher, wanted a peaceful settlement of the affair, but two members of the commission, General William Tecumseh Sherman and General "Kit" Carson, preferred a military solution. It was not these concerns that I became preoccupied with as I studied the old documents which I had come upon. It was, rather, the pleasure which the youthful Nathan Tucker took in the adventure that immediately caught my eye. How quick he was to identify with his own father's Christian spirit! How he deplored Generals Sherman and Carson's cruel intentions, but it was something more memorable and lasting in effect that made its impression on me. Everywhere Grandfather turned there was something to be admired, some adulation that possessed and delighted his soul, something that bespoke his generosity of spirit. And in most cases it was the behavior of some fellow creature that stirred him.

The first friend he made on his Kansas adventure was a young newspaper reporter very near his own age, a Washington correspondent of the *New York Herald*. He was Henry M. Stanley, one and the same Stanley who would one day be famous for searching out Doctor Livingstone in Africa. Nathan at once recognized the other young man's adventurous spirit of fun. Together they rode the plains and explored remote regions of the wild landscape. Differences in their temperaments and backgrounds were not even momentarily a barrier. The fearlessness of this strange lad inspired Nathan with unaccustomed fearlessness on his own part, and he gloried in the experiences they shared. In his memoir of those days Nathan Tucker recounted how they came upon a grove of sacred birches—sacred to a certain Indian tribe. To the branches and limbs of every birch tree was tied some little totem that the Indians had fastened there. The two boys, thoughtless of any sacred element, made a collection of these fanciful objects to take home with them. As they were returning to their encampment they presently heard the sound of hoofbeats on the plain behind them. A band of savages was in hot pursuit. At Henry Stanley's instruction, the two boys commenced hurling the totems to the right and left of the tall grasses on either side. Having divested themselves of all booty, Henry Stanley—to Nathan Tucker's everlasting delight—led the way himself, shouting like a wild Indian and laughing joyfully at the top of his lungs. They made it safely back to camp, and under the blanket of his cot that night Nathan could occasionally hear Henry still sniggering at the memory and making Nathan promise not to tell the older newspaper reporters about their close call. For Nathan, Henry's pleasure in all events of the expedition possibly constituted his own greatest pleasure. But he delighted, too, in observing all the other people he encountered on that expedition. He took pleasure from his own acquaintance with Kit Carson and even more from the brushes he had with the unfriendly General Sherman, whose notes to other members of the commission Nathan described as being invariably written in the "most exquisite prose." He cherished the character of all the Indian chiefs he came to know, relished particularly their special forms of humor (which I have never seen made reference to in any other account of the period), especially the very names by which they elected to call themselves: Fish-e-more, Woman's Heart, Stumbling Bear, One Boar, Wolf's Sleeve, Bad Back, Ten Bears, Painted Lips, Dog Fat, Black Kettle, Heap of Birds, and many another which he carefully recorded on the pages of his memoir of that time. But most of his remarks about Indians were more of the following nature:

Towering above all in native intellect and oratory, Little Raven, chief of the Arapahoes, was there. His speech before the Commission on the question of damages, back annuities, and the cause of the recent war, would have done credit to any enlightened statesman. His reference to the Chivington massacre and the ill-treatment the Indians had received at the hands of the white men of the frontier, who, he alleged, had been infringing upon their reservation rights in the past, were scathing, and his plea for protection and better treatment in the future was the most touching piece of impassioned oratory to which the present writer has ever listened before or since. And when his oration was concluded he was seen by onlookers to have mounted a white stallion, provided by I know not whom, and vanished into the Black Hills of the Dakotas, forever beyond the reach of General Sherman and his ilk.

At the time of the funeral, of course, I could have had no concept of what my grandfather had been like. My principal impression during the services in Nashville, as later during the ceremony in Knoxville, was of the huge crowds that gathered wherever we went. And for long afterward large gatherings of any sort meant only one thing—Grandfather Tucker. I remember that my interest in the funeral ceremonies had been exhausted pretty early and that I spent much of my time draped over my father's shoulders with my eyes closed. I heard Mother say more than once that bringing me along on such a trip had been an "ill-conceived idea." It had of course been Father's "idea," and he kept replying to Mother that it was an experience I would remember as long as I lived. What I most distinctly remember about the Nashville "parade" was the cadre of National Guards (or so I must suppose they were) moving at a stately pace with drawn sabers just ahead of the casket. After the procession had passed along Broad Street and down Fifth, it continued at snail's pace up to the steep incline to the capitol, where the Senator's body would lie in state for two days—allowing the stream of citizenry to pass by and view the remains. After that, the whole of the funeral party that had journeyed from Washington would reboard the same train for an overnight ride to Knoxville. Word had come a while earlier that Aunt Augusta and the Senator's widow were so indisposed that they had been removed to a Nashville hospital, but they were now recovered and were able to rejoin the party aboard the train. I was taken by Mother to see the two old ladies again, and I remember how astonished they both were to discover that I was still of the party. By the time we arrived at the Knoxville cemetery I was so weary of events that I refused to take notice of anything that went on. I insisted on being carried first in the arms of my mother and then in turn in the arms of each of my two aunts—the husbands all being occupied as pallbearers. I saw little of the ceremony and did not take notice of the coffin being lowered into the grave. In fact I have no memory of the event at all, unlike the occasion of the gruesome event twenty years later when, during the exhumation (and before its second interment in another cemetery a hundred miles up the valley) I witnessed the breaking loose of the clay-covered coffin from the crane lifting it from its grave. But although I didn't remember any of the earlier event, in later years I was told I behaved strangely, as if in a presentiment of that second event. When the first clod of earth was cast down on the coffin at that first interment I began to groan so loud in my aunt Bertie's arms that she placed a hand over my mouth to stifle the sound. And at that same moment my mother burst into tears and had to be comforted by my other aunt.

At Knoxville there had been a general misunderstanding by members of the funeral party. They had assumed the train would return them to Nashville after the graveside ceremony or possibly even to Washington. But that was not the case, and it ultimately became known that all passengers—all mourners—would have to fend for themselves. This was disturbing news, of course, and even before they reached the cemetery everyone began trying to make private arrangements. When the service was concluded and space had been provided for nearly everyone either in limousines or in carriages, the undertakers in charge discovered that Cousin Aubrey Bradshaw was *not* provided for and that he could not be found anywhere on the cemetery grounds. At last the assembled party had to go ahead without him. One of the undertakers remained behind for a while, even searching in the woods that skirted the old graveyard. But it was reported at the railroad depot that the man was simply not to be found. It was reported that he had altogether disappeared.

Part Two

BECAUSE MY OWN father died when I was just nine (scarcely five years after the journey on the funeral train) I used as a boy to fantasize that Father, too, like Cousin Aubrey, had merely gone away somewhere and that when his whereabouts were discovered he would come back to us again. I knew better than this, of course. I remembered too well the sight of my young father lying in his coffin, his face emaciated by the many months of his mysterious illness, the illness whose name I was never to hear mentioned. And so long as I was living at home I used to go with Mother every Sunday to put flowers on Father's grave in the local cemetery, which was only a few hundred yards from our house, and to gaze upon the gargantuan, rough-cut tombstone erected there to his memory. Sometimes I could imagine I saw the profile of his handsome, rugged features chiseled into the planes of the variegated stone. And sometimes, only a few years later, I would imagine similarly that I saw the smooth, even features of my Uncle Hobart's profile etched into the grave surface of his own marble monument in the Nashville cemetery. I must suppose that I only failed, still later, to imagine Uncle Lawrence Todd's profile on still another tombstone somewhere in an East Tennessee burial ground, because he outlived the other two men by a number of years and because I would by that time be well beyond any such fanciful flights of the imagination.

But Uncle Lawrence Todd outlived the other two only in the most literal sense. Like Uncle Hobart—and like my father too, before I was even born—Uncle Lawrence very early came to lead a dissolute life. Uncle Lawrence ended his years locked away in an "institution." I knew for a certainty, of course, that neither Father nor his two brothers-in-law would ever come back to be found alive in any familiar place. Yet this early awareness of the finality of death remained boxed up within me for the greater part of my young life, unrelieved by any outward expression on my part. While sometimes indulging myself in fantasies about my father's and my uncles' return, I think I never for a moment lost sight of the true state of things. And this inner conflict between reality and fantasy no doubt had some bearing on my being driven, at an advanced age, to seek out the aged Cousin Aubrey's whereabouts and to confront his actual presence if ever and wherever he might be found.

Sometimes I think I have no memory at all of what my father was like during his lifetime. There are only snatches of memory. I seem to recollect only what I was able to conjure up afterward. I suppose that while he was alive it never occurred to me to try to observe what he was like. But after he was dead memories of him would come back to me in flashes. I would be walking along one of the dusty lanes around the old West Tennessee town of Thornton when suddenly an image or images of him as he had appeared to me in his lifetime would surface. Or sometimes there would come a memory of what some stranger had said of him or how graphically he had been described to me by someone else. Or it might be a random piece of information I got from my mother or one of my aunts.

Even as a child I could recall lying on the floor of our downstairs sitting room with a pencil and large piece of paper before me trying to make a drawing of my father's profile. In retrospect it was a very disconcerting recollection. In the first place I was naturally unskilled at the age of five. But even more troubling was the frown Father inevitably wore on his face then and his disapproval of any artistic effort on the part of his small son. I do think I remember his trying to distract me from my drawing and trying while my attention was drawn away to slip the large piece of paper into the wastebasket. And what I seem to remember most distinctly is the pained expression on his face as he did so, as though it was, so to speak, hurting him more than it did me. I had very early developed some instinct for drawing faces—more than most children, I believe. And I believe my father's behavior at these times could only represent his own dislike and distrust of such an artistic instinct in me. All the while I remember my mother's continuing to provide me with large pieces of paper and the large tablets that I liked to do my drawing on.

Once when I was six or seven I lay on my cot in what we called the "little middle room" behind the downstairs sitting room. It was nap time for me, and Father had not yet gone back to his law office after lunch. I could hear my parents talking in the room beyond, and through the half-open door I could catch a glimpse of Father's figure as he paced back and forth in there. I could hear Father saying, "I am just afraid you will make some kind of sissy of him after I am gone." And I heard Mother say, "Sh-sh-sh." Then she came and closed the door between the two rooms. But I could hear their voices distinctly still. I put my pillow over my head, though I could still hear them well enough. "I hope that after I am gone you will see he spends half his time in the households of Lawrence and Hobart. He will need some such model of a man after I am gone."

And my mother's quick reply was: "I do not acknowledge that your death is so imminent as you would make it out to be!" She uttered this denial in her very loftiest tone. Father gave a genuinely hearty laugh. In later years I would always remember Father's laughter more clearly than any other sound of his voice, and to my ears it would always sound derisive. But even if it was sarcastic or uncivil, his laughter was the liveliest and most winning thing about him. Presently they began raising their voices, and I was afraid that Mother was going to cry, though she was a woman I would rarely see give way to tears—even in our long lifetime together. I began sliding down under the piece of cover that had been spread over me, and so managed to block out most of the sounds I heard after that until I heard the door slam behind Father and heard him go down the steps from the side porch. Pulling myself from under the cover I expected a glimpse of him beneath the partially drawn window shade of the sash beside my bed. Again it was his profile I saw. It was nearly always in profile I saw him wherever he was, almost as if he were trying to impress it upon my memory. I remember crossing the Courthouse Square with my nurse (whom he thought I was too old to go about with) and seeing him stepping onto the square from the shotgun law office which Father shared with his father and two other quite elderly gentlemen of the bar. He carried under his arm, as so often he did when I chanced to see him downtown, a great stack of law books. (My nurse told me once that he was known sometimes as "his old daddy's book toter." I did not understand that the word she had heard—without herself understanding or perhaps only understanding in essence—could not have been other than "factotum.") I recall seeing him out in the traffic of the square with the sunlight shining on his head of glossy black hair, parted as it always was in the middle (though that style was very much out of fashion by this time). The part was made by what seemed like a straight, white scar down the center of his scalp, finding its way to the back of his high handsome head of hair and thereby somehow calling attention to his strong jaw and generally to the overall good looks of the man, though suggesting even to his small son something of a past time—especially of the Civil War tintypes in the old albums which my father himself collected.

Very often, though, it was hard for me to recall my father except in the company of my uncles. In my memory, at the age of nine or so (after he was dead), it was not easy for me to disassociate the three men. It was not that I had seen them together so often in the past. On the contrary, I saw them rather infrequently together. They were always so intense about every interest they shared—whether it be current politics or Civil War history or quail shooting or simply their judgments of various friends and acquaintances. They had been close friends since college days. They had matriculated at Vanderbilt University just after the turn of the century, where they had been fraternity brothers and even roommates. It was only by chance that they had been thrown together there, each having hailed from a different section of the state's three Grand Divisions. Father had been born and brought up in the town of Thornton, the county seat of a large cotton-growing county. He was the son and grandson of lawyers and landowners. His grandfather had "taken up" land at the time of the Purchase in that westernmost Grand Division of the state, and his own father had ridden with "old Forrest's cavalry in '63."

Father had met my mother while himself a student at Vanderbilt. I used to be told by friends and neighbors of an earlier generation that even in Father's boyhood there had been wide speculation in Thornton as to whom he might take as a bride. It seems there was nobody quite eligible for a young man of his standing in the entire county or even in the whole Grand Division. I would never know what, in the last analysis, may have had weight in his selection of his bride, though he and my mother thought they had spontaneously fallen in love at first sight. One could but acknowledge that in the daughter of a senator, a senator himself from one of the state's oldest families, Father had, so to speak, met his match. And ironically—perhaps one should say inevitably—a similar account must be given of the marriages of my uncles Hobart and Lawrence. My uncle Lawrence's lineage in Upper East Tennessee seemed to cry out to the daughter of an incumbent governor. One must bear in mind what was most prestigious in that day and age and in that place. And one must also bear in mind the very attractive appearances and personalities of the Governor's three daughters. Uncle Hobart was already courting the Governor's second daughter, Felicia, and it was he who took his former roommate in the college to meet the first daughter. Uncle Hobart had been the first on the scene, no doubt, because he was a native of Nashville and therefore knew the social ropes in Middle Tennessee, which was the most powerful province of the three Grand Divisions. And then finally these two fraternity brothers brought my father to meet the youngest daughter, Gertrude. It was a very happy outcome for all. Or certainly it seemed so in the earliest days of the three marriages. Uncle Hobart and Felicia were soon wed in the West End Methodist Church. (So many people had not yet become Episcopalians in Nashville.) Uncle Lawrence had to wait a year or two before he finished medical school. My father had to wait still longer. Grandfather Nathan Tucker had already been sent to the Senate by the time his daughters were married. But long engagements were not unusual in those days and were scarcely frowned upon at all.

PERHAPS MY FATHER'S love of horses was the thing that in my mind most distinctly set him apart from the other two men. It was the trait which most clearly linked him to his own father. But the love of horses was something that my father also shared with each of his four brothers and to which was ascribed the "ruination" of the four older sons. This was not necessarily the case. They were all enamored of horse-flesh, so to speak, but that was not surprising in view of their father's near fame as one of General Nathan Bedford Forrest's most daring cavalrymen. I would so often hear it said that though my father had followed in my grandfather's footsteps, his brothers had only followed the horses—"the ponies." One after another, Father's brothers had left home, though not to disappear like Cousin Aubrey or the vanished men before him. Someone was always reporting to have seen one or another of them at some racetrack—in Memphis or Louisville or Vicksburg or even New Orleans. Possibly this was why my father's father was at first so distrustful of Father's serious and permanent interest in the study of law. All that "schooling" counted for little with him since he had himself done nothing but "read law" in a certain old Squire Humphrey's law office. Surely that was why he had made my father come home and prove his ability as a lawyer before committing himself to the incumbent Governor's youngest daughter.

ONE OF THE CROSSES that my mother had to bear in her young married life was my father's attractiveness to all the other young females in town. She never told me this herself, but I gathered it from things that were said to me by aging beauties later on in life. And I deduced from all the things they said that his charm lay partly in his aloof manner, indicating that he would never be available to the likes of them, and also possibly could be attributed to his long legs and erect carriage and even the cleft chin that he held so high when he strode across the public square. A good many years later when I knew more about my father, I would wonder to myself if it were not the knowledge of his reformed character that so attracted those girls, for some of them at least must have known that as a young stripling he had for a time imitated the ways of his older brothers and that then at seventeen or so he had given up all girl chasing and bourbon whiskey and even horse racing and had taken his father as his model. He confined himself to his concern for his own saddle horse, which he kept in his father's stable.

UNFORTUNATELY my last two memories of my father were unhappy ones, and alas they both had to do with horses. They still come back to me like dreams, with all the mixed emotions that characterize dreams of my early boyhood. I hear my father's quick steps on the porch as he comes around the side door of the house. From what I know of his ways I assume something unusual has happened. I get up from the floor in the sitting room where I've been lying on the carpet, listening to Mother read *David Copperfield* aloud to me, and simultaneously Mother puts aside her book and rises from the platform rocker which she has been occupying. Possibly she, too, has guessed that something is amiss. Father's habit is usually to enter through the front door of the house and to call to Mother from the front hall. And now he begins speaking even before he opens the screen door from the side porch.

"Two men have spoken to me today," he says, "about the rate of speed at which you were driving my filly through the square!" That's how I remember it, usually in the present tense as the memory begins, and then it slips easily into the real memory of the past.

Mother first gave a challenging little laugh, exclaiming ironically, "How people do talk! That's what it's like to live in a little town like Thornton!" (One has to remember that Mother had lived in Washington for two years with her papa, the Senator.)

Now, it happened that my mother was in her way as fond of horses as Father. She particularly liked driving about in the old-fashioned chaise which Father kept in the shed beside the stable. With me beside her she often went flying along the dirt roads outside of town with both of us singing at the top of our voices, or sometimes Mother reciting poetry. On this day when I was trudging home from school I saw her, with one of my father's sisters as a passenger beside her, come trotting at top speed up the street and then turn into the little driveway beside our house.

It was easy for me to imagine how she would have appeared to the other townspeople who had seen her that day. I remember particularly how she stepped forward and kissed my father on the mouth. But then she quickly stepped back from him and turned away as though she were afraid of him. I recognized a strange fury in the expression on his face, which so often seemed immobile. I saw his two hands were drawn up into fists.

But I'm sure that in his entire lifetime he never struck Mother, any more than he would have ever struck me. He was always too much in control of himself for that. He was too much the reformed perfect gentleman. It was a part of the control he had achieved as a young man. Yet Mother did continue to take several steps backward, as if to be sure she was several steps beyond his reach. I got up from the floor now, and she stood looking at Father as she held my hand close to her side.

"Two different men stopped me on the street today," he said very nearly repeating himself, "to say that they wouldn't let any woman ruin a horse of *theirs!*"

My mother took still another step backward and said, "Indeed! Indeed!"

My father said nothing more except once to repeat her "Indeed!" He only stood there opening and closing his fists in utter frustration, it seemed.

I have another memory of Father during the last year of his life, which I would often call to mind in the years to come. He had already stopped going regularly to his office. He must have lost much weight because I remember how his trousers were looped beneath his belt, which was drawn tightly about his waist. Because of his enforced idleness he was currycombing his own horse in the stable when for some reason the dappled gelding he had just recently purchased turned about and bit him on the upper arm. Without hesitation he hurried off to the house to dress his wound but stopped at the kitchen door to call back to the stable boy not to put the horse away. And when he returned twenty minutes later he tied the beast's halter by ropes from one side of the stable to the other. Then taking up a rawhide whip he proceeded to give him a dozen or so terrific lashes across the buttocks. I remember the horse rearing and snorting and whinnying wildly as he received those lashes and sometimes pawing the earthen floor of the barn.

Recalling my father's frustration, particularly during his last illness and more particularly after he was bedridden, and also later on when I saw his two surviving brothers-in-law, I often thought that the three of them were like veterans of some war that they never got to fight in. They had been brought up, of course, on talk about the glorious days of the Civil War, and they had heard accounts from their older brothers of the fighting in Cuba and the Philippines during the Spanish-American War, and then they had been too encumbered by marriage and children to freely enlist in the First World War. Perhaps they would have pulled up stakes and gone West, except that it seemed too late for all that kind of thing, and now they were too involved in the modern community they knew, and they believed too much in the meaning of history as they and their kind had come to understand it.

AFTER MY FATHER died Mother and I did go to spend time in the households of my uncles Hobart and Lawrence, but life there was never what my father would have expected. At Uncle Lawrence Todd's, the master of the house was seldom to be seen. He was always spoken of as a practicing physician. But one had to suppose that he was always on duty at some house other than his own, and all the while one actually knew that he was indeed on duty at the nearby state penitentiary, where he was retained as physician for the inmates. (I can only guess that it was a political appointment—from my grandfather's hand.) Whereas at Aunt Felicia's house in Nashville Uncle Hobart seldom left the premises. At thirty-five—or scarcely even that—he was already said to be retired from the large wholesale business firm he had inherited from his mother's side of the family. They lived in a rather large stone and stucco house, a pseudo-English style, in the Belle Meade section of Nashville, overlooking Richland Creek.

From their house I used to go down to watch the minnows and frogs that abounded in the rocky creek at the foot of the lawn. When Mother and I were visiting, Uncle Hobart made some show of taking me under his tutelage. We would walk for a little while around the premises, and he would tell me the Latin names of all the shrubs we passed among as we strolled there. Or sometimes after he was dressed for lunch or dinner (Uncle Hobart always dressed in different clothes for each meal) he would take me up to his room and have a little "man-to-man talk." I think this was done for Mother's and Aunt Felicia's benefit—and in memory of Father—and I could never remember anything he said to me upstairs. Principally I can remember the display of clothing to be seen there in the closet and on the clotheshorse in his room. Sometimes there would be a black servant picking up the clothes he had strewn about. What I found most impressive and at the same time most ridiculous were the dozen or so velvet smoking jackets in a far corner of the big bedroom, hung on a rack beside a full-length looking glass.

Since my aunt Felicia had been enamored of fashion and the "great world" of Nashville and Washington, D.C., it was inevitable that when she married, her husband would be a man from that world. Certainly there was never a man more so—more *from* and *of* that fashionable world—than was my Uncle Hobart Washburn. His father had been a Confederate veteran, a Confederate officer, of course, who had gone to Virginia before Tennessee seceded to join Fitz Lee's army in the Valley of Virginia. The late Captain Washburn's distinction in the War had been that he led the first charge at the Battle of Bull Run as well as having been the first Confederate officer killed at Antietam. My uncle Hobart, son of this Captain Washburn, might be said to have spent his life celebrating that victory at Bull Run and mourning the defeat at Antietam.

Uncle Hobart Washburn was also in continuous celebration of his father's wartime friendship with the famous and beloved Gallant Pelham, who fell at Brandy Station, and with that elegant Baron von Borcke, who was wounded at Antietam and was subsequently repatriated to his father's castle in Westphalia. (Daguerreotypes of those heroes still hung on the walls of Aunt Felicia's house, even after Uncle Hobart's deplorable suicide, and I once saw copies on the wall of my uncle's office downtown.) Uncle Hobart graduated from Harvard Law School with highest honors, though he never bothered to take the Tennessee bar exam. Instead he returned to Nashville to marry the daughter of the newly elected Senator, who it was always added (by Uncle Hobart himself) was a descendant of one of the founders of the Lost State of Franklin. He and Aunt Felicia had two little daughters. There was a third child, a son, stillborn. But by that time Uncle Hobart, who was only a medium success as a businessman, could no longer conceal his successive affairs with various low women of the town. The couple had been married only about ten years when my uncle took his own life.

When I went with Uncle Hobart to his room it was easy to imagine him admiring himself there and making decisions about what to appear in at breakfast or at lunch or at dinner. And in the great armoire with its doors thrown open, there was visible row upon row of brown and black wing-tip shoes —each shoe with its own wooden shoe tree inside. (I remember what a problem it became after his death to dispose of so many shoes—along with the smoking jackets and the three-piece suits.) Before dinner when my mother and my aunt and my little girl cousins were gathered in the front living room my uncle would beckon me to come with him, and we would go to the billiard room where, taking two cues from the rack, he would give a minimum of instruction in how to hold a cue, though not instruction in the rules of the game. About what the rules were I never had any idea. Finally he would lead me into the hallway behind the billiard room, which he referred to as his armory. There were the glass-fronted gun racks in which he housed his quite remarkable collection of old guns and pistols, most of them dating from the time of the Civil War. When we were there he was apt to be reminded again about the role his father had played in the War Between the States (he never spoke of it in any other terms). He would impress upon me that his father had fought not with General Forrest or the Army of Tennessee but with the Army of Northern Virginia, and his father had been Chief of Ordnance under General Fitzhugh Lee in the Valley Campaign and under General Longstreet at the Battle of the Wilderness. I think this was meant to imply that the War in Virginia had been the *real* War. Some of the guns, though, were from a more recent time and even quite contemporary.

My uncle had fairly recently been a member of the Davidson County National Guard unit and Chief of Ordnance there. Even the National Guard uniforms were among the pieces of his clothing that had to be disposed of when he died. I took little interest in the guns at the time. But at a later date I did remember that there was a Napoleon gun and a Belgian rifle among the lot, as well as a number of Enfield rifles of the Civil War period. Ah yes, and there was a thirty-pound Parrot gun from those days. After his death—always described as "Uncle Hobart's accidental death"—I could not help speculating upon which of the guns he had used in taking his own life. I could not but believe it had been a certain antique revolver that I saw out of place on the bottom of one of the gun cases.

UNCLE HOBART WASHBURN'S death was something that was never discussed within my hearing. Perhaps that was why it came as a greater shock to me when nearly a year afterward I was told that Aunt Felicia was to be married again. I know that on the night I received this news I had one of my recurring dreams about Cousin Aubrey. It was my mother's silence on the subject of Uncle Hobart's suicide that first made me become objective about the complexities of her character and motivation in a way that I could not have been earlier as a small boy. It may have been merely the silences themselves that determined this. But the fact was that I had reached an age at which I was mature enough to make such judgments of Mother and my two aunts as well. It wasn't that I loved my mother less after this occurred, but that I understood better the two sides of her nature and, I must add, understood the different aspects of my two aunts' characters.

My mother, for instance, in addition to being a very reserved person, was known in the family for her wonderful memory of lines from Shakespeare's plays and her knowledge of other poetry of almost every kind, all of which seemed sometimes out of character for her. She had often accompanied herself on the piano singing old songs from her girlhood for my special benefit. And she had recited great quantities of poetry for me. But not till now had I heard her willingly give recitations for the family group. Though I was always well acquainted with whatever she recited, her recitation seemed strangely unfamiliar and even foreign when given for other ears than mine. There were certain pieces that my little girl cousins would always call for; more often than not they were the very lines I liked least to hear. In fact some of them I found no less than excruciating. It seems probable to me now that they were lines she would have learned in some elocution class when she was indeed a very young lady and even, I can say in retrospect, lines that she might possibly in her time have recited to Cousin Aubrey Bradshaw. Just at twilight one December late afternoon I came upon my cousins and my aunt and my mother assembled in the front room of my aunt's great house in Belle Meade. Mother was in good voice, but what she was reciting was the opening passage from the old poem "Lasca," containing the most painful of all lines to my ears. It was a passage in which Mother's voice assumed a wonderful serenity but which seemed totally foreign to the placid, sweet, comforting mother that I knew. It began:

> "I want free life and I want fresh air
> I sigh for a canter after the cattle,
> A crack of the whip like a shot in a battle
> With the green below and the blue above
> And dash and danger and life and love."

At this point in my mother's recitation I immediately withdrew. I withdrew from Mother and from the other children, my five little girl cousins, and I moved away to the opposite corner of the room. I could not endure the timbre of my mother's voice or the wild, excited look in her blue eyes. But once her recitation had begun there could be no interruption. It was as if another spirit had entered into her body and taken possession. There we were at my aunt Felicia's great suburban house—amongst all the amenities and luxuries of the rich. Mother stood before the assembled guests in her ankle-length crepe de chine dress with her hands clasped demurely before her. She made no gesture, but how vivid for me was the image in that scene now being depicted in the poem:

> "She was as bold as the billows that beat.
> She was as wild as the breezes that blow.
> From her little head to her little feet

She was swayed in her suppleness to and fro
With each gust of passion. . . ."

It was the alliteration and the pounding of those rhymes that somehow destroyed my equilibrium. Even at my tender age it made me sometimes wish to burst into derisive laughter, though it would not be until years later that I could see anything at all comical about the poem. And even to this day I do not know how much humor Mother found in it. As I hurried off to hide myself somewhere beyond the reach of her voice, her high rhetoric seemed to pursue me "like an ominous bird a'wing." Certain lines stirred my emotions into a frenzy, particularly the lines that contrasted my mother's composure and serenity with the passionate nature of the heroine of this poem:

"She was alive in every limb with feeling
Even to her very finger tips.
Little she knew of books and creeds
An Ave Maria sufficed her needs."

I threw myself on the sofa in the far corner of my aunt's living room and pulled one of the hard pillows over my head. I wished to shut out all sights and sounds until Mother's recitation had finished, but I could not quite muffle it. It was as if I were halfway into a deep sleep. I hoped, of course, that my withdrawal would not be noticed, as so often it had not been noticed on similar occasions. I had the image of myself as an invisible being while still in the room with the visible others. But now I felt the arm of my oldest cousin, Josephine, slipping about my waist. I knew that I had been observed and knew that Josephine had tiptoed over to sympathize with me. I sat up and leaned my head against her shoulder and pretended to listen with indifference to what remained of the recitation. Then at last Mother concluded the final passage of the poem. I could not help hearing her:

> "I wonder now why I do not care
> For things that are, like the things that were."

From amidst applause of the other children assembled there—the four little girls who were scattered about the rug at her feet—Mother made her way across the room to where I was. At once I shifted my head from Josephine's bony little shoulder to my mother's warm bosom. And immediately it seemed that my mother's real self had reentered her body. My real mother had returned from her dazzling fantasy and presented her real self to me.

On another occasion the following summer I had a similar experience at my other aunt's house, which was on a farm situated on the outskirts of the small Tennessee town of Petrach. We were all visiting her there, and during the afternoon we gathered on the lawn for a big picnic when something attracted my attention to one of the upstairs windows of the house. It may be that I had looked off in that direction because I knew that Mother was slated to give a recitation that afternoon. The house was a big brick farmhouse built in the style of a Tuscan villa, with wide eaves and a simulated tower at one end. Just as I looked up I saw the tall figure of my uncle Lawrence Todd who I had been told was not at home and would not be present that day.

My aunt Bertie's tastes were different from Aunt Felicia's. Yet she, too, had married the son of a Confederate veteran. His father had been a doctor in the Confederate Army and as such had participated in General Kirby-Smith's East Tennessee Campaign. Though a doctor and a gentleman, his father had been a famously rough character and was greatly admired by Kirby-Smith's staff. As a young man Lawrence had been given to strong drink, and my grandfather had warned Aunt Bertie against marrying him. Uncle Lawrence was, as I have indicated, a medical doctor in the nearby state penitentiary at Petrach, and the hours he had to keep were unpredictable. As soon as I saw his figure in the window I began to move toward the house without any special plan in mind. When I got inside, my uncle's manservant, a prison trustee, I believe, tried to prevent my going upstairs, saying there was nobody up there except some ghosts who might be "scary." I continued, paying no attention to his warning. I found the door from the hallway to the so-called tower room standing open and saw my uncle now stretched out upon his large mahogany sleigh bed that was arranged rather catercorner to the front window. That tower room had a higher ceiling than did the other upstairs rooms and a row of little eyebrow windows across the top near the ceiling and, when stepped down into on entering, seemed a room made for giants like Uncle Lawrence. I had never before been so aware of the chaos and disorder in the room. Perhaps it had not existed on my earlier visits. Several of the big pictures which hung in the upper regions of the room were askew. I don't remember what the other pictures were, but one was a print of the school of Athens with figures of Socrates and Aristotle in the foreground among the throng of people represented there. Perhaps I remember it because some small object had been hurled up against it at one time and the glass had been splintered. But perhaps the print of that painting returns to my mind more readily nowadays because in later years I was destined, when I would be teaching art history at the University of Virginia, to sit before such a magnified version of the same painting. (It hung in a concert hall where my wife and I would attend many a concert and many a lecture.)

I had been able to tell from his tremendous height as he

stood in the deep recess of the high window that it was Uncle
Lawrence. I had recognized him at once by his height, especially by his extraordinarily long arms. He used to brag sometimes about the great height of various members of his family
and about their arms, about the advantage it sometimes gave
them in battle during the War. His family had come from
Upper East Tennessee, near Bristol, where the Solid South
was not so solid, and a good many soldiers had fought on the
Other Side. They were always careful to speak of the Confederacy as Our Side and sometimes of the War for Southern
Independence. His father had fought with General Kirby-
Smith and General Longstreet in their efforts to take East
Tennessee for the Southern Cause. He seemed ashamed, my
father used to say, of the *r*'s that crept into his accent and the
flat *a* sounds, and so he took every opportunity to use the
Tidewater diphthong. But there still remained something always about the *r*'s in his speech and a certain harshness to
remind everyone that no matter how genteel his people, they
were from the mountains.

On the top step, as I was just inside the door, I observed
a broken-down morris chair in the center of the room and a
lamp turned over on the dresser as well as articles of clothing
strewn about the room. More than anything else, I suppose,
I was aware of a quart bottle of whiskey on the floor beside
Uncle Lawrence's bed, and I believe I detected its odor immediately upon entering. Presently he sat up on the side of
the bed, waving his arms about. I particularly noticed that
there were cuff links rattling like castanets in the starched
cuffs of his shirtsleeves. "Come here to me, male child," he
addressed me warmly. "You're the only person I could have
been glad to see here today!" But before he could finish his
sentence I had fled the room and was again on the stairs. I do
not remember seeing the manservant as I left. Outside I found

that the whole party of the picnic had moved down into the orchard beyond the rail fence.

I saw my uncle Lawrence only one time after that, and that was several years after he was certifiably insane. He had long since been committed to the asylum in Knoxville. I spent one long afternoon with him there in my middle teens. During that time he did nothing but make paper birds out of sheets of paper by folding them in a cunning way that he had no doubt learned sometime in his childhood. And it seemed to me then that he expected me to be excited by the process as if I were still some child. . . . As a grown young man I did attend my uncle Lawrence's funeral. I remember that two of the former prisoners from Petrach testified that my uncle had been the best doctor they had ever had, and, as one is apt to say on such occasions, they said they would rather have had him as a doctor drunk than most other doctors sober.

Where we were picnicking down in the orchard there was a strong mountain stream running through the property. I could hear my mother reciting, and I immediately placed my hands over my ears, but I heard her anyway, as clear as could be:

"I sat by her side and forgot, forgot
Forgot the air was heavy oppressed,
Forgot the cattle taking its rest,
That the Texas Norther comes sudden and soon
At dead of night or blaze of noon . . ."

Once again the deafening rhymes seemed unbearable to me, but they went on apace:

"And that once let the cattle at its breath take fright
Nothing on earth could stop its flight.
And woe to the rider and woe to the steed
That falls in front of its mad stampede."

The gathering there actually amounted to a kind of a family reunion. All manner of cousins were present—cousins of every degree and age, and from all over the long state of Tennessee. My mother had been charming to everyone that day with her reserved yet affable manner and her grave, pretty face. I remember how other women kept coming up to compliment her on the "stylish" way she did her hair and on her handsome dress. Her dress, as a matter of fact, was a black moiré and was indeed strange attire to be worn at a picnic. But Mother had a dignity that made all things acceptable, a reserve about her in all matters that her two sisters did not possess. I had heard my two aunts commenting on Mother's appearance that day. Nobody else, so they said, could have "got away with" such attire at a mere family gathering. And they felt that the black garment that she wore attracted too much attention, which, as they said, was "the very worst thing" that my mother, their dear sister Gertrude, normally would wish for. My father had died just two years before, and my aunts felt that Trudie ought to have given up mourning long before this. Actually it was only upon hearing Aunt Felicia and Aunt Bertie say so that I first realized Mother was still wearing black whenever she went out in public.

Because Mother had been widowed at such an early age her two sisters were extremely sympathetic and attentive to her in the first years of her widowhood. They were continually inviting her and her small son for protracted visits with first one and then the other of them. During these visits they sought to provide her with every comfort. They pampered her in all things. My aunt Felicia lived in her splendor in Belle Meade, in suburban Nashville, and was immensely fashionable. Aunt Bertie was relatively poor, but lived in picturesque comfort in the sort of Tuscan-villa farmhouse in the Cumberland Mountains that I have just described. In either of these places Mother was afforded all the comforts and amenities the house had to offer. She was perfectly at home in either place, and she always behaved with such propriety and such consummate thoughtfulness and consideration for others that she was loved equally by the inmates of both households.

WHEN I WAS away at Webb School in Bellbuckle, I was not far distant from my aunt Bertie's farmhouse at Petrach or from Aunt Felicia's place near Nashville. Bellbuckle was much closer to either place than to Mother's cottage in West Tennessee. To visit either of my aunts in those years was a relief from the austere life I knew at Webb School. I was a good student and adjusted quickly to our strictly disciplined existence there. But on my weekend visits to Aunt Felicia's or Aunt Bertie's sometimes Mother would travel over from West Tennessee to meet me at the house of one of her sisters. But it was when Mother was *not* there that I had the most to learn —to learn, that is to say, about Mother herself.

I SUPPOSE THIS was the period when I had my first glimmer of understanding of Mother's nature and of what her early experience had been. In her absence, Mother's sisters would speak sometimes of what she'd been like as a child. Until then it had not occurred to me to think of her as a child. In my mind her relationship with her son was the great reality of her life. The revelation made by her sisters that she had once been the darling of the widowed father gave me an entirely new perspective. The fact that she had once been the well-disciplined wife of such a man as my father, whose stern character began to emerge in the anecdotes told by my aunts, deepened my perspectives further. That was when I came to realize—or at least suspect—that there had been another man in Mother's life. I refer, of course, to none other than her cousin Aubrey Bradshaw, that illegitimate cousin who had declared his love for her when she was but fourteen and he was himself but twenty-one.

I'm sure that my aunts did not set out to enlighten me on my mother's past life. But the two women were inveterate talkers and fond of their own reminiscences, and in the course of many weekends I spent with them they must often have forgot—or not taken into account—my mother's reserved nature. It would not ever have occurred to my aunts that my mother talked not at all to her little son about any other man in her life. My aunts, having no little sons of their own, must have assumed that one spoke just as freely to them as one did to one's little daughters—that is to say, of whatever romance there had been in one's life. In Mother's case, moreover, they would have done well to reflect that in all probability Mother was not one who would have talked more openly to a daughter about any matters than she would have to a son.

In my aunt Felicia's grand suburban house, there in Nashville, was a large portrait of my maternal grandfather painted when he had long ago been Governor of the state. At first glance the portrait looked all black and brown. Then if you peered into the picture for a time you began to detect the flesh tints of the bald head and the scowling face with its drooping, black mustache. And you could faintly make out the more-or-less-white collar and shirtfront and finally below the white shirt cuffs the two hands gripping the brown oaken chair arms. The old portrait in its well-preserved water-gilt frame hung above the sideboard in my aunt's dining room. Below it on the sideboard was placed an enormous silver punch bowl (with embossed silver grapes decorating the brim of the bowl) and a pair of silver candelabra, which pieces had seen use at every entertainment given by my grandfather in Washington.

The heavy oak sideboard with its silver vessels and silver candelabra was unmistakably like an altar beneath the holy icon of my dead grandfather. Somehow from my earliest memory I found that arrangement of picture and ornaments a depressing spectacle. But also I realized early that my aunt Felicia did not find it so. For her the portrait was an object of veneration. But, more than that, it served nearly always whenever Aunt Felicia contemplated it to stir recollections of her own and her two sisters' girlhood under the Governor's protective roof, in the motherless household in which the three sisters had known such happiness together, despite the early death of their mother.

As a matter of fact, at my aunt Bertie's old farmhouse there was a similar arrangement in *her* dining room. But there the portrait of my grandfather was a simple crayon drawing, and on the sideboard were pieces of antique crockery and a blue glass compote dish. The pastel colors in this picture were as cheerful as the blacks and browns in Aunt Felicia's oil portrait were gloomy. In this picture, Grandfather wore a broad-brimmed tan fedora and had his arms folded with a certain casual gentleness over his chest. There was something of a twinkle in his eye and the suggestion of a smile on the lips which his silky mustache partly covered. His mustache and goatee were now white. Clearly this picture was done at a later and happier period in his life, perhaps at the very peak of his career or even just before he died, during his very last year in Washington.

Whenever I stood before one of these two portraits, alongside whichever aunt I was visiting—or sometimes both of them would be present—it more often than not drew some remark about my mother. "Your mother was always Papa's favorite!" Either of my aunts was apt to begin a reminiscence with those words. "Trudie was much the prettiest of us," one of the sisters might say. It was something on which they were in complete agreement. "And, of course, Trudie was the youngest. Possibly her being the baby could, alone, have made Papa partial to her. And then, too, of course, she was named for Mama. But more than anything else—and there's no denying it—Papa favored Trudie because she was smartest of us all." On one occasion Aunt Felicia told me that before she was three years old Trudie "knew her numbers." And she said that before Trudie could read she'd memorized the Beatitudes and "any number" of psalms. "She learned it all from Miss Duncan," said Aunt Felicia, "who was the governess we had for a while after our mama died. But little Trudie learned it because she herself *demanded* to be taught, whereas Bertie and I learned only what we were made to learn and after we were already of school age." . . . It seemed wonderful to me that they were never jealous of Mother. Perhaps it was in part because she was just a little baby still when their own mother died, and because ever after they had felt abnormally protective of her and were able to understand their father's special affection for her.

On the other hand, it would occur to me many years later that on the occasions of those family gatherings at my two aunts' houses both of them were then actually envious of my mother. They were envious because by then their own husbands were either divorced or institutionalized, whereas Trudie's husband, my father, was unalterably, literally dead.

Perhaps all of this accounted in part for the deference and attention they showed Mother during that period. But regardless of that, there was something in Mother's customarily serene manner that made all of us treat her with more deference than we treated other people. Even as a small child I perceived marked differences between her and her sisters—differences in speech and in manner and in their behavior toward others. The three women were each of them highly individual beings.

As is frequently the case with such people they bore little psychological resemblance to other members of their family. It was as though they had been brought up in entirely different environments. Being a child still, I oversimplified this in my observations. I loved my two aunts equally well, the one and the other, almost as much as I did my mother. And my two uncles were at that time, despite their infirmities, the objects of my profound admiration. Yet to myself I said that Aunt Felicia and Nashville were "too fancy," by which I meant too grand and even too pretentious. And I told myself that my aunt Bertie was "too plain," by which I meant that she was too modest in her dress and demeanor. (Even when entertaining the family with the rather elaborate picnic, she appeared not in black moiré but in a gingham dress and apron and did not have her hair done in an elaborate way for the occasion but drawn back tight over her ears.) My mother, on the other hand, except when she was reciting, always seemed the picture of perfect propriety and good taste, one who always struck the right note on any occasion and in any case.

On that day at the picnic, when finally the rest of the guests had departed, my mother sat down on a lawn chair and sipped the lemonade that had been fetched for her. My two aunts, in their striking dissimilarity, walked together at the far end of the orchard near the house. They paced up and down rather energetically and even far down in the orchard we could hear them reviewing events of the afternoon and analyzing the characters of the various relatives who had been present. Mother, on the other hand, had slumped down in her chair, as she often did when she was depressed, and sipped her lemonade. When addressed by one or another of the female cousins, she answered lethargically, clearly exhausted by all the afternoon company. I sat at her feet, and as I looked up into her drawn face I wondered if she weren't about to drop off into sleep. When one of the little cousins asked her to recite the poem "Lasca" again, she at first did not seem to hear the request, and then she burst forth so suddenly it startled me. I sat up from the relaxed position in which I had been leaning against her chair, and I remained there very erect, with my eyes fixed on her—and tense in every fiber of my being. It made my flesh break out in goose bumps to hear the vigor of her voice:

> "Never was fox-chase half so hard run.
> Never was steed so little spared.
> We rode for our lives—
> You shall hear how we fared."

I slowly began pulling myself up from the ground, and when presently I stood beside my mother it seemed she hardly saw me there as she continued her recitation:

> "And what was the rest?
> A body spread itself on my breast.
> Two arms that shouldered my dizzy head
> Two lips that close on my lips were pressed . . ."

I thought I might faint whenever I heard Mother speaking those particular lines. On the present occasion I imagined myself floating out of my mother's presence and away from the little girls gathered about her, as though I was an invisible guest in their midst. As I moved off in the direction of the rail fence at the bottom of the orchard I could hear Mother's voice, and although at this age I felt I knew the lines of the poem perfectly well, I somehow could not bear actually hearing the words from her lips. It was as though she were speaking in a trance, as though she were a medium for some other powerful spirit that I had to hear. And now her words struck terror to my soul:

"And there in earth's arms I laid her to sleep
And just where she's lying no one knows.
But the summer shines and the winter snows
And the little gray hawk floats aloft in the air
And the sly coyote drifts here and there
And the black snake slides and glistens and glides.
And I wonder now why I do not care
For things that are, like the things that were.
Does half my heart lie buried there
Deep in the prairie's soil with her?"

At last I was over the rail fence and had concealed myself in an abandoned and half-rotted woodpile. And I remained hidden in the woodpile until after it had grown dark and I could hear my two aunts and the tremulous voices of my little girl cousins calling out to me again and again, "Hallou! Nat! Hallou! Nat! . . . Come on in! Come on in! It's time to go to bed!"

MY MOTHER'S recitations always affected me this way. They had done so since the earliest times, and they would continue doing so throughout all the stages of my growing up. She was a woman who had almost total recall of almost every poem she had ever read, especially poems she had set to memory as an adolescent, as well as entire scenes from plays she had seen produced by traveling repertory companies when she was a young lady. Sometimes she would tell me how she, her two sisters, and their papa had lived for a time—it was just after their mother died—in the small town of Bristol, on the border between Tennessee and Virginia. In that town two railway lines were joined, the Southern and the N&W, as she always explained in telling me about it, as though it were a fact of great interest. The place *was* an important railway junction in the days when my grandfather brought his daughters there to live. It was there that all travelers going from the Northeast to the Deep South were required to change trains and that most traveling road shows and stock companies would often stay overnight and give a performance at the old Bristol opera house before journeying on to New Orleans. My mother and her sisters were taken there by their papa to see plays they would remember always. My mother would go on recalling lines from those plays until the end of her life.

My mother's sisters did not remember the plays so well as she. It was Mother alone who would forever be quoting lines and reciting entire scenes for me and my cousins. At the time of seeing those plays, however, she—according to my two aunts—had seemed totally unresponsive. Their papa, who was *the* great man in the community, sometimes arranged as a special treat for his motherless daughters that they be taken backstage and introduced to members of the cast. But Mother would actually hang back and even seem reticent about so much as shaking the hand of an actor or actress whom she so recently watched striking some dramatic pose on the stage or heard muttering what for her had obviously been unforgettable lines. I suspect she did not wish to acknowledge to herself the reality of the other moment. And yet twenty years later, when the mood came on her, Mother could delight her nieces (if not her son) by giving a thrilling rendition of those very lines. Tossing back her head of dark brown curls and throwing her lovely hands to her bosom she would exclaim: "Ah, Monsieur, you do me a grave injustice!" As she began I felt my face go warm with blood. I was filled with a fierce resentment of some imagined injustice. "You come to me at this hour of the night," she proclaimed, "and say things to me that my most intimate woman friends would not say to me!" And from the same scene, no doubt: "Ah, Monsieur, a little house in the country with violets leading up to the doorstep! A pretty fancy—just mad enough to tempt me! But for how long, Monsieur? How long? You're just as the old monk said of you at the St. Moritz Abbey. You're the soul of a predatory butterfly! You're the child of the air, of the wind, of the sky! But I am your leaf in the wind! Do with me as you will, Monsieur!" Fifty years later, I myself can still recite those lines and with no idea who the author was or what play they came from, but always when she completed one of these rather bizarre renditions Mother again became the sweet, serene person I knew and could count on for affection.

Ever since my father died, although my mother and I stayed with first one aunt, then the other, occasionally we would remain—just the two of us—for long lonely periods in the isolated cottage which, just before he died, my father had caused to be built for us on a stretch of barren land he owned in the West Tennessee countryside. I do not remember that my mother had ever given a recitation during Father's lifetime. Perhaps in those days she had reserved the recitations for her husband's ear alone. I first remember hearing them during this period when she and I were staying by ourselves at the cottage. And that was not an unhappy time. I was a small child, and she and I had many delightful little adventures together. Once we had passed a happy afternoon strawberry picking at a nearby farm, accompanied only by Mammy. Suddenly on the back porch of the cottage my mother dropped down into her old rush-bottomed chair and began: "Go back, oh Abraham!" She seemed to be addressing neither me nor Mammy. "Go back, I say, for I am thy faithful servant, Sarah! Sir, I have taken nothing that belongs to you. Why do you follow me to the door of my humble tent? Do you think I have taken something, Abraham? See, my hands are empty, as is my heart of all the love I ever bore thee. Go back, Abraham! Do not seek to enter my humble abode!"

Until that moment on the back porch she had seemed her usual serene self, but now again for a time she was estranged from me, and I felt myself alone in that isolated cottage in the dismal stretch of washed-out cotton land.

As I grew older and was sent away to boarding school, during the winter months I would sometimes try to recall passages of poetry Mother recited and try to reconstruct lines from the plays. I half filled pages of my notebooks with fragments that I could not entirely recollect. But it was surprising to me how little of it all I could remember with any accuracy. It was during this time that I developed my first serious interest in drawing and painting, and several times made efforts to do line drawings of my mother's face from memory. I was amazed and annoyed by my total failure to capture anything in the way of physical resemblance or any suggestion of the serious expression she ordinarily wore. There was always some element that seemed to be altogether missing from the picture. Or rather there seemed to be diverse elements that I could not reconcile and which would have made the portrait complete and given it a likeness to my mother. The passages from her recitations that I was able to write in the pages of my notebooks were never those most outrageous and disturbing lines that so often set me racing away to get beyond the sound of Mother's voice. For the main part they were the usual sentimental lines that anybody's mother of that generation might have quoted to her son. They were lines from "Snowbound," or

> The woman was old and haggard and grey
> And bent with the chill of a winter's day

I believe the poem was called "Somebody's Mother." I felt it ought to be called "Somebody Else's Mother," for it did not at all resemble my own.

Perhaps I shed a dutiful, filial, self-indulgent tear as I recorded such lines in my notebook, but in reality they brought no image of my real mother. Rather, the conventional thoughts and images they did conjure up served more to stand between me and any actual image of her. Momentarily I had no perception of what she was like at all, and I felt a sort of self-contempt for my own artlessness, for my own failure, that is, to capture on the drawing board of the lined page whatever my deepest feelings and my true emotions about my mother were. I did not fully understand then that art is long and that a lifetime might be required if I were to derive satisfaction from it.

I'M AFRAID I must admit that within a year or two after Father died he became a rather shadowy figure in my memory, somewhat like that of my maternal grandfather, whom I had actually not seen at all. Sometimes I would go and stand before a large "studio portrait" of him in Mother's bedroom, imagining that if I stared long enough and hard enough my memory of him would come back more clearly. And again, as I have mentioned before, I would sometimes delude myself with the thought that perhaps he had, like those other Tennessee men, only gone away without saying where he was going and that unlike them he would at last come back home again. But I could never capture a clear memory of him any more than I could capture those of my deceased uncles.

By this time I was already making friends among other boys in my class at school. The so-called High School at Thornton, Tennessee, consisted actually of all of the eleven grades of schooling therein offered, and students came from all over the county. Even so, it was a small school by modern standards. One knew students who came there from remote farms and various crossroads in distant parts of the county. One was apt, moreover, to find a great disparity in the ages of students in any one schoolroom, because attendance was not very strictly required or enforced at any age. Country boys and girls frequently dropped out of school for long periods and returned at their parents' convenience, depending on the sowing or the harvesttime for whatever crops were raised. Since Thornton County was then known for its crop diversification the range of ages in each class may have been greater than in most counties. It goes without saying, I suppose, that in all education in our time and place the races were strictly segregated. And so it goes without saying that in the Negro high school, half a mile beyond the courthouse in the square and in the center of town, the disparity of ages was even greater and the total number of students was still smaller. In any case, from the first grade through the eleventh there were small children who because of their remarkable aptitude and performance in the work had received "early promotion" each year or even each term, and there were great, gangling youths and maidens who had been kept home on the farm for as much as half of every term. I am only trying to indicate how wide was the range of my acquaintance by the time, after several extra promotions, I had attained the seventh grade.

When I was first entered in the upper school at Thornton, my aunts Felicia and Bertie warned Mother that I might be slow in adjusting. This was because I had been kept so close by Mother's side so much of the time—especially since my father had died. Whenever I was staying with Aunt Felicia in Nashville or Aunt Bertie at Petrach I observed how frequently the one or the other said to me: "Why don't you run outside and play?" But I would reflect that neither of those good and sympathetic women ever told me what and how to play. That was what I yearned to have them do, so that I might grant their wishes in this as in all other things. Little did they dream that in my head I was playing nearly every moment of the day and night or that sometimes my kind of make-believe was continued in my nightly dreams. The fact is that from an early time I had designated every room in each of their houses (and in my mother's house also) as a separate, sovereign country ruled over by one or another of a variety of figurines or decorative pictures or objets d'art to be found there, of which there was the greatest plenty. Between these ceramic creatures and the like in their separate rooms (or countries) there was a constant state of warfare. In my imagination they fired cannons or were perpetually leading masses of troops against one another. Meanwhile, I sat in my chair (or, in the earliest time, on somebody's lap) listening seemingly with rapt attention as my elders told and retold their same old stories and anecdotes. I had learned the childish phraseology of warfare from books and from the idle talk of my father and my uncles. For this silent play of mine the phraseology was all I needed or wanted—the use of which lasted me for a number of years after all three of those men were dead. But even as a little fellow when I was still saying my prayers at my mother's (or one of my aunts') knees, I would feel the urge to thank the Lord for the warlike vocabulary which I regarded as my chief heritage from my father.

I think I had a very happy childhood, and in my early teens I was always reminding myself of things I ought to be thankful for. It seemed I had only to think of something I wanted or needed for it presently to come to me. I could even imagine that my uncles' and my father's military talk had verily existed so that I could borrow their vocabulary for my daydreaming. I didn't *actually* believe this, and yet in retrospect it would seem so eerily like other fortuitous things that did come my way, as if for the purpose of making my life better, that I could almost believe that it had been arranged by Divine Providence for me.

I went through an especially religious period when I was twelve or thirteen, the last years before I was sent away to Mr. Webb's school at Bellbuckle. And I'm not sure but *that* was why I *was* sent away. My aunt Bertie urged it, saying that Mr. Webb would knock some practical sense into "the boy's head." But Aunt Bertie was rather a skeptic in all matters—especially religious matters. She had observed that Mother and I had been holding evening prayers before going up to bed at night. She told Aunt Felicia that she was embarrassed by it. "No such foolishness," she said, "was tolerated in the house where you and I grew up."

"That's because we were such a race of heathens," Aunt Felicia had replied. "In Papa's house we only believed in politics, as you very well know." Aunt Felicia had embraced Uncle Hobart's preference at the time of her marriage to him, and after his death she began attending what she termed, I believe, the High Anglican church. And I confess that once while visiting her in Nashville I came so under her influence I allowed myself to be baptized in that faith and even on a later visit confirmed by the Bishop.

It was during this period that I began thanking God formally every day for my great good fortune in life. And after my religious zeal had passed I continued to be glad always that my exposure to the rituals of the church came exactly when it did. It is during those years of adolescence that ritual and aestheticism are most useful and most accessible to us. I might never at any other time have appreciated so profoundly the value such experience can have for someone of an artistic temperament, which I was even then beginning to recognize in myself.

When I was in the sixth grade at school, in Thornton, there was a big, robust fellow in our class named Norman Hardiman. Norman must have been nearly six feet in height. His coal-black hair was parted in the middle and usually hung down limply on either side of his wide, high forehead. I realized very soon how closely he watched me when I was reciting in the classroom or how broadly he beamed whenever the teacher commended me for having given the right answer to some question she had asked the class. At recess I soon observed that he had seemed almost to be shadowing me. Particularly when I strolled about along the playground. One day I noticed he was walking some distance from me with a football held loosely under his long left arm. Presently when he caught my eye he seized the ball with his right hand and passed it directly to me. It hit me with its pointed end directly in the chest and fell to the ground before I could receive it. And before I could retrieve the ball from where it had bounced away on the ground Norman had dashed up and swept it into his arms. He trotted a little way with it and then returned to me, saying, "I thought just as much! You don't know how to catch a football or how to play any ball at all!" He looked me in the eye and I shook my head. "Well, I'm a-goin' to learn youans."

· I had never before heard him speak, and I realized afterward that the teacher out of kindness never called on Norman to recite in class. She didn't wish to attract attention to his great height and his generally mature appearance; she feared the other pupils might howl with laughter at his up-country accent and his bad grammar. Yet I think she probably made a mistake in thus shielding Norman. It seems to me that after a few minutes of conversation with him I never again noticed his defections of speech.

That day we went back to a certain nook in the playground and at once he began showing me how to hold and how to pass the ball—this being something that my father had never taken the trouble to show me, or possibly in his short life had never had the time for. Norman went home with me after school that day, and while my mother and my dearly loved and affectionate Mammy looked on with delight and admiration, he began teaching me the rudiments of football.

Other afternoons he came home with me and coached me some in baseball as well as basketball. Finally we even put a basketball hoop above the wide door to the stable. Norman was very businesslike about it all and with the instincts of a good teacher would not let me beg off or slacken my effort until he began to see signs of improvement. Whenever he came to the house my mother and Mammy would first of all make him sit down in the dining room for his big snack, and when he began his long walk home they would load him down with other store-bought edibles. They treated him with such appreciation for what he had undertaken with me, and they looked upon him like some long-lost son of their own. And when it began to grow dark after he had left us late on a winter's afternoon, they would speculate just how far Norman would have got by that time on his way to the Hardiman farm. Though neither of those two women was native to the place (Mammy had been my mother's own mammy over in Middle Tennessee when she herself was a little girl), they nevertheless seemed to know every inch of the dirt roads that crisscrossed the undulating surface of Thornton County. And I suppose that I absorbed by a kind of osmosis everything that I would finally come to know about Thornton County and which would live forever in my memory. If ever one of the two women didn't recognize the geographic point the other made reference to, then the other began to compare it ever so laboriously with some similar point in the geography of that Middle Tennessee county where both of them first saw the light of day. And as a result I soon came to feel that I knew Hamlin County in Middle Tennessee as well as Thornton County in West Tennessee. (And sometimes even, since Mother and Mammy spent much time visiting my aunt Bertie and my aunt Felicia, they would compare other spots in Thornton County with similar ones in Middle Tennessee where my two aunts were then living.) And it was not only all the roads and crossroads they seemed to know. They both seemed to know all the people who lived in Thornton and also those in every other township and precinct of the county. They at once knew who the Hardimans were, where their farm was, and what *sort* of people they were. They judged them as the very best sort of plain country people, which meant that if she went far enough back Mother could and probably would—through Father's family—claim some remote kinship. It meant, to say the least, that the Hardimans were a family that had come over the mountains from Virginia or from Carolina in the earliest days of the general thrust westward at the end of the eighteenth century. And somehow it was through my subsequent association with the Hardimans that I first came to imagine I knew who I myself was. I came to identify with the undulating hills and ridges of that old cotton-growing county which my father's great-grandfather had originally come out of Maryland to help settle and bring under the ax. My father's immediate neighbors and all those I came to know in that section of the county were warm and friendly people and skilled in all the specific agrarian arts and in general all arts of the homestead. I spent many a night under the Hardimans' roof that summer and many a night and early morning at Norman's side hunting raccoon and possum and squirrel. Two or three times I went with him to see a girl he knew on a nearby farm. He told me all about the girls he knew. He was, as I was later on to think, of the earth. He, the favorite of his girls, and I would sometimes keep walking about together in the twilight until Lillian was called in to supper. But I didn't like those times so much at the girl's house.

That fall Norman didn't return to school. I kept looking for him on the playground every recess, but he wasn't anywhere to be seen. Then one afternoon he and that girl Lillian appeared at our classroom door and told the teacher they had recently got married. I remember how the teacher blushed at first and said it was a shame he was giving up his education (she said nothing about the girl's education). Then the teacher got better control of herself and commenced shaking the married couple's hands and saying she was sure they knew what their best interests were. Presently Norman led the girl down the aisle between the desks to the place where I was sitting and told me to get up and kiss the bride. I did as I was told, but I couldn't make myself smile. Lillian was very pretty, and Norman Hardiman looked cleaner than I'd ever seen him before. That was actually the last time I ever set eyes on him for many years of my life, and it was only afterward that I observed to myself that his black hair looked cleaner that day. And the two strands were brushed back off his temple and onto the top of his head in a rather strange but entirely orderly fashion. I knew it was not really true, but I felt I had been supplanted by someone else. It seemed that his pretty young bride was taking him away to a place that defied all imagination on my part.

AFTER THAT I began more and more to play with boys my own age. And when they were choosing up sides for any ball game I found that I was no longer by necessity the last one to be chosen. But of course those games meant nothing to me, and I never thought so for a moment. Looking back on it, though, after I was sent away to Webb School where athletics were much more important, Norman Hardiman emerged in my memory as one of the guardian angels that made everything so much easier about growing up—easier, that is, than it usually was for boys of an artistic temperament. After I became advanced enough to read about someone like Percy Shelley I used to reflect that someone like Shelley brought a lot of his misery upon himself, and I was determined never to allow my classmates to call me "mad Longfort."

This was not to say, however, that I was the less determined to follow my own bent, whatever that bent may be. Another of those people whom I came afterward to look upon as one of my guardian angels emerged from what seemed an unlikely quarter. He was not a member of my family—or not a recognized member (I shall have more to say of him presently). Even before I began going to school I would spend hours of my young life trying to draw some objects and some people that seemed somehow appealing or significant to me. But, as I have indicated, even at preschool age I had been discouraged from this endeavor by my own father. I know now that this father of mine took utmost pride in his own drawings, though they of course were of a very different character from any that I might undertake at such a young age as I then was, and were executed by him for a different purpose, and from a different instinct, even from an entirely different inspiration than my own. My father's education before transferring to Vanderbilt had prepared him to be an architect. He had attended the Naval Academy, at Annapolis, and went on to work toward a graduate degree at the University of Pennsylvania in Philadelphia. He did not obtain his degree there, however, but because of his bad health he came back to Tennessee and took up the study of law as his father had originally wished him to do. He would eventually set up his law practice and take his bride back to his hometown to live. He said to me often and at an early age that I could never be an artist of any kind because I was "totally lacking"—I remember the words to this day, remember them all too well—"totally lacking," he said, "in any kind of manual dexterity!" He had observed this, I can only surmise, through some passing glance he must have made at my clumsy efforts to throw a ball or to catch one thrown to me (this before the days of my friendship with Norman Hardiman, of course) and which in my memory he never made any effort to improve or correct. But he was a well-intentioned father, or so I've always been told, and so I still believe. It was just that during his last years and during *my* early years he was always too preoccupied with his bad health to be attentive to anything other than the rapid decline of his ever-worsening condition.

That other person who emerged in this period as one of my guardian angels was a Negro boy who came to be my constant companion and playmate before I was sent away to Webb School. His name was actually the same as that of my own father and later as that of my son, Braxton Bragg Longfort, though he was always called simply BB. After I was grown my mother told me that he was thought to be the natural son of one of my paternal grandfather's brothers, who —like that paternal grandfather—had served under General Bragg at Missionary Ridge. At any rate his own father had formerly cleaned the stalls and fed the horses and milked the cows in Father's stable, and BB's mother was currently our washwoman, who came one day a week to do the washing on the back porch and hang it out to dry on a line in the backyard. I first got to know BB when Hazel, his mother, brought him along with her on wash day. He was an extraordinarily smart boy, and everyone recognized him as such.

Mother especially saw BB's intelligence and encouraged me to make friends with him. I soon looked forward to wash day on Thursday, and it wasn't long before I was discouraging my white playmates from coming to play on that day. When Mother took notice of this she asked me accusingly if I was ashamed to have them see me with BB. If so, she assured me, it was the purest nonsense on my part. There was such good understanding between Mother and me that I was shocked by any such suspicion from her. And so I confessed, a little belatedly perhaps, what it was I liked about BB's exclusive company on Thursdays. BB had been away in St. Louis that previous winter, staying with one of his aunties, because the Negro schools were thought to be so much better than the one at Thornton. He had music lessons there and could easily be persuaded to play Chopin on the box piano in our parlor. Better still, so far as I was concerned, he had received art lessons at his school. And from the very first time that he accompanied his mother on wash day he brought along his sketch pad to while away the hours when his mother was doing the washing in tubs on our own back porch.

Seeing what great interest I took in his drawings and sketches, BB generously tore out pages from his pad for me to use and gave me a choice of pencils from his pencil box. And excited by this enthusiasm of mine, Mother wasted no time in getting off a mail order for pads and pencils for me and even watercolors and pastel crayons for the use of the two boys. BB and I had a fine summer sketching, drawing, and painting together. He happened to pass on to me all the fine points that he had been taught in his art classes in St. Louis. He could repeat the exact words of his teacher with regard to shading, perspective, and such things as the vanishing point.

I believe he was the most generous and perhaps gentlest spirit who had until this time come my way—certainly so among any of my contemporaries in the town of Thornton. His modesty and his consideration were by any measure far beyond anything I experienced with my classmates. And yet there was nothing servile or weak in his makeup.

Once he and I were doing watercolors over in the pasture where Father's saddle horses had formerly grazed. There came a little gust of wind which simultaneously blew both our work sheets away across the meadow. BB was quick to run after them, and when he had retrieved both sheets and brought them back to our little encampment there he didn't immediately return my effort to me but momentarily pretended that he could not distinguish which was his and which was mine. And all the while, of course, his use of color and his skill at drawing were patently superior to anything I could attempt at that age. Another time when he was sketching in the back of the house, near my mother's kitchen garden, I was threatened by a hornet that was buzzing about my head and that I was too absorbed in my drawing to take notice of. Presently the hornet was just alighting on the back of my neck when BB, who had been keeping an eye on my would-be predator, shoved me backward to the ground out of harm's way. But suddenly now the angry insect struck home to BB's cheek, just below his eye. Clambering up from the ground I saw he had thrown a hand up to his cheek and eye and with one foot stomped out the life of the hornet which he had knocked from his cheek and into the grass. But he seemed actually stunned by the painful sting. I seized him by his free hand and quickly led him at a trot across the yard to the garden where Mother was at work among her flowers. Mother at once drew off her cotton work gloves and seated herself on the little folding chair that she always kept nearby to rest on when she was working there. She put her arm around BB, and pulling his hand away from his face she examined the area of the sting and made a try at pulling out the stinger. Presently she said, "Come with me, child!" Then together we ran to the screened-in back porch where Hazel was washing clothes. Hazel quickly dried her hands and tried to make sure Mother had got the stinger out, while Mother ran to the kitchen door to bring the baking soda. After the two of them had finished doctoring BB, Mother helped gather his pencil and papers and then insisted on taking him and Hazel home in the car. It was the week after that that I went for the first time to spend a night at BB's house. I went there to spend the night a good many times afterward. And it became for a time my favorite habitation away from my own house. I liked BB's neighbors quite as well as my own and felt that I knew them as well.

As at Norman Hardiman's house there was no inside plumbing at Hazel and BB's. The family there always spoke of the privy as "the Christmas tree." On my first visit when we had been playing up and down the dusty street with the other Negro children and had been around the corner to Mammy's place (where we found nobody at home), we then came back to BB and Hazel's to get a drink of water from the well beside the house. And I remember Hazel's calling to us out a side window, "Does one of you need to go sit on the Christmas tree?"

He answered her impatiently, "We're not any little tykes, Mama, we can go when we need to." I didn't know what Hazel meant that first day, but I soon learned. And it seems to me in retrospect that I spent many happy hours sitting in the privy with the door open, sometimes talking to myself about whatever I was playing in my mind. Sometimes when I had closed the door, Hazel's old yellow cur would yap to be let in with me, just to keep me company. Or Snow White, the cat, seeing the door closed would come and reach a long foreleg and paw along the floor under the door for me to make a game with my toe or a switch if I had one. But when the door was open, as it usually was, family members and even neighbors would pass by without so much as paying me any mind, and I could sit there blissfully looking into Hazel's cotton patch all the way to the picket fence that divided it from Mammy's patch, which was just around the corner on the dusty street next to BB and Hazel's.

Those are the kinds of things that someone who thinks he's going to be an artist or a poet remembers. Or perhaps I should say that someone who remembers things like that instead of the usual important things finally settles for becoming a painter or a poet because there is nothing else he can do with that sort of mind. When I now look back on my early years at Thornton I usually cannot easily recall the names of my so-called peers that I went to school or Sunday school with. They were nice enough people, but when by chance I happen to meet one of them nowadays—even those who came to my house every day or so and whose houses I went to just as frequently—I have to make a big effort digging back in my memory for the name. It is as though I were in the cemetery digging up a dead body, and when my effort is successful there is somehow no thrill in it. I was not unhappy with my usual schoolmates at Thornton, but when I came home after my term at Bellbuckle it was BB and Norman that I asked about. By that time BB had gone to stay with his father to continue his schooling up there in St. Louis. And Norman Hardiman and his wife had moved away and left no trace of where they were. It was a place and a life altogether beyond my ability to imagine.

But at Webb School there were plenty of other boys of

the kind I generally ran with at home, and they were nice enough boys, too.

It is only in looking back that I sometimes say that I was brought up by the three daughters of the late Senator Nathan Tucker. I would not have said so at the time when I was growing up. I had no question in my mind then about who my mother was. It is only in a manner of speaking that I say so to some stranger nowadays—some stranger who has had some acquaintance with my two aunts and has known something about them. And it was so that after my father died my mother saw to it that I spent time in each of the households of my uncles when my uncles were no longer there. I wonder if my mother would have been so scrupulous about my father's wishes if my uncles *had* been present still. I shall never know. I can only speculate. I don't believe she reckoned either of the uncles a real horror, any more than she reckoned the same of her own husband. As for my aunts, she never made judgments on them. I was left to make my own judgments if I chose to do so. One of my father's wishes, which she acknowledged and acted upon (and also by the urging of my aunts), was to see that I be sent away to Mr. Webb's school. However painful it was, Mother entered me there just as she had promised she would. At Bellbuckle, as I have said, I was about equidistant from my two aunts' houses, and Bellbuckle was a much better place to meet Mother than the cottage in West Tennessee.

Once when I was visiting at Belle Meade soon after my aunt had returned with her second husband, I stayed up much later than it was intended I should. Ordinarily I stayed up later there than I would have at school or at Mother's house, but Aunt Felicia never bothered about how late I might amuse myself with my reading or my sketching or even listening to my radio after I was sent up to bed.

Aunt Felicia's second marriage lasted only about three months. And had I been a little more precocious than I was I might have predicted as much. One night after I was already in bed with a book, I heard loud voices. I did as I had often done before. I clambered out of bed to close the register to the hot-air vent that came up to my room from downstairs by way of the front living room which was situated just below me. I did so in order to shut out the distracting sound of voices that entered the room through my register. There had been a dinner party down there, but the sounds that came up from the general conversation had not been so distracting as those that came now. All at once I recognized the assembled party had dispersed, and that the only voices I heard were those of Aunt Felicia and the new Uncle Lucius. I listened for a moment and abruptly shut off the register to prevent my hearing more of what was being said. What I had already heard were the angry voices of my aunt and young uncle. Somehow it was only at that precise moment that I realized how much younger he was than she. I suppose I had been somewhat disturbed by my aunt's having acquired a new husband so soon, but I certainly did not wish to know the details or the subject of any quarrel they might be having. In addition to shutting off the register I had managed to pull a small throw rug over the grating and turned on my bedside radio. With the volume of the radio turned up I climbed back into bed and began reading again. When my aunt came up to my room some thirty minutes later she seemed entirely self-possessed and even in high good humor. "You, you rascal, you book-worm, you jazz hound," she exclaimed all in one breath and with a wide smile on her lips. I quickly switched off the radio and lowered my book. "I guess you'll go on reading half the night," she said teasingly, "and so I won't even suggest that you put out your light." She came and sat down on the corner of my bed, pulling the book a little closer to her. "Ah, Thomas Nelson Page," she intoned. And then: *"In Ole Virginia*, ah, how he loved them—your uncle Hobart."

"I found it in the library," I said. "It has his name in it."

As she leaned back against the footboard she smiled radiantly at me. I could see she wanted to talk. It was hard to believe it was the same person whose voice I had heard through the register. Again there was great warmth in her smile as she commenced to reminisce. "His favorite stories were 'Marse Chan' and 'Uncle Edinburg's Drownin'.'" She sat there talking to me at great length about the library Uncle Hobart had inherited from his father. Evidently I didn't listen to her very intently after that, though I do know it was all about Uncle Hobart and the pleasure he had taken in the recollection of his boyhood days and his young manhood even when she first knew him as a student at Vanderbilt. "And how proud he would have been of you," she went on as though he were someone I had not known at all. But what I was thinking about meanwhile was how her face lit up as she talked of him. Though she was Mother's older sister she seemed at the time a much younger woman than my mother. I remember she was wearing a blue velvet dinner dress with silver brooches at each corner of the square neckline. There was a luminescence in her eyes that neither my mother's nor Aunt Bertie's eyes ever possessed. In my immature mind I reflected that it was no wonder that Uncle Hobart selected her above the other two girls when he first came calling at the Governor's suite of rooms at the Maxwell House. That night particularly she seemed to laugh adoringly at everything I said even when it was not my intention to be amusing. "Sometimes you seem so like Hobart, though you don't have a drop of his blood in your veins," she said, and then we both laughed aloud. And even now I can recall how pearly white were her teeth when she laughed this way with me.

At other times on other visits to Aunt Felicia's house she would pull out old photographs of her own papa when he was a lad my age and say how very much I did resemble him as he had looked at that age. However different my mother and her two sisters were from one another they always seemed to speak of their papa with one voice, and always there were suggestions of how I reminded them of him. Mother was scarcely ever critical of Aunt Felicia, but she would say of her three marriages that, alas, she was always trying to re-create the image of Uncle Hobart in each subsequent husband. I would later acknowledge this in light of the only outburst of Aunt Felicia's which I was present for and managed to overhear. It occurred on one of my visits to Belle Meade and after Aunt Felicia had been married to her third husband, Uncle Harold, for more than a year. Uncle Harold was as much older than Aunt Felicia as Uncle Lucius had been younger. Their lack of interest in me was most obvious from the way they constantly ignored my existence when I was about the place. I knew very early in each case that my presence in the house was not something they wished for. My aunt's two little daughters caused her husbands no discomfort. That was another matter. But there was more than just me they would have liked to dispense with.

One year at the time of my much-heralded spring visit to Belle Meade, Mother had journeyed ahead of me from Thornton and was present at my aunt's house before I arrived there. The fact was that she was there to meet my train when I arrived from Bellbuckle. I was much amused to discover her waiting in the uncovered front seat of my aunt's town car. The chauffeur had not turned up for work that morning, and

Mother had come herself at the wheel of this car that she had never driven before. I threw my bags into the backseat and embraced Mother with special affection. I was amazed along the way at her fumbling with the gears and the choke and the other alleged aids to locomotion. It was before we turned into the Belle Meade house that she gave me some idea of the unpleasantness that had been going on that morning between Aunt Felicia and Uncle Harold. "All is not well between the newlyweds," she said. And just as we turned up the driveway, here came Uncle Harold in his sedan, packed to the roof with all his possessions, going off on the shoulder of the driveway in order to pass us—himself not once looking up in our direction. When we came in view of the house there was Aunt Felicia on the front lawn carefully examining some flowers she had planted there, or making a show of doing so. As we drove up she beamed at the sight of us—that is, at the sight of us with Mother at the wheel and me there beside her. When I alighted from the car and ran toward her to embrace her, she threw out her arms to me and gave no sign of having been disturbed by Uncle Harold's departure. We went into the house together with me lugging my suitcase and my large portfolio of drawing paper, which I so laboriously took with me everywhere. "Doesn't he look like his father," Mother said rather solemnly, "that big chin and all!"

"Well, I suppose so," my aunt said without much enthusiasm. Presently I was allowed to take my "things" up to my room. Though I wasn't in the habit of eavesdropping, today I consciously made a point of not shutting off the register when I entered my room and closed the door. It had already occurred to me that Aunt Felicia had made no reference to having just sent Uncle Harold packing. I heard my mother's voice in the register saying, "He's gone?"

"And he won't be back," said Aunt Felicia. "You wouldn't

believe it but the last thing he said was: 'I shall return when you have removed that portrait of Hobart from up above the mantel and that portrait of your dear papa from the sideboard in the dining room.' " There was a moment's silence and then she said, "He'll have a long wait." Almost instantly I heard her follow this with her merriest peal of laughter, though there came no sound from Mother. "If he ever does return," my aunt presently added, and I'm not sure it wasn't for my benefit upstairs, "he'll find a portrait of my beloved nephew hung across the dining room from Papa and the sideboard. He can count on that!"

I didn't daydream about the teenage portrait of myself that was to be. Rather as I lay there in bed, I saw before my eyes, as if there on the ceiling, that portrait of my grandfather downstairs.

MY AUNT BERTIE'S tastes were altogether different from Aunt Felicia's. Yet she too, of course, had married the son of a Confederate veteran. And as I have said earlier his father had been a doctor in the Confederate Army and had served in General Kirby-Smith's campaign in East Tennessee. Though a doctor and a gentleman, he had been a famously rough character and was greatly admired by General Kirby-Smith and his staff. My uncle, the doctor, was also a very rough character. As a young man he had been given to strong drink, and my grandfather had warned my Aunt Bertie against such a union. But whereas Aunt Felicia was attracted to the fashionable world, Aunt Bertie was drawn to outdoor life, to horseback riding, to camping trips. Once, soon after they were married, she and Uncle Lawrence went off together on a camping trip in the Tennessee mountains and were missing for so many days that searching parties were formed and sent out to find them. They were keeping house, so to speak, just inside the mouth of a cave. Far inside the cave Uncle Lawrence had fallen down into a deep crevice. He had broken his leg just above the knee and broken several toes on each foot. His bride had managed to drag him up and out to near the entrance of the cave and tried to keep him warm with a fire she built there. It was speculated that Uncle Lawrence had taken along a great quantity of booze and no doubt had been drinking when he slipped. (It was Aunt Felicia and Uncle Hobart who told me about all this long afterward, speculating in my presence about the drinking.) Aunt Bertie and Uncle Lawrence had collected several bags of Indian arrowheads on their hike into the mountains and had deposited them at the cave's entrance. They had shared portions of the arrowheads with two mountain men who happened along with the understanding that they would report their plight and send someone with a stretcher to bring them back. But their plight went unreported, and it was a number of days before a searching party found them. From all I have heard, such adventures were part and parcel of the life Aunt Bertie lived with Uncle Lawrence. He was said to be a splendid doctor when sober, but after a few years his drinking destroyed his practice everywhere he went. That was when he took the position as prison doctor at Petrach. Nobody seemed to mind very much the drinking he did there, and he found he rather liked than disliked treating the rough inmates who were sent to him as patients.

From the very beginning my uncles Lawrence and Hobart had been specially congenial. What they had most in common was, of course, their great interest in the Civil War. Over a period of several years they made expeditions to the various battlefields. Sometimes my own father accompanied them, sometimes not. With them there was a certain snobbishness about which command one's father had and had not fought under. *My* father's father had fought under Forrest and under Bragg. I'm sure that was not considered so honorable as to have been with Longstreet or Fitz Lee. On several occasions I paid extended visits to Aunt Bertie's at Petrach. It was when I was twelve that Uncle Lawrence Todd was finally institutionalized. He was sent to the insane asylum at Knoxville. Aunt Bertie was left with three little girls to support. It was, of course, a very difficult time for her, especially since she insisted on keeping her daughters in Belmont School for girls in Nashville, where Aunt Felicia's daughters were enrolled as day students. Through some sort of influence dating back from the days of her father, I suppose, she was appointed postmistress of Petrach. Though her supervision of affairs at the post office and her attendance there were very irregular, I can but suppose it was some kind of government sinecure she received, for I know that when I would be visiting there her presence was not required every day. Since Mother remembered very well what a poor student Bertie had been in school, she took little stock in the so-called appointment at the post office. Whenever Mother and I were there together, Aunt Bertie was to be found working among the flowers and vegetables in the garden. Watching her from the back porch, Mother would say to me, "Bertie has buried herself in the garden since Lawrence went to Lion's View."

When I was alone with my aunt, I often as not worked right along beside her with my hoe. At those times she would talk to me about my uncle as though he were functioning normally in the institution and would presently be home for supper. Perhaps it was not that way, but that was how I seemed to understand it at the time. Since I had a bad bruise on my shin and complained of it, Aunt Bertie without looking up from her own row would say, "I'll ask Doctor Todd to look at it next time he's with us." Then she did look up and give me a wry smile. She was kindness itself to me and always seemed delighted to have me visiting. "It's nice to have a man about the place," she often said to me. "And I suppose this is what it would have been like to have your own grandmother, which I never had." One night when we were alone together there we were sure we heard somebody moving about downstairs. She fetched an old Winfield rifle for me, and together we got it loaded. Meanwhile she had taken a loaded revolver out of her pine chest of drawers. She proceeded down the back stairs while I went down the front stairway. Presently she called out, "Is that you, Doctor Todd?" She often addressed him as Doctor Todd, as was the way of a generation before her own. When we had got downstairs and had found no one or no trace of any intruder, she pretended to laugh and said she only called out "Doctor Todd" to make the intruder imagine there was a man in the house or that one would be expected home soon. But I was not sure that was the case. My uncle often had to make calls on patients other than his prisoners after all the rest of the family was in bed. "Not everyone knows that he is gone," she explained, "and that I am home alone." I didn't tell her that as I came down the front stairway it occurred to me to ask myself what if she and I with our loaded weapons should mistake each other for the intruder and shoot each other. After we got downstairs and the scare was over we relaxed in the kitchen, and she made us cups of hot chocolate over the few embers that remained in the range. She told me how on other nights it really had been Uncle Lawrence, coming home at a later hour than was usual, and how he would shake his head over the thought of some poor dying creature he had seen that night. And he would have, as she said with a bitter smile, something stronger than *this* just to bolster his spirits. She admired and loved him still, and she would stand by him always. Even in the past when there had been clear signs of abuse—a blow or a slap across the face, as I had heard my mother point out—Aunt Bertie spoke no word against her husband.

I MAKE NO COMPLAINT of the companions and the life I had at Bellbuckle. I was a fair scholar and behaved myself, and so I got no thrashings from Mr. Webb or any of the other masters. I learned to wash my face in a washbasin of cold water every morning at 6:00 a.m., and I learned to conjugate I can't tell you how many Latin verbs. Mostly though, I think, I learned how many Tennessee and Kentucky boys there were who had for some reason or other to be sent away from home to obtain a good schooling. The best part of the weekends and holidays were spent with Mother in Thornton or at one or another of my two aunts' houses.

Otherwise, my years at Webb School were a nonperiod of my life, as for that matter were the four subsequent years in Sewanee. Perhaps this is true for all layers of higher education for almost anyone. Perhaps one is learning all these years that one must conform, or drop out and disappear from the familiar world. Looking back, I could see the tragedy was that I had learned that I *could* conform. The worst of it for me was that I had learned too early that I was *able* to do so. For six years I had, or so it would seem to me afterward, buried my head in the sand without coming up for air. It seems to me now that during those years there were only four real events for me. They were the funerals of my two uncles and my two aunts. At each of these events Cousin Aubrey made his covert reappearance.

Uncle Lawrence's funeral was held at Aunt Bertie's house with the local Presbyterian minister presiding. We were all present. Aunt Felicia along with my new uncle Lucius, in fact, came by way of Bellbuckle to pick me up and take me with them in their car to Brush Mountain. It took us longer to make the trip than it took the hearse to travel a much shorter distance, and so other mourners had already arrived at the house before we even got into town. The chauffeur, who was recently employed, had some difficulty in finding the house. And even Aunt Felicia was uncertain of how to get there, though she had, of course, been there a good many times before. Actually it was I who finally had to tell the driver what turns to make and in what direction and how far to go. Aunt Bertie's farm was on the edge of the small town, and as a little boy I had rambled all through the neighborhoods of the town—enough to feel myself very much at home in the place. I remember I felt quite exultant when we came to the big two-storied brick house with the black hearse and numbers of other cars parked in the front yard. It was, just as I had predicted to the driver, situated on a stretch of dirt road just beyond the point where the town asphalt paving ended and with an old-fashioned hitching post near the front gate. People were already on their feet singing a hymn when we went into the front rooms and hallway, where the rows of little wooden folding chairs were set out.

Aunt Bertie herself greeted us at the front door and kissed the three of us. At once Aunt Felicia began explaining in a whisper why her two girls—now quite grown-up—couldn't be present. Aunt Bertie kissed *her* again and then pointed out Mother to me. Mother was seated in the front row close to the casket and with an empty chair beside her, obviously reserved for me. As I went on tiptoe down the center aisle, arranged between the folding chairs, my attention was somehow caught immediately by the dark head of hair of a man sitting three or four rows behind Mother and on the opposite side of the aisle.

Even before I saw his face I knew instantaneously and with utter assurance that he was someone I had known. Before I sat down beside Mother I had got a glimpse of the unfamiliar and yet at the same time indubitably familiar features of that face. It was the expression in the eyes that was absolutely familiar. I was in my chair beside Mother before I could say the name or positively identify the resentment and even malevolence I read there. But then before there was any greeting between us I whispered in Mother's ear: "Have you seen Cousin Aubrey! He's back there!" Without looking at me and without making any pretense of even glancing over her shoulder but rather looking straight ahead at the casket, Mother said under her breath: "Nonsense! What a child you are still!"

And yet when the funeral service was over and the members of the family were invited by the minister to leave the room first, I could see Cousin Aubrey nowhere and could not even locate the chair on the aisle that the man must have hastily vacated. Among the handful of people at the graveside in the cemetery Cousin Aubrey was not to be seen, and when the family had returned to Aunt Bertie's house afterward, I asked each of my three cousins present that day—Aunt Bertie's daughters—if they had noticed the man with the black beard. But they had not even seen him. Mother overheard me asking Letitia, the youngest of the three, and shook her head at me severely. Before I departed for Bellbuckle she made an opportunity to tell me that it was not nice on such an occasion as this to be imagining and talking about "spooky things" that brought back unhappy memories for everybody. It had not until then occurred to me that it was anything like a ghostly apparition I had seen. And I believe it wasn't. But it did occur to me then that it might all have been in my head. And that possibility worried me even more than any real look of resentment or malevolence could do. It set me to trying to deal again with the old stories of disappearance so often heard by me as a child.

On our way back to Bellbuckle I found myself trying to steer the conversation to that subject. I got no response from Aunt Felicia. She seemed somewhat abstracted by the events of the day and even a bit bemused. My new uncle Lucius fell in with my scheme, however, and gave liberally with anecdotes on the subject I was angling for. What I noted first was the coincidence that I had heard most of his stories before and that they had come to me from Uncle Hobart, his predecessor as Aunt Felicia's husband. But I fully understood that Uncle Lucius and Uncle Hobart had grown up together in Nashville and had been fraternity brothers (Phi Delta Theta) at Vanderbilt. And what I realized that day was that probably all of Aunt Felicia's husbands had to be cut of the same excellent cloth. She was destined to have only one husband after Uncle Lucius—Uncle Harold—but he was indeed cut of the very cloth of his forerunners. And he might easily have passed on to me the exact anecdotes I had heard that day in my aunt's car. I think they might properly have been said to be typical Nashville anecdotes. At any rate, among Uncle Lucius's memoirs was that very banker in Nashville who left the office in the middle of one afternoon, without so much as taking his hat and cane, and whose whereabouts would not be known by anyone in Nashville for more than twenty-five years.

When my uncle Lucius had finished that story I noticed that my aunt sighed and that her eyes misted over. "It is a very sad story," she said. And I cannot help thinking now that Aunt Felicia had heard this story a good many times before—perhaps from Uncle Hobart as well as Uncle Lucius. And likely as not she would hear it, or stories much like it, from Uncle Harold within the next two or three years. Because Uncle Lucius died the next summer, and Aunt Felicia was widowed less than a year before she took to herself a third Phi Delta Theta. . . .

When I got back to Webb School at dusk I was too late for the early supper they had there, and I was happy to climb right into my little cot and slip between the sheets that I had made up that morning. I didn't go to sleep for a long time, though. I lay there on my back until total darkness fell and the other boys came trooping into bed. I was thinking about the sad occasion of the funeral. The funeral had been a rather happy time for me, seeing my mother and my aunts and my affectionate cousins and my aunt's old farmhouse which I remembered so fondly from earlier visits there. What kept me awake and mystified me were the thoughts about the man who had gone away without taking his hat and cane with him. It really frightened me to think of how much I identified with him and how happily I pictured in my mind the place where he might now be living. It even occurred to me then that I might someday wish to make a move for myself, and I doubted even then that I would find the energy, the motivation, the courage it would require.

These were years when funerals seemed nearly the norm for our occasional family gatherings, both when I was at Bell-buckle and later when I was at Sewanee. I soon taught myself never to think of the dead person in the coffin but only of the warm living souls by whom I had been surrounded when I was growing up.

I sometimes find it hard to believe or realize that during the period of six years everybody but my mother had been swept away. Only my five young lady cousins survived, and three of them were already married by that period. They made but little effort to keep in touch and very rarely attended the various funerals, except in the case of their own mother's. But *I* was always present, along with my mother, of course.

The only thing that seemed in the least extraordinary about all this funeral business was Mother's insistence upon attending the funerals of her sister's three husbands and her insistence on my meeting her in Nashville for those services. But Mother had had a genuinely sisterly affection for her brothers-in-law and had maintained to me that in the instance of each divorce the uncle concerned had not been entirely culpable in the charges of infidelity that Aunt Felicia brought against him. Mother never explained further than that. But my mother was a woman of a puritanical nature, and at the same time was given to great flights of fancy. She was a person whose literary bent and ambitions for a career on the stage had been thwarted early in life by the conventions of our world. Of her older sisters and of Aunt Felicia's husbands she was alternately and sometimes simultaneously adoring and disapproving.

I must mention that at Aunt Felicia's funeral, at Grace Church in Nashville, I saw again in the congregation someone that I believed I recognized as the vanished Cousin Aubrey. The church was crowded with Nashville socialites and other persons of local consequence and prominence. It seemed to me that just before the service began I saw the familiar bearded man being led in by one of the ushers. He was being seated in a folding chair among other similar chairs which had been placed at the chancel in order to accommodate the overflow crowd. At first I discounted what actually I saw plainly enough. I told myself that it was only predictable that I should have imagined I identified just such a man here today, since at previous family funerals I had momentarily and quite mistakenly (according to Mother) made such identifications. "Look there in the chancel," I whispered to Mother. "Is that you-know-who?" But she disabused me at once. She craned her neck and let her eyes roll over the faces up there. Then she settled back into the pew, cutting her eyes at me and shaking her head as at a nuisancy or too playful little boy. Aunt Bertie was seated on the other side of me. She had ever been the most trusting and unquestioning of the three sisters. When I looked at her with my question she said by way of reply: "Ask your mother. I see who you mean, but I don't know." She clearly didn't care. It was not till a year later at the funeral of Aunt Bertie herself, and in the Presbyterian church at Brush Mountain, that I could feel really sure. I made certain I was the first person out of the church when the service was over. I was a pallbearer, but I told the undertaker in charge that there was a relative from out of town whom I must see before he drove off to Nashville. I could feel my mother's critical eye on me as I hurried up the aisle before the coffin or anybody at all had passed through the front portal. When they had brought the coffin out on the stoop and down the flight of steps, I helped them lift it into the waiting hearse but told them that I had not yet found the Nashville relative and that I would have to meet them at the town cemetery. When I turned around there stood Mother with Aunt Bertie's daughters and their three husbands. Without allowing my eyes to meet Mother's, I hurried inside the church.

He was standing there alone, waiting for all the family to be gone before venturing out. I met him halfway down the aisle. He was carrying his homburg hat but had already pulled on his overcoat with its fur collar. My first thought was how very prosperous he looked. "Do you recognize me?" I greeted him in the most affable of tones.

He didn't hesitate a second to say what he did say. And he kept his eyes fixed somewhere up on the choir loft at the back of the church. "I never saw you before in my life," he said flatly, "and this is not an occasion for making new acquaintance." He made a gesture as if to put his hat on his head but instead drew the hat back to his side, and stepping quickly around me he made his way up the aisle to the entry doors which still stood open and allowed me to see how quickly the funeral party was moving away.

I drove my own car through the town to the cemetery, and when I got there I could see Cousin Aubrey Bradshaw wasn't going to join us. I didn't offer to drive Mother or anyone else back to the house. Instead, I rode around town for twenty minutes or so. Perhaps I thought I might discover him somewhere. But I'm not sure what was on my mind except that it occurred to me once that I might just keep on going after I got to the edge of town and not come back to the gathering of mourners which was sure to be at my aunt's house afterward.

I did go back to the house, though, and there in the familiar living room, crowded with fifteen or twenty of Aunt Bertie's neighbors, stood Cousin Aubrey, still with his hat in hand and still wearing his fur-collared overcoat. Mother was nowhere to be seen, and immediately I went back to the kitchen to find her. I asked her at once with a certain naïveté, "Have you seen Cousin Aubrey?"

And she answered at once, "I don't want to see him if he is present. Nobody has any business disappearing for all those years, then turning up at a time like this."

I turned again and went back into the living room, but he was gone by then. I ran out onto the porch just in time to see him getting into the backseat of his chauffeur-driven limousine. As the long, plum-colored car pulled away on the dirt road, I began running after it, calling out for the driver to stop. But as the car reached macadam paving at the town limits, it at once took on considerable speed. When I gave up the chase and turned back I realized I had not even noted what the state of the auto tag license was. Many years later I would learn what kind of life Cousin Aubrey lived, but that day at Brush Mountain and through all the years—I was destined first to be a graduate student and then to continue the research for my books while actually supporting myself by teaching (when not living and traveling on foundation grants)—through all those years, quite literally, the mystery of my cousin's whereabouts and his manner of life remained with me and held for me some unnameable significance. In later years possibly the wife of my bosom and possibly every one of our four children would suspect what this unnameable significance for me was—or at least before I, indeed, came to know it all too well myself.

THERE WERE other things I didn't understand about my own experience through all those years and which became apparent to me only later. First of all, I did not know how I endured or survived all those family funerals at my tender and impressionable age, from fourteen to twenty. I think I can say now that I bore the experience of those years by almost total withdrawal from and rejection of all my innermost and perhaps profoundest feelings. I think from the time I was sent away to Bellbuckle and during the whole time I was at Sewanee I had to relinquish my deepest feelings about anyone and anything. I no longer allowed myself to *feel* what I had once felt about my parents, my aunts, my uncles, my cousins, my friends Norman and BB, the town of Thornton itself, the whole landscape of the Tennessee country we inhabited. I allowed myself to know but not to feel. Very similarly I came to read and know about painting but no longer painted except in the most superficial sense. It ceased to be for me an expression of what I felt about what I saw with my eyes. I did intellectual exercises to explain and interpret what was taught by my teachers and my friends. For there was one master on the faculty at the Webb School who liked to see me paint and obligingly taught me a few principles, and at Sewanee we were permitted to paint, and there was an ignorant professor there who lectured on art history and who was allegedly a painter himself. My friend and roommate, Robin Maury, painted a little also, though not seriously, and his wild theories about the arts I used to enjoy by the hour. He had a gift for language and could sometimes be cruel to the all-but-illiterate art history lecturer. After class one day Robin said to him of his paintings that hung on the classroom wall, "I like the picture, sir. I think it has quite meretricious detail!"

"Thank you very much, Maury," said the art history professor. "I pride myself on that."

It was in my senior year that I went home with Robin for our long winter holiday. My mother didn't want me to go. She often had strange presciences. She always liked my being at Bellbuckle and Sewanee because there were no girls at either place. It may be why she chose those schools for me. The town of Bellbuckle was a mere crossroads, and Sewanee was not even that. Whenever I went home to visit other boys, it was the girls I might meet there that worried her. She disapproved of early marriages, and she maintained that I had an "intense, romantic nature" and was sure to want to marry the first girl that "batted her eyes" at me.

Melissa Wallace, in Sussex, Virginia, would have been the last girl in the world to bat her eyes at anybody or anything. I recognized at once that she was stubborn and decisive about all matters. I think she only finally accepted my proposal of marriage because she honestly believed I needed her to help make decisions "in life." Her attachment to Robin came only from his being the "boy next door" when she was growing up. At any rate, I did propose to her on the third evening of my visit to Robin's. On the fourth evening she gave a tentative acceptance contingent upon our mutual feeling two years later when she would have finished college at Fredricksburg.

I did feel that upon our first meeting Melissa Wallace somehow batted her intellectual or perhaps temperamental eyes at me. At any rate, our intellectual or temperamentally opposite natures attracted each other. I cannot say how immediately our sexual attraction was in operation. Perhaps the one was simultaneous with the other. Both came soon enough anyhow. On the third day we wrapped ourselves in our warmest outer garments and went for a long walk together through the countryside in and around Sussex. I expressed my concern for the coming decision I had to make between an academic teaching career and that of a professional painter. She at once halted her step and stood stock-still in the frozen roadbed where we had been walking. Without looking up at me or staring ahead at the dull disk of a sun, low on the horizon before us, she said abruptly: "Now, that's the kind of decision you will have to make for yourself—always. That's between you and God, not between you and your wife!" I knew then what Melissa Wallace was like and what she would be like—always! There in the middle of the frozen country road I threw my arms about her and kissed her on her now well-beloved lips. I came back to see Melissa three times before spring, staying each time in the house with Robin Maury's parents. And in the spring she took a bus over to Thornton primarily for the purpose of meeting my mother. They became fast friends at once. The three of us—Mother, Melissa, and I—talked endlessly about nothing but plans for the future. Mother was ever insistent that I had to be a painter. In private Melissa continued to maintain that the decision was mine alone. I realized at once that that was what she counted on and that it would be true for her always.

IN THE EARLY fall I went to New York, where I was enrolled at Columbia University as well as in the Art Students League. I went in my own car and stopped by at Fredricksburg where Melissa was still at college. She would not even allow me to talk about our getting married. She would not even agree that we were engaged. All decisions must wait another year.

She was so firm in her resolution that I was thoroughly convinced there was no engagement. I found bachelor quarters on 114th Street and soon saw that I would have no difficulty living on the small trust fund my father had established for me on the day I was born and that was open to be drawn upon on my twenty-first birthday. It seemed so improbable to me that at last I was free to paint that I waited ten days before registering for art school. I wanted to savor the taste of the thing I had waited so long for. But once enrolled, I found that all time between these days and the days when I had painted with BB seemed as nothing. I can't be sure how long this sense of exhilaration and exultation lasted. I was incredibly productive and shipped two canvases out to Mother in Nashville, where she had gone to live in Aunt Felicia's house after my aunt had died. I sent one canvas—the best of the lot, I think—to Melissa. I suppose my high spirits lasted until about Thanksgiving. I took a train down to see Mother at Thanksgiving and found her ecstatic about the turn my life seemed to have taken. I was doing what I was born to do. For the Christmas holiday I planned to see Melissa and go on to see Mother again. But after my Thanksgiving with Mother, my mood and my enthusiasm had altogether changed. I was bored with the instructors and with my friends among other students as well as with my own efforts to paint. The instructors and the other students seemed ignorant of everything in the world except how to mix paint and put it on canvas. I began to frequent the museums—everything from the New York Metropolitan Museum to the Museum of Modern Art— and the libraries at the art school at Columbia University. Soon I had reams of notes, and before long I was writing articles which I submitted to the art magazines and the learned quarterlies. I did it almost without contemplating what I was doing. I told myself only that I was doing it out of boredom and I hardly knew what to make of it, when I began receiving letters of acceptance and even adulation. I didn't go home for Christmas, and I didn't go to see Melissa. By midwinter I had a three-hundred-page manuscript to submit to a publisher. To Melissa I wrote, "It is easy as pie this research business!" The New York publishers, of course, showed no interest, but by spring I had a contract with a university press and the offer of a teaching appointment at the same university if I was willing to work toward obtaining my Ph.D. at that same university. When I went out to the Middle West to begin my teaching career the next fall, with a book already accepted, I was treated like some rare phenomenon, a sprouting genius.

Again and again I wrote to Melissa, repeating that this research and writing business was easy as pie. And it is, compared to going to your blank canvas and taking up your brush with serious intent. Think of merely comparing two paintings you have seen in a museum or the work of two painters whose intentions are either quite simple or the very antithesis of each other or even two traditions of painting which are not just the same. Relatively, you put nothing of yourself into it; it takes nothing from you. It represents merely knowledge. But the decision was not so easy as I make it sound. I knew that Melissa preferred a straight course, once the course was taken. And I knew how disappointed Mother would be by my giving up the thing I was "born to do." More than that, moreover, someone else had entered the picture since I had come to New York.

Within weeks after my arrival, I began to realize that there was a huge number of Southerners on the New York scene—even a sizable colony of Sewanee people, of one kind and another. It happened that the very professor who had lectured to us in art history was living in a cold-water flat down in the Village. Several times he invited me down to party there. I succumbed to the atmosphere and the rather famous people that one met at his place.

IN THE COURSE of the professor's party I was introduced to Linda Campbell, a beautiful and herself rather famous Broadway actress. She was a woman much older than I. In fact she was actually a woman of my mother's generation, but from the moment we met she had the very strongest attraction for me. I was not yet married, of course, and considered myself only vaguely engaged to Melissa Wallace. I did not really at that time believe that I would ever be able to afford a wife. I was, as I have said, still an aspiring painter and had not yet settled for becoming a mere art historian. I had not yet accepted that role as my respectable lot in life.

The party at which Linda Campbell and I met was one of those Greenwich Village parties that one went to in those days at which the intellectuals, serious artists, poets, and composers and even highbrow actresses mixed together rather freely and profitably—profitably in every good and civilized sense. Indeed it seemed for a time in New York that there might be developing an intellectual society like those that had existed—or at least that one reads had existed—in all other great world capitals and power centers of the past. The very idea of it excited me at that age and at that point in my development. But all too soon things would begin to split up and fall apart, as they always do seem destined to do in that city, and soon enough when one went out socially it would be once again only artists and musicians or only literary and political people that one met. During that brief little epoch, before the inevitable split up into cliques began, Linda Campbell flourished. Linda was created, so to speak, to shine forth and excel in such diverse gatherings as we had then. She especially liked the adulation of people possessing talents different from her own. And since her own intelligence proclaimed itself in her very responsiveness to their attention she was of course the more appealing to them. No doubt this was part of her attraction for me from the first.

But I mustn't give the impression that I was in any way attracted to Linda because she reminded me of my mother. It did not occur to me that there was any similarity between them, and at first it didn't occur to me that Linda was nearly twice my age. As a matter of fact, I had seen her in several Broadway and off-Broadway plays before that night when we met, and I admired her style in acting immensely. At the beginning, and afterward when I came to know her, it seemed to me that her lines on the stage were as spirited and spontaneous as her speech in conversation. No doubt I seemed to be following her around that night at my teacher-friend's party. It was a night toward the end of June, and it was noticeably warm in the apartment. All at once in the middle of a conversation with two of her actor-friends and with myself, Linda turned about and threw up a window that we were standing near, and then to no one in particular—perhaps mostly to herself—she muttered under her breath with a smile: "I want free life and I want fresh air!"

My eyes must have widened at what she said. Almost without thinking I took it up:

"I sigh for a canter after the cattle!
The crack of a whip like a shot in the battle!"

She looked up at me then with those jet-black eyes of hers, almost as if she were seeing me for the first time. She held her little mouth very tight at first and then presently she burst out at her two actor-friends, "God bless us, here's a young man who knows 'Lasca'!"

She knew the whole poem from beginning to end. It was a well-known specialty of hers amongst her friends, and I was the first person of her acquaintance who had heard of it before being introduced to it by her. Later that night she called the party to order and announced the discovery of this "knowledgeable young person" beside her. By popular demand she was forced to give her rendition. Someone provided "background music" while she recited, and it seemed quite magical to me to have the familiar old poem presented in this context and in this company. There was a certain amount of sniggering during the recitation. Although most of the audience had heard Linda give the recitation before, still everyone seemed to be made uncomfortable by it and was unsure of how to respond. I was not sure myself what was expected of me. Of course I kept remembering my mother's rhetorical interpretation and was actually struck more by the similarities than the dissimilarities between the two renditions. It was almost as if they had first learned to recite it under the same tutelage —in the same elocution class, as it were. It amused me to observe certain variations in the two texts. Whereas in Mother's version there was the line

She drew from her bosom a dear little dagger,

in Linda's version it ran

She drew from her garter a dear little dagger.

It was hard to say which version represented the gentrification of the text.

But in Mother's case the poem seemed to come to me in little bits and pieces over the years, as though portions of it had been censored according to the occasion. In Linda Campbell's case it all came out in one hearing. And it seemed significant to me that never again did I hear Linda make any reference or allusion to the poem, never again except in one instance, and that but briefly and in passing. Linda was, you see, perhaps inordinately proud of her remarkably good-looking legs and graceful ankles. Admirers were forever commenting on this mark of her beauty. Her usual reply was: "Ah, yes, they are as good as ever they were." But once when some admirer complimented her in my presence, she winked at me rather flirtatiously and repeated certain lines describing Lasca, which I had altogether forgotten till that moment:

> "Her eyes were brown, a dark, dark brown.
> Her hair was darker than her eyes.
> Something in her instep high
> Showed that there ran in each blue vein
> Mixed with the gentler Aztec strain
> The royal vintage of old Spain."

Though Linda would often refer to herself as a native of East Texas—speaking of the region as of a different province from the rest of Texas—this was the only allusion she ever made to the possibility that she might have Spanish or Mexican blood in her veins. During the months that we knew each other she told me many things about herself but never anything, I believe, about her origins or about her childhood. It was not the kind of subject which interested her. Very late in the evening we left the party in the Village together. We went down the three flights from my teacher's old cold-water flat and out into Bleecker Street and began trying to hail a cab. When finally we succeeded I found to my surprise that it was not her intention that we take the same cab. In fact, when I opened the door for her she stood a moment blocking my way before climbing inside. "We're going in different directions," she said.

"But I will see you home," I replied, momentárily confused. I believe I had no preconceived ideas, but it had not occurred to me certainly but that we would take the same cab. She stood for a time opposite me, shaking her head while the driver waited.

"I always go home alone," she insisted cheerfully. "It's an old habit of mine." After a second she added, "I'll come to see you some afternoon in your loft and watch you paint or sculpt, whichever you happen to be up to. And you must come to lunch one day at my apartment. I'm an excellent cook." She hopped into the cab and was off and away. I think I understood perfectly even then the platonic nature of the friendship which Linda Campbell and I were going to have. Or perhaps she had not quite made her decision then. Perhaps she was waiting to learn more about me, as she would in the months ahead. But anyway it was only friends that we did become, no matter what everybody else at that party expected ·and no matter what they may later have believed.

And she did come to my "loft" and watch me sculpt, since that mainly was what I was up to at the time. She came the very next week and would come many times after. And we talked not about her childhood or about mine but about what we had achieved thus far in our adult lives. She insisted that that was what mattered to people like ourselves. She said that what she felt the day she had had her first adult consciousness was the most magical experience in her life and not some awakening in childhood that so many people went on about.

She told me (what I already knew and all the world knew) that she had five times been legally married and that among the lovers had been two world-famous Mexican muralists. Two of her *husbands* had been artists, too, and two had been literary men of sorts, and one had been the director of the first Broadway play she was in. She told me about those men in the most natural way as they came up in her rambling talk, and I told her what little there was to tell about myself— about Melissa, of course, and a couple of college romances, and even about my mother and about my aunts. But she had little enough interest in what I had to say about that. She was only interested in whatever I might say about my painting and sculpture—however casual it might be. She was very free with any criticism she had to make or any praise she had to give. It became plain to me fairly early that her admiration was nearly all for my skill and method. She had little to say about the end result. But I felt that it mattered hugely to her. And I began to reflect that in reference to her former husbands and lovers it had been more the art she was in love with than the man. She had fallen in love with art at an early age and had given herself to it forever at that early age.

This was apparent in everything she did and said about herself. I did have lunch at her place many a time during those months, and just as she predicted, she proved herself an excellent cook. She prepared all my favorite dishes. She did a fillet of sole Marguery that was the best I ever had—before or since. She didn't try to conceal that for the time being I was the center of her interest in life. She was between plays during this period, waiting for the right one to come along. And we had time for all kinds of expeditions. We went to concerts and to plays, often only staying through the first act. We went to the galleries, public and private, and of course spent a day up at the Cloisters. She seemed to know all about any play that had ever been produced in New York or in the whole country and was able to identify some of the lines from the traveling road shows that Mother used to quote. Her memory was her special genius, so to speak, and she did not fail to understand that this was so.

At last one day when I came to lunch she told me that she'd accepted a role in an off-Broadway production that was opening next month. It was a production of Chekhov's *Platonov*, at a theater on Fourteenth Street, directed by a man she liked to work with. I attended rehearsals with her from the very first read-through. It is such a long play that it inevitably has to be cut dramatically for any production. I noticed that the director conferred daily with Linda about where the cuts should be made, and that other members of the cast did not object to the deference shown her and did not seem surprised by it.

I had not until then dreamt that she had such authority or was regarded with such respect by other people in the theater. But everyone seemed to understand her complete commitment. When I asked her if she had ever thought of becoming a director, she only laughed and said, "If you can act, why would you ever think of directing?" But when the play had been in rehearsal for two weeks, she did not know her lines at all and still had to read from the script. I found this shocking and thought that the other actors must surely find it annoying. She paid attention only to her blocking and her gestures. I felt that she was remiss and not a little arrogant. But I made no mention of it. And then on the second weekend she went home and returned Sunday night knowing her lines from beginning to end. After that I questioned nothing about her method or judgment. And from the time she knew her lines she seemed single-mindedly concerned with her own role and that of Platonov, the young scholar who had gone to teach in a remote Russian province. This actor was a man approximately her own age and, like herself, playing the role of a younger person. One could see at once there was a great empathy between them and that each was as concerned as the other not only that they give the illusion of youth but also that they present precisely the kind of experience that Chekhov had in mind. At one point, for instance, when the director wished to omit a line and a gesture of Platonov's, Linda interrupted. She proceeded to illustrate exactly what needed to be done. At center stage she stopped abruptly and there struck her heels noisily on the floor exclaiming with great feeling: "Parquet!" We were all silent with admiration. Presently she glanced down at those of us sitting in the front rows of the otherwise empty theater and said in her sweetest East Texas voice: "If you had grown up in the East Texas country as I did and got into New Orleans just once a year"—here she stomped her foot sharply again—"then you'd know how good the sound of parquet under the foot can be."

The play opened to a full house, then closed after a run of less than three weeks. Linda asserted it was the best performance she had ever given, and some of the notices agreed. But in New York two weeks will exhaust the number of Chekhov enthusiasts. There was only half a house on the final night, but Linda Campbell was still enraptured, and alongside her Platonov, she came back to take seven curtain calls from the faithful little band who merely half filled the theater.

But well before the final night there came a rupture between Linda Campbell and me. There was nothing dramatic about it. There was just a little supper that she prepared after the Saturday night performance at the end of the first week. As usual the two of us had walked from the theater to her apartment. The supper consisted of a crayfish bisque and shrimp St. Augustine. We didn't usually have a salad. Somehow the salad, when it appeared unheralded and unannounced, gave me the message as clearly as if she had declared in her softest East Texas voice: "Nathan, I have to tell you there's going to be a radical change in things."

And thirty minutes later Linda had told me she was in love with her leading man, that she had been seeing him on weekday afternoons, and that no matter how innocent our friendship was, her real-life Platonov wished me to stop coming so regularly to the performances and to stop seeing her home afterward. Her middle-aged Platonov, it emerged, was not only an accomplished actor. He was in fact a licensed pilot and the owner of his own airplane. On the Sunday morning after the play closed the two of them flew away in his plane to the little farm Linda Campbell still owned in East Texas. And in the course of her last token supper in her apartment she took pains to tell me in the very gentlest way that she thought I would be wise to marry that girl from Virginia. It seemed to me later that I had had little to say about Melissa Wallace as well as about my two aunts and my mother and that she had paid no attention to what I had said. But that last night over the supper and the liter of wine we polished off, I discovered I had said much more than I imagined and that Linda's phenomenal memory had inevitably registered all of it. Most of my discoursing had certainly been on the subject of Mother, and I distinctly remember saying that in comparison with herself and the path she had chosen, or been given, Mother's losses in life were not altogether the greater. What I remember with clarity is her saying that Mother's path (whether it was chosen or allotted) had been the path of dependence—dependence upon the system, upon men. Whatever I did with myself, she instructed me, it was my business to remain dependable. And then she said what came nearest to wounding me at that last meeting: "For you, my darling

Nathan, you along with everyone else were born to be reliable, to be dependable." I felt that she had censored her speech in midsentence and had come very close to saying "if nothing else" instead of "along with everyone else." On the Sunday morning after the play closed, she and her husband of twenty-four hours flew off in his plane to East Texas. But the "smart-looking little plane," as I had heard him describe it, crashed in fog while passing over the Cumberland Mountains of Tennessee. I was called upon to go down to Tennessee and identify the bodies. At first I thought I wouldn't possibly be able to do it. But I did go. After hours of dread and uncertainty on the long overnight train journey to Tennessee I took a taxi for I don't know how many miles to the coroner's house in the county seat, where the bodies waited to be identified. I found it hard to realize that I was actually in Tennessee. And the names on the special legal paper shown to me might have been any names. I scarcely bothered to read them. At last I was taken into the room where the bodies were lying. The face of the actor-husband looked very familiar to me, but the face of the dead Linda Campbell seemed strangely unfamiliar. Like the face of someone I could not place in the receding past of my boyhood. After affirming to the coroner that they were who they were, I remained on his premises not longer than twenty minutes. I had no other business there. At any rate, I took the opportunity while in that part of the world to go and pay a visit to my mother for the first time in two years. Then I came back to New York, where Melissa Wallace and I were soon married.

AFTER OUR FIRST child was born the following year—Melissa's and mine—Mother was with us more and more. Her admiration and enjoyment of our little Walter was wonderful and was a great satisfaction to Melissa and me. Mother was sure from an early age that Walter was going to be the artist that I never became, but then she would later be sure of the same fate for each of our boys. Very much later she used to tell me how gratified she was, especially for our youngest son, Braxton. "It is because of Braxton's naïveté," she would say to me more than once, "that he will become an artist. It was apparent in him early." She had never talked so directly to me about anything before, anything that so concerned her hopes for the future. "Unlike you, Nathan, at the age of fifteen Braxton knows nothing about life. He has everything to learn, and it is all there *for* him to learn through art." Sometimes what she said seemed perfect rubbish to me. At other times it seemed almost like something that Linda Campbell might have said, for I do believe that for an artist knowledge can be a dangerous thing—at the outset anyway. Discovery in art must somehow or other be linked to his learning about life. But if what Mother said were true, how on earth came she to such knowledge? How, living alone as she had for so many years in that cottage in the barren, washed-out Tennessee countryside? Does one learn from experience or merely from reflection, I asked myself. (And at any rate I was fond of adding one piece of wisdom as if to complete what Mother had said.) "Whereas *I*," said I impudently to Mother, "have from the earliest time understood almost everything—everything but you, yourself, Mother." But I would smile at her tenderly as I said this.

"Yes," she would say, smiling blithely, serenely, at me, "that is true, Nathan. . . . You were a long time in coming to understand me, I think. I suppose it was someone else in your life that finally made you do so, but I will never know, most likely. Perhaps it was someone you knew that I didn't know. It was something you were *taught* to understand by someone else and not something you perceived for yourself. And that, Nathan, is a very different matter, isn't it? I think so, at any rate. Perhaps it is the difference between the artist and the scholar. Perhaps I'm only an ignorant old woman without education or experience and it is not easy for me to say."

It just happened that it was scarcely twenty-four hours after Linda's crash, when I had to fly down to identify the body, that my mother communicated the plans to remove Grandfather's body from the Knoxville cemetery. Since I was already in that part of the country I could not refuse to accompany her on that awful journey she felt she had to make. She had not wanted to consent to the removal, but cousins of hers in Upper East Tennessee had already signed an agreement for the transaction. These very cousins were investing money in a new cemetery and simply wanted Grandfather's presence there as an attraction to other possible clients. They made the claim that they had not known she was still alive. (She was so out of touch with relatives in that part of the state that they imagined they were themselves the nearest of kin.) And there were extenuating circumstances that caused Mother to yield to them. There was a real threat of a new highway being put directly through the old cemetery, and so any protest on her part would likely have served no good purpose. Under those circumstances I joined Mother at the grave site on one hot September afternoon. I have referred to the terrible thing that happened that day: When the coffin was in midair, the chains connecting it to the great red-and-yellow crane gave way and dropped one end of the coffin back into the slime of the grave. The coffin did not actually burst open, but I knew what images must be going through Mother's head with regard to the decayed body inside, and I didn't fail to recall what thoughts this mother of mine had entertained that day in the Washington funeral procession. Moreover in my own morbid state I

could not help seeing in my mind's eye the bruised face of
Linda Campbell when I had to look upon it in the morgue for
the last time.

And in the first moment after the chains' breaking I heard
a car door slam not far behind where we stood. I looked back
with suspicion, I suppose, and I saw a man who had clearly
just stepped out of the car running toward the grisly scene.
But when the coffin came firmly to rest on one end, I saw the
man turn back and quickly step inside the car again. Rightly
or wrongly I had imagined it was Cousin Aubrey I saw. But
knowing how Mother would likely respond to such an idea of
mine and not wishing to wound her, I spoke not a word. By
the time I turned back again, the car and its passenger had
departed. I will only add parenthetically that when Mother
and I stood together at the second place of interment, in Elizabethton, a hundred miles up the broad valley of East Tennessee, I had a somewhat similar experience, but I was in
such a disturbed frame of mind during those days that I not
only didn't mention to Mother what I believed I saw but I do
not even now insist upon it to myself. It could well have been
an illusion on my part.

" . . . A REMARKABLY wide knowledge in his field and
profound insight on every page." So ran one of the blurbs on
my book. Whether or not the words made sense, they were
strong words for a young man not long out of college and still
working toward his doctorate. The book was well received by
all the academics, and with such encouragement any young
man—no matter how great his latent talent for painting might
be—would be unlikely to give up the course he had chosen.
As a matter of fact I used often to speculate about what made
my essays and art histories have such a wide appeal to a rather

large readership. At last I decided it was the enthusiasm I was quite capable of developing almost simultaneously about the various schools and modes of painting. Something like that at any rate. It seemed to me that I was less biased than other art critics whose work I knew or that came to hand. I approached most schools of painting with spirited approval and moved from school to school and from painter to painter with a certain easy ardor. It was my special delight to be able to speak about opposite kinds of work almost in the same paragraph with this ardor and enthusiasm—that is, the work of abstract expressionists, say, right along with that of traditional representationalists. It was gratifying to be able to point out precisely the same themes in paintings of very different sorts, and somehow that gave satisfaction to many of my readers and gave me a popularity with a wide range of readers, though not perhaps with the majority of my colleagues. In fact, once when I found myself "closeted" in the men's room, I overheard two of my colleagues standing at the nearby urinals refer to me as "old on-the-other-hand." I did not find this particularly offensive chiefly because it gave me an unwonted insight into what it was I was judged for by these colleagues —gave me a new and welcome insight into the nature of criticism that was being voiced about me. It was not till years later when my own son Braxton was setting up as a painter in the city of Washington that I might find it necessary to reexamine many of my aesthetic theories—the tenets of my faith, as I allowed myself to call it. I would by then have perceived that this extraordinary son of mine had at his various stages of development found it necessary or perhaps only convenient to embrace with a passionate intensity one view or another on the successive steps of his program as an artist—one view or another of his aesthetic understanding. I would see that with him it had to be a huge discovery that he could believe in devoutly for the time being. And I would even understand how the narrowness of Brax's artistic vision at his various stages meant all the world to him.

Melissa and I were married a few days after the publication date of that first book of mine. The first baby was born the next year. The other babies followed in quick succession, all but Braxton. Melissa and I used to sit talking for hours over coffee on the porch at night about how different our life would have been if I myself had become a painter. It wasn't with regret exactly that we spoke of it, more with idle curiosity; as if we were speculating about two other people, two friends perhaps that we had come to know at the university and whose lives had followed other lines from our own.

AFTER WE GOT MARRIED—and almost before, I might say—I set about establishing us in what I believed was going to be our idyllic academic life. To some extent it was just that and would always remain so. I worked out this new life with a certain vengeance. I began trying to reeducate myself in all practical matters in a sense I had not bothered about before. My two sections of Art History I and Art History II I generally taught wherever it was I was located in any given academic year—along with my more advanced classes. That was my usual procedure except sometimes when there was a baby on the way in the family—in which case, being then too nervous for extensive research projects, I offered all my classes in the summer term as well, and so added a little to my income. Moreover I soon began to dabble in academic politics. An older member of the faculty had said to me that it was simply part of the job and that one should never neglect any element of one's career. Somehow it was the first time I had thought of my being committed to a career in the sense that a doctor or a lawyer was. And my main concern would remain the production of those art history books that were going to contribute importantly and without fail to our income and that would so sustain us through any hard times that might lie ahead.

There was such a sameness about all the places I was to go and teach in the years that followed that I cannot always distinguish between them in memory. If Melissa could tell them apart, it may be because her experiences in every case were more sharply drawn and in the end were more significant than my own. I must confess that I was not aware of the immensity of Melissa's growth and progress. At times I was mystified by whatever it was she was undergoing. How could it be otherwise? In reference to certain of those happy instances in our life I can only express my astonishment at having been so blind. And my blindness of this particular sort does indicate how far apart were my past and previous experiences in this life of mine—in the kind of life which I had been involuntarily catapulted into. When I first became aware that Melissa was concealing some area of her life from me, I was currently embroiled in trying to settle into my first teaching appointment at Indiana University.

Upon my arrival in Bloomington I had been at once saddled with the chairmanship of a committee of six, whose business it would be to develop an extensive creative arts program. Nothing had been said to me in advance about these administrative duties, all of which were bound to interfere with my own writing and research. Moreover, our proposed quarters, which consisted of a walk-up apartment that the deans euphemistically represented as "university housing," were totally unsuitable to us since we were then expecting our first child. Here I was, having arrived on the scene with a pregnant wife and a rattletrap secondhand car, along with a rented trailer that contained all of our worldly possessions, to be told forthwith that our "apartment" was the second floor of an old converted army barracks, a temporary building, so to speak. One climbed the steep stairway to get to this apartment, a stair not unlike a stepladder in a barn. The only means of heat in this three-room affair was a large butane gas stove in the center of a so-called living room. The beds in the other two rooms consisted of double-decker bunks made of two-by-fours and a sort of wire mesh and pitiably flat little cotton mattresses. In the kitchen there was no electric refrigerator, only an old-fashioned icebox and a sign we had to place in the window for the iceman, indicating the number of pounds of ice requested for any particular day.

While waiting for our delayed occupancy we had been temporarily put up at an old-fashioned rooming house in the town, but I made my way at once to the Dean's office to register a complaint. I had already written a letter to the University of Iowa, where it had been indicated to me that there would be a similar job opening in the art department. Every day that week I hung out at the Bloomington post office, waiting for the mail to be put up. I considered that the letter I had sent to Iowa had been an inspiration on my part. I had no idea how such things were done in the academic world, but I discovered then that I was a fast learner. The morning when the letter from Iowa actually arrived Melissa did not accompany me to the post office. And lo and behold I found that the job was actually being offered to me.

As I ran across the square in the direction of the Dean's office, already it had occurred to me that I had a worldly talent that I had not dreamed of possessing. I realized that if I were not going to be an artist, I was at least going to be one of the world's best finaglers, and that there were other works of the imagination that I could fill my life with, other schemes and opportunities that would present themselves. I took the wide steps leading to the stone archway two at a time. At the Dean's office I was received without delay or any hesitation and without being kept waiting for a moment. Before I could speak the Dean read through my letter and picked up the telephone. I had no idea of what call he was making, but presently I heard a long-distance communication with the Dean at the other university. It didn't occur to me for a moment that this Dean at Indiana could be checking my story. That was not the way people behaved in the world I was used to. But addressing that other Dean simply as Harry, he asked what interest he had in bringing me to Iowa. And in the moments of silence that followed I saw my own Dean's face reddening, and from the other end of the wire I heard the title of my recent book being pronounced slowly and clearly. It was my book whose prestige they were bidding for. And when the conversation was presently concluded, the Dean of my school replaced the instrument on its cradle and looked across the desk at me with lifted and questioning eyebrows. "And what exactly is your criticism of our treatment of you?" At once I told him about the six-man committee and the unsuitable apartment. Then I told him something that Melissa and I had scarcely been able to speak of to each other before. On the day previous to that one we were taken to inspect the proposed apartment a terrible accident had occurred. Only twenty-four hours before this the small child of the former tenant had been caught in flames from the butane gas stove and had been burned to death. The marks of the child's burning, so I informed the Dean, were still visible on the splintery floor.

An attractive little prefab house, recently erected on the edge of the campus, was offered to us while I was standing there in the Dean's office. And I was told that I could forget about the six-man committee that I was supposed to head up.

The next morning Melissa and I inspected our new premises. I was wildly happy over the changes in our luck—over the way *I* had changed our luck. Melissa seemed mildly happy about it, but was clearly more amused about the enthusiasm I expressed and the pride I took in my success. Once we had walked through the house for the first time, Melissa looked at me and said, "I fear this may be the first step in your corruption. And all for me, alas." I laughed at the very idea.

B u t I m u s t confess that that night as we slept in our rooming-house bed I dreamt that I was pursuing a man mile after mile but that I could never quite catch up with him. I felt it imperative that I catch one good glimpse of his face. Yet in the dream I could never get quite close enough for that. He continued always six or eight feet ahead of me, never to be overtaken. It was a dream that would remain with me for many a year afterward. It was a dream that I could never entirely forget, no matter how often other dreams might be repeated. It was the beginning of a dream life that would never leave me until its final meaning would become to some extent explicit.

I ' m n o t s u r e now how successful my teaching was in those first years, but my publications were all that the administrations everywhere seemed to care about. But even in those days I began seeing how much I was learning from teaching itself. From having to lecture on the paintings of Hogarth, who began as one of my pet abominations on my list of artists, I discovered he was one of my favorites, and even the French Impressionists, who were one of my bêtes noires, became the subject of my profoundest enthusiasm. . . .

My next academic appointment was at another large

middle-western university. The irksome thing was that I had no students at this second place, and so I had to devise some other means of occupying myself. But somehow it could never be with my own efforts at painting. I spent many lonely hours in my office and in the studio that was provided me there. Sometimes in my loneliness I would call Melissa at home just for the company. She was always warm and said she was happy I had called, though I suspected always—I knew, in fact—that the call must be interfering with her activities and her cherished isolation, or with the care of the children perhaps.

I began to suspect moreover that the department itself did not like me. All the other professors had an abundance of students in their workshops, in their studios, and in attendance at their lectures. On several occasions I overheard my fellow professors in my own department saying that I was their "window dressing" and that consequently I had no need of students of my own. During that year my production of highbrow "art criticism," of articles in the slick magazines and coffee-table picture books, was prodigious. During the second year, due to my great productivity, as I can only suppose, I was repeatedly asked for lunch at the President's house whenever there was a celebrity or near celebrity in town. It didn't matter whether or not the current celebrity had any relevance to art or art history. I was simply a bright name toward the top of the administration's list.

SOON I WAS spoken of by the other members of the Art Department, and by other members of humane studies in general, as "the President's Pal." Indeed I began almost to think of myself as that. I had his confidence in many matters. I even listened to his talk about what was the matter with the

Political Science and Mathematics departments, subjects about which I was almost totally ignorant. Near the end of that year there came a crisis between the President and the majority of the faculty. The differences of opinion were principally centered around whether or not a particular speaker should be asked to appear before the student body on Campus Day. It was a certain Hyram Crosswich, whose politics were far to the left of the President's and even to the left of most of the faculty, I suspect. But the outcry over the principle was what stirred up so much feeling—the right to free speech on the campus. I was inevitably aligned with the President's party and stood by his right to make whatever decisions were involved. A great deal of campus politics came into play. Feelings ran high. The fire spread from department to department.

Now, at this branch of the university only the President can call for a general faculty meeting; otherwise a two-thirds majority of the faculty must express demand for it. Placards were posted all over the campus calling for such a meeting. Finally there was a roll call of faculty opinion, held in the university auditorium. A petition was circulated and an official meeting was called. And meanwhile I had been more than once heckled by groups of graduate students while crossing the campus. In some ways I considered it—and still do so— the high point in my academic career. At least it was the most exciting point. Melissa said facetiously that she feared for my life. And indeed I was induced that week to sit on the stage with the President when the meeting took place. But I had no fear about the course matters would take. For it was I who had to be credited with making the brilliant suggestion which the President would never forget, and for which, I'm sure, he would never fail to be grateful to me no matter how long he lived. . . . I came up with the reminder that all the doctors in that midwestern city had faculty standing and that they were all very conservative men and would certainly vote against Hyram Crosswich's being allowed to speak. But even better than that I pointed out to the President that all the ninety-odd counties in the state had that many county agents in the agricultural program and that all these agents and their assistants had faculty status in the university Agriculture Department and all of them received notice of the meeting. Consequently, when the hour for the appointed meeting arrived that afternoon, hordes of shiny black state-owned cars began to roll onto the campus, bearing one or more of these agents who had come to take his seat in the auditorium and cast his vote as a member of the loyalist party.

About the outcome of the vote there could be no doubt. And when I picked up the afternoon paper, I saw the headline which obviously had been set up before the meeting began: "Communists Defeated at State University." When I read it aloud to Melissa, she burst into tears, though she held our second boy, John, in her arms at the moment. I took her into my arms along with him and tried to comfort her. I was perplexed because I had not yet perceived what her fear was, and what her passion for hours of isolation meant. She was so successfully secretive about it, and would be so for several years yet—her passion, that is, to be alone through certain hours of the day. But I knew already that it had some connection with the direction my own career had taken.

At last I was able to comfort her, to have her saying how silly she had been and that I must not take any notice of it. My success in supporting the President in the challenge of the faculty was a Pyrrhic victory for me, of course. And I knew well enough it was not going to increase my popularity on the campus. The President must have felt he could do no less to repay me than to promote me to Provost or Chancellor or

Vice-president of Internal Affairs. I didn't want any of that sort of thing. It was enough to have prevailed over the general run of the faculty who had, I felt, treated me so shabbily. It would be satisfaction enough to see such people changing their tune with me, which would be bound to happen, in the hope that I would lend a hand in their advancement. I knew I was going to pay a price in this period of my life.

Yet I was already restless and began to speculate about what other fields there might be for me to conquer in this academic world I had fallen into. I still remember how I had exulted in that line of shiny black cars I had seen pouring onto the campus. And I seem to remember still better the unhappy dreams which I had soon afterward. I dreamt I saw those same black cars unloading, each person a crooked, stooped figure wearing a different sort of felt hat, but all their faces complete blanks.

IN THOSE DAYS I would sometimes spend a whole evening describing for Melissa tactics that our side was employing. She often seemed absentminded and didn't attend much to what I said. We didn't quarrel about it, but sometimes I would have to snap my fingers before her eyes to gain her attention.

Eventually my published articles on contemporary painting became so well known that I was invited to no less a place than Harvard for two successive terms. Then I was invited to the University of Chicago for a second term. I also lectured at Stanford University. I became so jaded with this kind of performance that after subsequent trips to Oxford and the Sorbonne I went into a depression for a time and sometimes resorted to tearing up the manuscript of my lecture as soon as it was delivered. These lectures were a challenge, and I succeeded sufficiently well, but the exercise seemed somehow degrading—so much so that after a lecture at University College I went behind the little paneled doors and shredded each lecture so that I would not be caught delivering them again elsewhere. And each night when I returned to the quarters we occupied in University College I knew perfectly well that when I had kissed the children goodnight and slipped into bed beside Melissa I would again have one of those dreams of mine. More than once in fact I called out in my sleep and had to be awakened by Melissa. The dreams that I had that summer were all very much the same and sometimes I would be in such a deep sleep that Melissa would have to put on the light and even shake me. Once she had to sit beside me on the bed and tell me what country I was in and at what university I was lecturing.

IT WAS ON my tenure at Oxford that I began first to suspect the nature of Melissa's preoccupation. For some time I had guessed it was a diary she was writing. But after she insisted on taking her own little typewriter with her on her journey, I knew it must be something more than a diary or journal. It was not likely that she would make the entries in her diary on a typewriter. I knew that in college she had had a serious interest in literature and that after a while she was reading every novel that came to hand. But it didn't occur to me for some reason that she was continuing this interest. She never once talked to me about literature or particularly about fiction. In fact she made a point, as I realized afterward, of never discussing in any way the novels she was reading. By this time we had three children that we took with us everywhere we went, no matter how far afield we journeyed. Once my suspicions were aroused to the true nature of the writing she was doing, I made a point of not intruding upon her. By this time—with the care of three children—she would snatch little moments that I would never be aware of. Insofar as I wondered about it at all, I tried to imagine why it was so important for her to keep a secret from me. I remember that as I was bringing the baggage into the house after our recent trip to England I said to Melissa about her typewriter, "I hope you've made great use of that on the trip since you insisted on taking it."

And she replied, "I did," and she wore an angry expression on her face that I had never seen before and that I would never see again, I believe.

AT LENGTH an invitation to teach at a little Ohio college came along. With my inflated reputation it would not ordinarily have occurred to me to consider such an invitation. But Kenyon College had been described as being very much like my own alma mater, Sewanee. I was teaching again at the University of Chicago that winter and I lay awake that night thinking what a joy it might be to take my family to live in a small rural community where an Episcopal seminary was the only thing that bore any resemblance to a graduate school. I was also aware that a former teacher of mine and a great favorite with me always—a Professor John Paul Randelman —was now teaching at Kenyon. It didn't fail to occur to me that he might have been the person who suggested my appointment. That is, I felt sure it must be he. I was also acquainted with the head of the Art Department at Kenyon— until now a department of one. He had been a bright student when I was doing my first teaching at Indiana. I could well imagine that the two of them had put their heads together and cooked up a plan to bring me to Kenyon as a resident lecturer in art history. After a brief exchange of letters with the President of Kenyon I one day got in my car and drove the three hundred miles to the village of Gambier, Ohio. As I drove up the hill through the stand of giant sycamore trees I was overwhelmed by the natural beauty of the place. I came to the spot just after having driven along the beautiful Kokosing River, and I drove along above the river route, which is known as the Bishop's Backbone. It was almost dusk, but I met the first flushes of spring everywhere I turned. In facing the light I felt anew the old, familiar urge to put paint on the brush and to get to work on my neglected palette. At the very top of the hill in the village of Gambier, even more than in Sewanee, I could imagine myself in the surroundings of some remote English crossroads. There was only the lovely white weatherboarding and the red rooftops to alter the image.

Before turning into the gate at the guest house where I had been directed to go by the President in his most recent letter, I took a turn about the center of the village in my car. Peering up at the Middle Path toward Bexley Hall, where the seminary was, I mumbled under my breath, "Eureka!" I imagined that at last I had found the place I would love to settle with my family, to work and live out my life. Here was the place one dreams of, away from the squabbles and distractions of the faculty world.

Presently I turned into the driveway that led to the guest house. Going inside I was greeted by a white-haired woman who struck me as nothing less than angelic-looking. She had a certain air about her. Her long white hair, coiled as it was in plaits on the crown of her head, seemed fairly to glisten as she stood in the dark vestibule. The truth is, she had a grandiose way and yet the most simple charming manner. I imagined she all but curtsied as she acknowledged who I was. And as we traversed the hall on the second floor, walking side by side, I could not help imagining that she was a vision of the little old lady that Melissa might someday be. Why such a notion should come into my head I shall never know. As we were standing face-to-face in the doorway of my room, I suddenly seized her by the hand and wished her a cordial goodnight. Simultaneously I felt the blood rushing to my cheeks and saw that the lady was blushing also.

The next day she did not appear again. She never appeared again during the entire visit to Gambier, and I could only suppose that she was purposefully avoiding me, that I had frightened her with the strangeness of my behavior. But my feeling was that she had not been real, only an illusion, some sort of symbol of a new life I was about to enter. Alone inside the room I stood thinking of Melissa and wondering if I had wasted her life and if there had been an achievement I had interfered with. And I wished only that I could make amends for whatever I had been guilty of. Had I allowed her to sacrifice her divine talent for my pursuit of a worldly career? I vowed then and there that after we had moved to Kenyon her literary aspirations and my academic career would have the same claim upon our energy and time. And I remembered this afterward as a turning point—a turning point at least in my intention, though I might later fail in my resolve. My first impulse was to take up the telephone there in my room and call Melissa in Chicago and tell her of my new resolve, but as always I was distracted by my immediate surroundings and by the excitement that this step toward settling in Gambier meant to me—that is, by the petty demands of any one moment in life. I did pick up the telephone, though, with the intention of calling the President's house. But instead I could not resist calling Mr. Randelman, my old teacher from Sewanee days. He was astonished to hear from me, as was also the onetime graduate student of mine who now constituted Kenyon's one-man art department. The two men happened to be in company together at the very time I called. Contrary to what I expected they had not been consulted by the President about my possible appointment, and it turned out that the President was very much in opposition to any candidate who was likely to be brought forth by the faculty. Both men urged me not to mention my having called them on the telephone and not to say that I was going to see them the next day, as they now invited me to do.

BY THIS TIME in my life I was so accustomed to various political maneuvers in the colleges and universities that it was second nature almost for me to fall in line with one faction or another. I believe in that moment I forgot again about my renewed interest in painting. I did then as my two old friends bade me to do when I went to the President's office the next morning and did not say a word about them. Within half an hour the President had made me a firm offer. And I accepted his offer most gleefully, recognizing full well and possibly relishing the battles that would lie ahead. I was already anticipating my new life on Gambier Hill. But halfway to Chicago the next day I began remembering the dream of the night before. It was the kind of dream I might have expected to have after such a day, except that I had seemed to be learning to repress these dreams, they became so predictable after moments of exhilaration. In the dream this time there were figures on a distant horizon. They became smaller and even smaller until they would almost vanish—though never quite disappearing. And then they would begin to be enlarged again.

FOR THE NEXT six years that I taught in the tower room above Pierce Hall at Kenyon College I'm not sure I taught the students anything to speak of, but it was my most prolific period for my writing and my traveling. I went all over the world during our summers—pushing always at my research. It was at the end of these six years that I received a call to the University of Virginia. I'm aware that I sound like some Methodist parson announcing that he has had a "call" to some rich congregation, and I do suppose it was not unlike that for me. At any rate, I had satisfied the ambition that drove me on and kept me from asking unanswerable questions about myself. It was at Kenyon that my three older children did their real growing up, and it was in this place that our last child, our youngest boy, Braxton, was born. Significant or not, it was here that our elder children's talents started to flourish. And it was the time when Melissa began to publish her short stories in the little magazines of university presses. Her stories represented the work of a lifetime, really. As soon as she began publishing she ceased to write other stories. The stories were obscure and private, but they had some following among readers and writers of those little magazines. And I think she derived real satisfaction from having produced them, sometimes under very trying circumstances. I told myself that from this time forward I would get *my* satisfaction from the creative productivity of my family in the life that I had more or less provided for them. I suspected already, as would turn out to be the case, that my greatest satisfaction and my greatest amazement would be from my wife's stories. She revealed in them a sense of color I would not, as a painter, have suspected she possessed. And there were bold, linear effects that one does not expect from short fiction. There was always a wonderful oneness in her design of the stories, elements that are seldom seen so well developed on the printed page. It was as though she had carefully suppressed a tremendous feeling for painting and had unconsciously allowed it to seep through on that printed page of hers. But what were inevitable were the obscure and dazzling effects that she managed to get in writing about commonplace, everyday characters. Overnight she had revealed she was a person with this remarkable sense of color and line and a feeling of oneness. It had always existed within her, as such things always do exist and are held back to be expressed at some good moment of development. What seems most incredible was that those of us around her could seem so naïve as to marvel at someone so intuitive in her art. It made me face certain things about myself and come to deal with them realistically. In fact it was about then that I left off trying to paint seriously. After that, my painting became mostly an exercise to remind me of what the process of painting and its techniques possessed as their most serious concerns —that is, whenever I set out to write something on the subject. From time to time I might imagine I was serious about painting again. But essentially it was over for me.

Part Three

IT IS SOMETIMES interesting to recall the mystifying behavior of one's children in their infancy, because so often they
were already exhibiting characteristic traits that would be
confirmed later in their adult behavior. When this Braxton of
ours was a baby, before he could crawl on his hands and knees
even, he could with his stout little arms pull himself over the
side of his crib and land himself—headfirst sometimes—on
the wooden floor. At last we got so we would place a protective pillow on the floor when we put him down at night. But
after thus dropping himself on the floor he could worm himself out of sight underneath a nearby bed or table. Many a
morning I heard Melissa give a startled gasp when she found
him gone from his crib and altogether to have vanished. But
more often we would find him in the upstairs hall where he
seemed to be making his way not toward our room but clearly
toward that of his two big brothers. We lived in fear that he
might one morning tumble down the stairs. With screws and
a screwdriver I finally set up an accordion gate attached to the

newel post. But I suspect there was never any real danger of his falling down the stairs. Though he did often seem to have had a hard time finding his way out of the room that served as his nursery, once in the hallway some instinct seemed to direct him toward the older boys' room. Looking back on those episodes, I see now a foreshadowing of how things would be when he grew up.

After he learned to crawl and then to walk there was still further difficulty about keeping him in his crib and confined to his room. The older children were a great boon to us in sharing responsibility for their baby brother and appreciating the boundless joy and affection which he inspired in us. Though his sister, Susan, was barely more than a toddler herself when Brax was born, she was as adept as Melissa and I at changing a diaper or giving a bottle or patting his bottom to put him to sleep at nap time. By the time Brax was two or three years old she would read to him by the hour on the side-porch swing in summer or by the open fire in the sitting room in the winter. It was not often that we did not have a part-time nursemaid and a maid-cook as well in the house, both of whom doted on our blond cherub. But his sister insisted on having him under her wing much of the time. Even his mother had almost to fight the other females of the household to have the baby to herself during mornings and afternoons of the week. The boys had their turns too with the baby. They were quite as efficient as Susan with the diaper and the bottle. And when I came home from the University and turned into the driveway I was apt to confront any one of the three older children pushing Brax up and down the asphalt in his pram or stroller.

When Brax got a little older we found even more remarkable the tolerance and forbearance shown by his big brothers when he insisted upon joining in their games. He would be out there running the bases before he had any idea what base-ball was all about. Or he seized the basketball and heaved it upward above his head and not at all in the direction of the hoop above the garage door. The two older boys never complained of his interference. Yet if by chance they failed to give him a turn at tossing the ball or running the bases he would throw the worst kind of temper tantrum. The same was true with their games of checkers or cards. There would be moments in all these games when Brax would come running to Melissa in a flood of tears—tears of fury—and have to be taken up in her arms. He would seem absolutely inconsolable and have to be held for some time, heaving deep sobs until at last he fell asleep upon her shoulder. And with Susan, when he was scarcely two years old, he would insist that he take turns with her at reading aloud from the book she held. For an endless period of time he would babble away, imitating the rhythm of Susan's voice and turning the pages at approximately the same speed Susan would have done. Then he would look up at her and say obligingly, "Your turn."

When the little lad was four or five he would tiptoe into our room in the early morning, and we would find him there in a chair watching us sleeping together side by side. It seemed to interest him that we were the only members of the family who slept together in the same bed. When we began to stir he would come to the edge of the bed and say, "I want to get in bed with you guys!" I would lift him over between us and he would bury his head beneath our pillows with his little rear end in the air. One of us would pat his bottom until he fell asleep there.

But more must be said here of what seemed a prediction of the sort of person he would become. Melissa and I thought that his ambitious and competitive nature suggested that Braxton was going to be precocious and a great achiever in school. But it didn't turn out so exactly. He always excelled in the first part of any school term, but after the first months he wanted to get on to the next term of the next grade or to work with the teacher in a class above his own. He stopped doing his homework at this point and could barely pass the classroom tests that were given. By the time he was twelve or fourteen he wanted to read grown-ups' books. It was hard to know what he made of books like *Madame Bovary*, say, at the age of thirteen. And then, as I've said, before he even left high school he had taken to painting and refused to attend college anywhere on the grounds that it might "damage his vision"!

For some time it had been my habit to excuse myself from the breakfast table before the others had finished. As they were all well aware, I liked to hurry up to the attic, where I had a small studio, and put in an hour or so on my abstract watercolors, perhaps, before going to the University. It was not that I any longer took these efforts of mine very seriously, but I did like to keep my hand in with the crayon sketches and watercolors and sometimes with oils. This was understood by everyone, though I don't recall ever explaining precisely what I did with those precious early hours of my day. Of course Melissa knew, and she was ever protective of my devotion, permitting no noise or roughhouse by the children until I had descended from the attic and set out for the University. And for almost no purpose would any one of the older children have presumed to follow me above stairs.

Yet one morning before I left to go up to the studio, suddenly Brax drew back from the table and announced under his breath that he was going up to his own room. From the breakfast nook we saw him mount the back stairway just as I might have done, and heard him close the door to his room behind him. Then on the following day we saw him repeat the performance. I am not sure the other children knew what

was going on. In fact, I'm really not certain that either of the
two older boys was present, because they were both already
upperclassmen at the University then and stayed in the dor-
mitories about half the time—whereas Brax was still in junior
high. But Melissa and I could not resist smiling about it afterward.

And it was no more than a week or so later, when I got
settled at my desk easel one morning, that I heard his footsteps on the steep attic stairs. When he came up to the studio,
I didn't look up. Presently he sat down on the straight chair
only a few feet from me. When neither of us had spoken for
several minutes, I glanced at him quickly and then looked
back at the picture that I was daubing away at. I realized that
Brax had not come up there to talk to me about some problem
of his. He had come up simply to look at me, to watch me, to
see what precisely I was up to when I shut out my family this
way. And when he went downstairs nearly an hour later, I
assume that he had decided it wasn't much—that it wasn't
much I was up to. He repeated this silent invasion of my
quarters a good number of times during the following months.
But he and I would never speak of it afterward. And I don't
believe I ever spoke to Melissa of his coming up there, though
I'm relatively certain she must have known what was going
on better than I did.

Before long Melissa discovered that he was charging art
supplies to my account at the supply store, and by then he
had already begun showing us examples of his work. He was
also beginning to make the whole family escort him on expeditions he had planned to the art galleries up in Washington.
We all wanted to go, but it was a matter of suppressed amusement that little Brax himself had developed such an interest.
Until this moment of his growing up his interests had all been
in the sciences. He had gone from dinosaurs to airplanes to

radios, et cetera, and on to the inevitable electronics. On earlier expeditions to Washington it was to the Smithsonian that he had dragged us all. He had often slept in the car while the rest of us—all but Susan perhaps, who stayed behind to keep him company—went to the Mellon and Corcoran. But now he led me back through the rooms of great pictures, and it became apparent to me how well he knew my own textbooks on art history, though not necessarily what he thought of them. My final certainty about this came one day when he insisted on giving us a lecture on how wonderful the Turners were. I knew from looks that the older boys gave me as we passed those self-indulgent swirls on canvases that the other children were all expecting a rebuttal from me. But my actual perception that day was that Brax knew how little enthusiasm I felt for Turner and how little room I gave him in my textbooks.

As an adult there would be much about Braxton's physical bearing to remind me not of my own youthful self or even of my father as I remembered him, but of my maternal grandfather as I vaguely pictured him in my own mind's eye. As Brax grew into young manhood, even distant relatives, those who well remembered the old statesman, would remark the strong resemblance. Perhaps it was his erect carriage, so unlike my own or my mother's, for that matter, through whom he would have had to have inherited a likeness to the old Senator—perhaps it was the erect carriage that so suggested the resemblance, this along with his high coloring and the reddish tint to his hair. But the fact is that even as a child —even when he was quite a little boy—there had been characteristics that sometimes made me think of my maternal grandfather. Because of his preeminence in the family there

were, of course, seemingly a myriad of anecdotes about the
boyhood of my distinguished grandfather. Nevertheless there
would have been no particular reason for me to associate this
child of mine with one or another of my forebears, though
now and then a trivial incident did suggest it. I had been
brought up on the anecdote in which the little Senator had
climbed upon an apple crate and for the benefit of his brothers
and sisters delivered himself of a childish lecture. The incident related was regarded as an omen of his future career as a
politician, though of course it relied for comic relief ostensibly
on the childish subject matter of his lecture. That little Senator began his moral preachment with these words for the
country cousins gathered round him: "Don't leave the gate
open when you go through! Don't let the hogs get out of the
pigpen! Don't leave the gate open to the chicken yard! Don't
interrupt your mother when she's on her knees in prayer!
Don't break up the chamber pot and don't let it spill on the
carpet!"

The parallel incident in Braxton's behavior was when he
crawled up a little set of library steps and commenced waving
his hands about. What he said really meant nothing, yet he
did seem to be railing forth at someone about something. No
actual words came forth, but like Mercutio he threw a hand-
kerchief over his face and gave way to bawling forth: "Blah,
blah, blah, blah, blah, blah, blah . . ." When I told his
mother about this performance, which he had given to me
alone, she immediately said he thought he was mimicking me
the day I let him audit one of my classes. But to me he seemed
too like my grandfather for it to be denied.

However, at the time of which I want to speak mostly,
Brax was a grown man and like his two older brothers and his
sister, Susan, he had long since left home. He had not, however, gone so far afield as the other children, and consequently

he came home more often than they. This youngest son of ours had set up shop, so to speak, in the city of Washington. He was scarcely two hours up the road from the university town of Charlottesville, where his mother and I continued to live after my retirement from the University there. It was as a painter and a sculptor that Brax was already trying to establish himself. Moving into Washington was not a very good idea, though I would not have presumed to tell him so. And just why he chose such a philistine place as Washington for such a endeavor was beyond all comprehension. I have had a lifelong acquaintance with that city (both sides of our family having been in politics whenever their politics was right or their luck was good), and I knew that Washington's appreciation for art, as for nearly every other aspect of life except politics, perhaps, is at best only skin-deep and to say the least only superficial. Everything there is transitory and soon out of favor. But my son Braxton Bragg Longfort was never one for listening to advice from his elders, even though they might be ever so experienced or learned in the subject at hand. And so it was that after Brax was no longer living under our roof, I ceased trying to offer him counsel of any kind. He went his own way in the city of Washington.

But on those weekends that Brax was back home with us, he and I passed peaceable hours together. We did, that is, until I began my incessant, excessive talk about my cousin Aubrey Bradshaw. "Incessant, excessive" was how Melissa termed it when she was out of sorts with me. It was Brax's strong negative response to the mention of that cousin's name that set me analyzing anew this oversensitive and capricious lad that Melissa and I had brought into the world. And over the months the more negative he became to the subject the more persistent I grew. I found I couldn't somehow leave the subject alone. Ours had been a close-knit family always, and after the dispersal of the children we were always much given to long-distance telephoning. Even over the long-distance wire—between my house in Charlottesville and his studio apartment in the District—I could easily detect the tension in Braxton's voice. It was not that I was unused to contention and opposition on his part. Brax was a child of the sixties. He *must* be allowed to do his thing in his *own* way! But I was mystified by his insistence and, later on, his persistent opposition to me in the matter of Cousin Aubrey. In this instance it seemed a particularly infantile business. I'm afraid that is how I put it to myself. Yet continue he did with his discouraging and pejorative remarks in the months ahead. He would go on even after the evidence became clear that our ancient cousin Aubrey Bradshaw was not only still alive but was residing from time to time in our very own part of the world. It appeared that that old man was actually now in the vicinity of Washington and Charlottesville. I could not resist speaking of it to Brax now and again, though Melissa warned me against doing so. If she were nearby whenever I myself brought up the subject on the telephone with Brax, she always made silent ugly faces at me. For Brax didn't even like me to mention Cousin Aubrey's name and would sometimes pretend on the telephone that he couldn't hear me or that he didn't know to whom I was referring. He would make me repeat the name several times, and yet, sometimes, I felt quite sure that the young fellow was making his weekly call home just for the purpose of finding out if his father was still running on about the "old Tennessee relative."

Let me say here that the three oldest children were eminently supportive of my every effort to discover what I could about Aubrey. The rest of the family had always stood behind me in *all* things. They might laugh at me and suggest that my concern for this cousin of my mother's was supplant-

ing my scholarly interest in the English Pre-Raphaelite painters (about whom I was allegedly to write a book during
retirement), but my older children's good nature and my
wife's understanding heart had seen me through the many
trials of academic life and made me able to endure the pains
of it. They had indulged me in everything. My having been
brought up by my widowed mother and those two aunts of
mine made it inevitable that I would often enough be told that
a man so reared—by women alone—would all his life remain
spoiled and difficult. Well, my wife and daughter, as well as
my two older sons, had taken me as they had found me, so to
speak. After my mother's death they shouldered the legacy
with such apparent ease that when Mother's death actually
came about I scarcely noticed this transfer to their able shoulders. I should say here also that although all of them have
always listened to my Tennessee stories with infinite patience,
neither Melissa nor any of the children is in any sense a son
or daughter of the Volunteer State. Nor has any of them ever
resided there for more than ten days or two weeks at a time.
Instead, my children spent their earliest years in the half-
dozen towns where I taught before settling in Virginia. And
as I have said, they and their mother would be dragged by me
through Europe and half of Asia on the various research projects that I undertook during summer recess.

From my own lips they must all of them have heard my
entire stock of stories—many times over. With the oldest children I felt this created a certain bond between them and me.
We had a field of common reference when any difference of
opinion or misunderstanding arose. In conversations my
daughter, Susan, ever since she had become a grown woman,
would frequently refer to my Tennessee anecdotes. And, of
course, she has observed how much this pleases me. When
she used to come home on weekend visits from her Angora-

goat farm in Southside Virginia (where she also worked at her sculpture in those days) she often told me about some rustic characters down there who reminded her of the people in my stories. One day she winked at me and said that she would keep an eye out for Cousin Aubrey in case he should turn up in her neck of the woods. My two older sons, Walter and John (born while I was doing research on Walter Pater and John Ruskin and named for them), were no less indulgent than their sister with me and no less sympathetic to my interests. Those two older sons along with their wives and children were now living in New York City, and together the two of them owned and operated a rare-print shop on Fourth Avenue, near Union Square, as well as a very elegant picture gallery on Sixth Avenue near Seventeenth Street. They, Walter and John, were more amused than annoyed by my talk about Cousin Aubrey, and presently they began sending me a series of comic Japanese postcards relating to Shintoism and ancestor worshiping in general.

My first exchanges with Brax on the subject of Cousin Aubrey were actually over long-distance telephone. Brax, as I've indicated, is an artist—primarily a painter. He has great facility, as everyone observes. When he first set out as a painter he was so changeable that it was hard for me to tell from one picture to the next what school of painting his allegiance could be traced to. I believe he was an abstract expressionist at the time. And as abstract expressionist he was passing his impecunious existence in that most expensive place in the country, which is Washington! Between the two of us there had been many contests of will. This I cannot and would not attempt to conceal. Braxton being mine and Melissa's only *true* child of the sixties, he had come into manhood in that infamous era. He declined to do any kind of apprenticeship with one or another of the various accomplished artists that I, myself, knew and could have afforded him access to.

Sometimes it was with the support of his mother that Braxton made fun of me, and sometimes he stood alone, as if he were pitting himself against the whole world. Often when I was in Washington on some errand at the galleries, I would go and stay overnight at Braxton's place. I would always call him from the gallery, of course, and ask him if it was convenient. He would say for me to come right on up. Either he would be there to welcome me or would leave the key under the mat. But suddenly now it became very different. If I let it slip that I was trying to follow up some clues as to Cousin Aubrey's exact whereabouts, he would say he had a friend staying overnight with him and that it wasn't exactly convenient. I would assume that it was a girlfriend, which in all likelihood it was. One night he insisted on taking me to dinner as his guest, and it turned out to be for the purpose of introducing me to his Russian girlfriend, Masha. Masha was discreet and did *not* spend the night that night. I took note of the fact.

On previous occasions there had been other girlfriends, and Brax had never before had scruples about their spending the night or not. He had even had me sleep in the kitchen one night when a totally strange girl—strange to me—was staying with him. I could never be sure, however, that this change in him did not come about because he had formed a permanent attachment to the émigré Russian girl in whose company I would see him on all subsequent visits. But not now—not when I was on my present business concerning Cousin Aubrey. During this period, besides following up on hunches as to Cousin Aubrey's whereabouts, which nearly always proved to be false, I was looking up information about other members of my family. My mother's family, of course, had its longtime official connection with the city, going back for several generations. I would suddenly remember some relative or other, all of whom had been aboard that fateful funeral train bound for Knoxville in 1916. I would wonder if that relative who came to mind was still alive and if he would know what had become of Aubrey. I knew that some of those people (or the descendants of some of them) still lived in Washington or its suburbs, but it would turn out finally that none of them recalled anything or cared at all about remembering him. He was not, after all, an important relative. If they vaguely remembered something, it would only be about the scandal of the irregularity of Aubrey's birth. "Wasn't he born of some Tennessee mountain woman and the Senator's older brother? And didn't the Senator kind of adopt him? Let me think. He *was* born out of wedlock, wasn't he?" I might even be reduced sometimes to looking up old addresses in the public library. And from there I would go on to the Library of Congress to find certain information about forebears that I shared with those people. As I have said, we had all manner of family connections in Washington. My Senator grandfather's own father had once come to Washington as Commissioner of Indian Affairs—a hundred years back. Descendants of the old Commissioner's appointees in the bureaus were actually still living around the District, and in the course of my researches at the Library of Congress I came upon a bundle of correspondence between that Commissioner's *own* grandfather and President Andrew Jackson himself when he was fighting in the War of 1812. The correspondence was mostly squabbling about the transport of supplies from Mobile to New Orleans.

It was my interest in all of this, as I have indicated, that most offended my son Braxton. Here I was wasting my time on such family trivia when I could have been off in London collecting material on Pre-Raphaelite painters! Once when I assured him that I was going over to London the very next year to conclude my research in that subject he replied directly: "I am sure you have every intention of doing so! But you will take your Tennessee research right along with you. Somehow you can't ever shake it, can you? Though you dragged the family all over the world with you when we were growing up, and skipped about from college to college all over the U.S.A., you've never left home, really, have you? Never left Tennessee, have you? You won't have it dragged out of you, will you?"

But ultimately it was not just Brax and I who were involved in this unpleasantness. If my wife, Melissa, answered the phone when Brax called, I could tell from her silences that he was haranguing her about my "tacky obsession with the past" and my obsession with Tennessee in general. While he was talking, either Melissa would fall silent or I would hear her saying, "Yes . . . yes . . . yes . . ." And I began to perceive that a certain complicity existed between them. Otherwise when she wasn't on the phone with Brax and she and I were alone in the house she would seem generally indifferent to the subject and would say with seeming candor that it was all much ado about nothing. That, of course, pleased me and was meant by her to do so. But I knew that when I was not present our youngest child could wrap his mother around his little finger and have her in complete agreement about anything. That is simply my wife's nature. And the same is true of our daughter, Susan. When Susan came home on a weekend visit, I could tell that Brax had been haranguing her, too, over the telephone from Washington about all this. If I asked her directly what she'd heard from Brax she would say simply, "Oh, he called. That's all." If I pressed her further for something he had said—asking her if he had talked about Masha Obolinsky, for instance—then Susan would look at me with disdain, as if I were a wretched old busybody. But Susan would never outright lie to you about anything. It was: "He said a little" or "Not much." Or: "He mentioned her only in passing, I think." But I knew better.

Through it all Brax remained considerate of me in most respects and was nearly always affectionate in his manner. After much reflection I saw his position as this: he had accepted early in life and with a certain degree of fortitude that his father *was* the merest academic and was in no sense a creative talent, but he could not and would not reconcile himself to his father's last days being spent "researching some such banal family affair" as Cousin Aubrey's disappearance represented.

Brax never put it to me in precisely those terms, of course. It seemed to him that the case of a missing person, whether down in Tennessee or elsewhere, was a private matter not to be looked into. It was a man's own affair if he wished to disappear! I might be opening a can of worms! said Brax with respect to what Cousin Aubrey's life might be like. He repeated again and again that if I was successful in my research the result might be disastrous for my old cousin as well as, somehow, for myself. Along with Melissa and the other children, Brax could remember anecdotes told about Cousin Aubrey by his grandmother. She had lived with us in Virginia during her last years, and he could recall her portraying this Aubrey always as a country bumpkin and a laughingstock to girls of her generation.

Nowadays my beloved, quite elderly mother was staying with us much of the time. She was no less interesting a person to me than she had ever been and was as much a favorite of Melissa and the children as she was of mine. But there was never any question about whom her attention was most focused on. During those times I would wickedly point it out to her, saying that she had eyes only for Brax. She would fuss and fumble, utterly denying all truth of the accusation. Her most usual riposte would be that I was only revealing my jealousy of my own child! She would appeal to the other children and ask if they didn't think she loved them all equally well. They, along with Melissa, reassured her, of course. But in private they would reproach me for teasing Gran and making her uncomfortable. They would also admit that I was right about it. Susan would even add that Brax was everybody's favorite, giving me an accusing look. "And why shouldn't he be?" she said. "The baby is always the favorite!" Nevertheless, my mother, who occupied our only downstairs bedroom, truly did keep her eye fixed on Brax as long as she lived. From her own room she watched his comings and goings with affection and approval. She never asked him where he was going and where he had been. But she always called him in her room and gave a big kiss to tell him goodnight or good morning—and, I suspect, to slip him a bit of money. To me she said she thought he would make a name for himself as a painter. She said Brax had the mixture of aggression and sensitivity it took to be an artist.

THIS WAS but a year before my mother died. Her death was, I think, a relatively easy one for her, and she had advanced at any rate to a very great age. During her last year I had begun to notice a frankness about her that I had not noticed before. She would say things about her family that she would not have said earlier. Little expressions of criticism of them that had been previously left unsaid. There were whole episodes that had been omitted in her earlier narrations. Most of them did not seem particularly significant, and I would find myself wondering why they had been left out in earlier versions. One night, apropos of nothing, so it seemed to me at first, she began giving me that account of the night she and Cousin Aubrey were going to elope. When she got to the part where Cousin Aubrey said, "We must not elope," she burst out again just as she must have done when she was a young girl, "Oh, Aubrey, you'll break my heart!" And as she sat beside me there in the downstairs living room of our house in Charlottesville her wrinkled old cheeks became suffused with deep blushes. Presently she turned her head aside pretending to readjust the pillows on the couch though actually to conceal her blushes. I think she had not, herself, known what she was going to say. And momentarily a silence hung over the room like something palpable. I tried to think of something else to say that would change the subject and relieve her from going on with her account, but some compulsion she felt about it would not let her stop here. As if recalling Cousin Aubrey's very words that long-ago night she continued to quote him. "I have been awake these three nights thinking about what to do," he had said to her. And as though trying to catch his own tone, she deepened her voice as she quoted him, "I must not take you away! I am thinking of *you!*" Then recapturing her own girlish voice, which was as distinctly different from her rasping, present-day voice, she represented herself as screaming, "You're thinking of *me?* You are thinking only of yourself! Oh, I'll go and throw myself out that window!" She went on to describe how she had run across the room, and now actually lifting her arms as if struggling with the big, heavy window sash, she told how he had followed her and made every effort to restrain her, seizing her by the upper arms and drawing her to him, and, looking me in the eye as if I might not believe her intention, she vowed that her wish to end her life had been so genuine and so intense that her strength was almost greater than his, but he held her in his arms so tightly that momentarily she gave way. For a time she had let her head rest on his shirtfront while she sobbed and presently began to wail in high deafening peals which he must have feared someone in the corridor might hear. As she gave her account it was almost as though she were reverting to her old dramatic presentations. It was so impressive to me that I felt that all her recitations had been but a rehearsal for this moment she was describing for me there on the couch. "Or perhaps even my sisters in their rooms might hear!" she exclaimed leaning her head a little to the side, though not comically—but rather so convincingly that I could not but be absorbed in the scene. And then slowing the rhythm of her recitation she went on. "At last Aubrey led me to the settee and managed to quiet me for a time. Then my sobbing began again. I can hear my own voice right now. Sobbing as if from inside me. I really don't know that I made any sounds."

For me it was as if I could see her long brown hair that had, that night, fallen about her chaste and virginal shoulders and over her tearstained face. But presently she continued her dramatic presentation. She told how he held her from him in order to talk to her, to reason with her. She described how she sprang up again and ran instantly to the window. She was quite serious about what she wished to do. This time she would be able to raise the sash a little way before he got to her. But again he took her in his arms. She closed her eyes momentarily, and as he held her there she could think only of how much stronger he was than she. "Trudie, what does this mean?" he asked her, almost shouting his words at her. "What does this mean?" As he looked down at her, she felt he saw her as a small child, a small child having its way. "Perhaps it occurred to him then that this was only the first onset of adolescence in me. Perhaps in that moment he felt the difference in our ages." However this might be, as Trudie had looked up at him from his feet she became aware that she had been suffering for a very long time from suppressed feelings and unnameable drives of some sort. At last she allowed him to take her to the settee again. And he went through the motions of comforting her.

Then Mother concluded by saying that she did not remember what he had said to her in the hour that had followed. She said she was never afterward to listen seriously to anything he said to her. Her papa returned at nine o'clock that night and neither her sister Bertie nor Felicia was ever fully aware of all that had taken place in the Governor's suite.

I do not know fully how I myself responded to this account of Mother's. I sat there in stunned silence. It was unreal to me. It was as if Mother had just now repeated some old nightmare she had had as a girl.

UPON MOTHER'S DEATH I think I suffered the same sort of shock I would have had if she had died when I was ten or twelve. It came at the end of a long day which I had spent shut away in my studio in the attic. Since it was early fall and there was already beginning to be a chill in the air at night I got up and closed the windows before I went downstairs. That was how I happened to see her. She was seated in a circle of plank chairs which we kept arranged on the lawn. She had pulled her chair a little off from the circle in order to be away from the shade of the apple trees that grew there. I closed the window and then I went directly down to join her. She had been sitting there very erect when I caught my first glimpse of her from the window. When I came out the side door onto the grass she had cowered down into her chair with her head a little bit to the right side. I'm sure that it took only the time required for me to come down from the attic to the side door for her to be taken away from us. Somehow I understood at once without any reflection that she was dead. As I took her in my arms and carried her through the side door to the house, lines from the old poem "Lasca" came to my lips, but I shook away the formation of the words as though they were a sacrilege. My wife had been watching, I suppose—as she would have done after one of the children when they were little—because she was there to receive us when I brought my mother through the doorway. Melissa and I didn't exchange a word until I had laid Mother on the couch in the living room. "Poor dear," Melissa said, addressing her words to me. Then she went to the telephone to call the doctor, and looking down at my poor, little, dead mother, I felt I ought to say something to my wife, but I could say nothing. Presently without a word I went back up to my room in the attic.

It was only because I hadn't bothered to put on a light in the shadowy room, but everything there seemed strange and unfamiliar. And it was as though I knew then that nothing in the world could ever look quite the same again. But presently I got up and went down the dark stairway that I had just climbed. I knew how inhuman it would seem to Melissa for me to go off by myself at this moment. When I arrived downstairs again Melissa told me not to go into the living room, but disregarding that I went to Mother and kissed her on the forehead for the last time.

During the first weeks after her death I was afraid to let myself be alone with my thoughts. I required that some member of the family be always beside me. I couldn't go up to bed at night unless Melissa led the way. And I don't believe I once darkened the door of my studio during all this time. Nobody was so inconsiderate as to mention the matter of my mother's will until weeks had passed. And only *then* because several taxes had to be paid. At that point it became incumbent upon me to open the drawer to her little desk. And the first thing I came upon there was her handwriting across a folded paper, and it said, "My last will and testament." While dreading the sight of it, it actually lifted my spirits as nothing else could have done. I presently took the paper into the living room, where members of the family were gathered. And because I could not ask anyone else to do it for me I opened her testament, so called. On it was written: "I bequeath all my monies and all worldly possessions to my grandson Braxton Bragg Longfort." It was a relatively modest sum, but for Brax it constituted a real fortune. It was something that would support him as an artist for the foreseeable future! My thoughts soared at the first sight of the words. It represented my mother's renewal of hope for the kind of artist I had never become. It meant that she had cherished that hope till the end. It bespoke her full and complete confidence in Brax. Moreover, it gave me a wonderful feeling of being let off the hook once and for all, and it altogether dispelled the gloom of that day and of depressing days I anticipated for the future. There was no black cloud in my life after that. It must have produced the same effect upon Melissa's spirits, because the very next day I saw her take up her notebook again and write with the old ease. It was as though Mother's confidence in Brax's talent also served to liberate her own articulation and power. And it was only then that I fully realized that Brax's aesthetic powers were something he inherited more from her than from me.

CERTAIN MATTERS in my past life seemed to weigh heavily on me at this period, and thoughts of Brax were always with me. What I counted on was Brax's not recalling, Brax and the other members of the family, for that matter, the actual ends to which the vanished Tennesseans came. Because the full truth is that before I left my Tennessee haunts I had done countless hours of research on the fates of those men. Even as a small boy I made mental notes of casual remarks dropped by my uncles and aunts and family friends on any subject related to the fate of the vanished ones. I climbed into my grandmother's attic and read all the old letters that might be pertinent. I read old newspapers and even dipped into local history books that were to be found in abundance on the shelves of various members of our family connections—when I was not yet twelve. In my teens during summer vacation, I made excuses to my mother to travel considerable distances in order to follow up clues I had obtained in my snooping. Anyhow, although those first efforts of mine at research and detection were eminently successful it did seem somehow to me demeaning, even shameful, in the light of opinions held by my forebears on this subject. And so I seldom mentioned my findings to anyone. To my own children especially.

Brax was so consistent and persisted so in taking his own line on this that I very early came to suspect that he somehow was quite as obsessed as I was—that is, with the question of whether or not I might find the man that was so on my mind. My other children, in their own easygoing way, had already accused me of harboring a secret wish to disappear from the scene of our Charlottesville life. With equal good nature I had told them that theirs was too easy and obvious a way of interpreting my obsession with Aubrey Bradshaw—or my profound interest in all those other lost Tennessee men. But on the other hand it wasn't long before I was questioning whether or not a very young man like Brax mightn't himself harbor some such wish to vanish into another atmosphere. Surely I could not myself have failed to recognize the power of my own son's imagination.

It crossed my mind very soon that this was not why he deplored any mention of my concern with Aubrey Bradshaw. I had long since, you see, come to the conclusion that there are days in the lives of all men when they harbor such longings. I suspected already that it was almost universal amongst men, the wish to lose oneself—especially amongst men of a certain cast of mind or temperament. And the more so since Braxton, himself, had become more or less obsessed with the tales and rumors concerning the ultimate fate of some of those vanished men, which he had picked up I know not where. (He certainly had not rooted around in the places I knew.) From somewhere or from somebody he had learned that my father's cousin who had disappeared with a woman from a neighboring farm had finally wished to return home. According to Brax, the wife's brothers, hearing of his, went to him wherever it was he had revealed himself to be and forbade his coming back home or even manifesting his whereabouts to his wife and children. Allegedly the poor man was never seen again in our part of the world. In fact according to Brax he spent the rest of his life knocking about from pillar to post, altogether penniless and homeless.

And then there was the Nashville banker. Brax had a version of the end he came to, too. The end of *his* story was that when at last he manifested himself again, he had overcome his difficulty with the demon rum and was regarded as a model citizen in his new location. Sad, though, was not the word for what happened after he was rediscovered. When he was at last hunted out by a Nashville newspaper reporter ("Just for the story in it," so it was reported), the two oldest children of the new family he had started locked themselves in their rooms and put bullets through their pretty heads. It turned out that that banker and his former secretary, with whom he had run off, had together opened a small hardware store somewhere in the Northeast and were operating a moderately successful business there. . . . And I can assure you there were other such instances in Brax's repertoire, all the details of which Brax had picked up and happily reported to me. As for my wife and this son of mine, they have always shown more interest in those stories with unhappy endings than in those that end merely in tantalizing mystery. My son, moreover, used to predict perversely that were I to find my cousin Aubrey it might do him irreparable harm. From the outset I felt that it was likely that the old man's rediscovery by a long-lost cousin, being myself, scarcely more than half his own age, might just as easily turn out to be a great boon for the old fellow—and might somehow inevitably be so for me. Yet in my nightly dreams about him throughout the entire period of my search it would turn out sometimes one way and sometimes another. Even now I cannot say for sure what our eventual reunion meant to either Aubrey or me.

IN MY REFLECTIONS I always find it curious and somehow significant to look backward and forward on my life. The thoroughfares and byways of the old town of Charlottesville seem to represent the years of my children's maturing and finishing off their education. Here they had ridden bicycles, learned to drive cars, done their first courting, had their first best friends with whom they had stood on one street corner or another, discoursing on what they would do and what they would not do with their lives. The town was theirs and the University was theirs, too, though really it was like something they had borrowed for the time being. All of them but Braxton had attended classes and graduated, but the University, as I walk the grounds nowadays, represents what at such moments seems *mine*—my very own. Rightly or wrongly it represented what I had done not with a particular talent but with an abstract ability to cope. I had met classes, done research, published books, given papers on Renaissance art at meetings all over the world. All this was finished now, but that was what I had done with whatever powers I possessed. That was what the handsome Palladian buildings and white colonnades of the University meant for me personally. In my early years I had traipsed around a half-dozen state universities, building a case for myself until I should receive the "call" I awaited and expected. In the course of things I had declined invitations to go to Harvard and to Princeton. But the Tennessee boy had known almost from the beginning at what institution he meant to do his teaching, bring up his children, live out his life with the wife of his bosom. Talk about singleness of purpose! He had certainly had *that!* Or had almost had it, or had near about had it. During this period I found myself going for long, solitary walks in the environs of the town. Sometimes it would be in the long summer twilight when afternoon traffic of all kinds had ceased, and night traffic had not yet begun. Or sometimes it was in the early morning, before breakfast, when there seemed to exist precisely the same crepuscular light and the same hiatus of all human activity in the streets. I don't know that that was why I chose those hours for walking—it was after I had retired and was now free to walk at any hour I might choose—but in those hours and in that light I seemed more easily able to search out the significance of things about me, and often at those moments I would imagine that I saw the face of one or another of my children in the people that went past. . . . When I talked to myself on these early morning or evening walks about the crossroads, I never asked myself why there was a haunting emptiness just outside the satisfaction I took at having *done* my career so satisfactorily, and the other me never reminded the present me of the particular painter or sculptor I had set out to be and that my doting mother never forgave me for not being.

It was true that my mother never forgave me for not going on to become a painter, but despite that lady's general knowingness, her enlightened views, and despite her eccentricities, she was still Southern woman enough to relish my having received the appointment at *the* University. Even my father would have approved. And it was not only my old mother or my deceased father who would take satisfaction from this appointment of mine. Relatives from all over Tennessee, some of whom I had never set eyes upon, wrote me letters of congratulation. Many of them said they had known this was where I had always belonged and had been confident that I would end up here. Sometimes I would be ashamed of the fact, but I have to confess I rather agreed with them. How could it have been otherwise? By my mother and by my aunts and all the other kinspeople I had been so tenderly looked after in my childhood; by my beloved Melissa I had been so lovingly tended and cared for and catered to in all things; by my children—even by Brax up to a point—I had been so revered as a father and looked up to as a great man (almost as great as my grandfather), as a supreme authority, that is, on the graphic arts to which they would each of them give himself in one fashion or another; how could it not be at last that our great Southern university should reach out and take me unto itself? Of course I laughed at myself for the very egocentric monstrosity of the thought. And yet. And yet. As I walked along the colonnade back across the terraced Lawn I knew how far back in my life went every reference to every foot of serpentine wall and every plinth and column and molding and architrave and every molded brick of every Range and Pavilion. I had never set foot on the place as a child. I'd been sent away to Columbia University on scholarship when post-graduate-work time came for me. But I suppose the sight of *the* University as it has always been was stored in my head. It was put there, I imagine, by all those who thought I ought to end up there. My paternal grandfather had attended classes there for one year. But most impressive to me was my father's uncle Hugh who had studied architecture like my father. Uncle Hugh had come home to West Tennessee after the War and built for himself a replica of one of the Pavilions on the Lawn. When I went there to teach I could never make out which Pavilion it was meant to duplicate. The most I remember was that even the inside walls of Uncle Hugh's Pavilion were made of brick. But this great-uncle of mine had been shot through the hand at Shiloh and could never pursue his career as an architect and had lived out his life in his brick Pavilion. I only went there once, and that is when I was taken to his funeral. But while he was alive I saw him every year at the Confederate reunion which was held at the fairgrounds in August. I would sit beside him at one of those long plank tables outdoors, where dinner was laid out for the veterans. And I always dreaded this, because that was when I had to see his hand that was shot through at Shiloh. The fingers of that hand were all fixed in a crooked position, and while I sat beside him he pulled out from his pocket in his gray uniform a specially made wooden fork that looked like a pair of wooden scissors.

When he was laid out in his coffin in his Confederate uniform, the coffin was placed with its lid leaning up against one of the inside brick walls. The wall was plastered, but through the plaster you could still make out the bricks. That gave me a certain satisfaction somehow. It made me imagine what the structure had looked like when it was new. But what I liked best that day was the fact that the undertaker had placed Uncle Hugh's bad right hand in his pocket, and so I didn't mind looking at him. It was especially easy to look at him, since my mother was holding my hand as we moved along the line of mourners who were looking into the coffin. Even that day I was reminded that the house was a replica of a Pavilion at the University. It all seemed a part of the warm and carefully protected world that was mine in my childhood.

And what is strange is that later very often when I had indulged in my memories and reflections about my own life, I ended up by turning my thoughts to Cousin Aubrey Bradshaw and to what I knew about the hours and days preceding his disappearance. The one recollection seemed somehow contingent upon the other.

THERE ARE SEVERAL ways of transporting oneself from Charlottesville to Washington. Brax always drove back and forth in his ramshackle car. He was too impatient to travel by any public carrier. When Melissa had had occasion to make the trip she generally went by Greyhound bus. I believe she felt that bus travel kept her more aware of her destination and of the true nature of the countryside through which she was passing. Being a native of that long-settled and still largely rural section of the state known as Southside Virginia and having as a girl attended Mary Washington Women's College, Melissa had some familiarity or at least some vague association with every mile of the journey. Either she had a relative or a onetime college classmate at each crossroad and village along the way. As for me, I nearly always took the train when I traveled alone, and there was actually a plane one could take —there used to be two or three flights a day before the hub system was introduced. But flying was not only expensive; it had made the Charlottesville–Washington journey into an unreal abstraction. Distance became a matter of no importance and no reality. Like a transatlantic flight there was insufficient time for the necessary adjustment from one culture to another.

At a quarter till five one spring morning, I got aboard the train at the picturesque Southern Railroad depot in Charlottesville. I remember particularly how rough and rude the conductor was as I mounted the metal steps which he had put out on the wooden platform. I suppose I knew exactly how he felt, because I could imagine momentarily that he too had been uncustomarily dragged out of his bed at an ungodly hour. It seemed, moreover, that he was justified in showing his rudeness to me because of my half-wakeful semicomatose condition. I could almost believe it was my own decision to take that morning train that had got him out of his berth so early. And the fact was it had been only Brax's insistent telephone call the night before which had brought me to taking the early morning Washington train instead of one at four in the afternoon.

I had actually been planning on taking the afternoon train, and had not even apprised Brax of this impending trip to the city. He had been so crotchety with me lately and so generally out of sorts—with the whole world in fact—that I had determined on this occasion to put up at a hotel near the Cosmos Club without even manifesting myself to Brax, whose studio was only a few blocks away. I could have been quite comfortable on that afternoon train. I knew the conductor on that run very well and often had dinner in the dining car just before arriving at Washington. But everything and everyone on the morning train seemed strange to me. Strangest of all, though, was the new and disturbing purpose which Brax's telephone call had given the trip. His mother had taken the call at first and for two or three minutes responded with a string of exclamations: "No! . . . Oh, no, Brax! . . . Oh, no, Brax, it is impossible!" I could hear Brax's rapid flow of speech but could not understand his individual words. Or perhaps I did actually catch the familiar syllables of Cousin Aubrey's name. Afterward I hardly knew whether I had or not. Presently I was reaching out to take the phone when Melissa turned in my direction, though still speaking into the mouthpiece, "You must tell him yourself," she was saying to Brax. "He would hardly believe it from me!" And then she handed the instrument over to me.

Brax's message was that he himself had inadvertently discovered Aubrey Bradshaw's exact present whereabouts. But it was a good deal more than that. He had seen him a number of times without knowing who he was, and now the old man was lying near death—or so Brax supposed—in the Georgetown Hospital. Brax was clearly quite emotional about the situation. He had already paid three visits to the hospital to inquire about the old man's condition! And now he was on the phone urging that I hurry on into Washington in order to join him, so that we could visit Cousin Aubrey's bedside together. Then taking the telephone by its extension cord I went to a comfortable chair and dropped down into it. I was not sure I could deal with the mixed emotions I felt. Of course I would support Brax in almost any mission he could propose. But it was as though never before in his life had he asked my support in any matter. And in recent months such a request from him seemed the last thing one could imagine. In addition to this shock, I had simultaneously to absorb Cousin Aubrey's actually being located—and located, moreover, by our own Braxton, he who had until so recently deplored every mention of the man's name. And of things in the world that might have brought Brax to asking for my help, surely this particular turn of events seemed the most unlikely.

At last I heard myself saying to Brax: "Of course I'll be there. And yes, on the morning train!" My beloved Melissa had by this time seized my free left hand and was patting it vigorously. She supposed from my ashen look that I might be suffering a cardiac arrest.

WHEN Aubrey Tucker Bradshaw resurfaced in my life at last—nearly fifty years after his first disappearance—he would resurface little by little, so to speak, inch by inch. And all this would be happening well before Brax's discovery. That is, I began first of all mainly to hear rumors of the existence of a man with a name much like his own, though not exactly like. The surname and the middle name had been reversed. And on the second occasion of my hearing of him it was indicated that the two names had been hyphenated—a most unusual practice for someone hailing from Tennessee. The old Cousin Aubrey in all representations of him had been so modest-sounding and unpretentious that I tended to dismiss the possibility of the two being one and the same. But once I had heard of the existence of this other man it registered indelibly on my mind. After the first report of him I was ever conscious of the remote possibility that this obviously different sort of man might still somehow be Aubrey.

Though it was always someplace other than Tennessee that I had heard his name spoken, it was inevitably added that his origins were there. It was this that made me first suspect that my mother and my two aunts might have been wrong in their assumption that Aubrey had fifty years ago merely disappeared into the East Tennessee countryside and had there resumed the role of a Tennessee bumpkin. It so happened that the first mention of his name reached my ears not in this country but while I was traveling in Europe. Since I was not over there on a pleasure trip and was not paying my own expenses, I was put up at a rather better hotel than I normally would have booked into. (My expenses were being paid by the University and by the Italian government for whom I was helping direct the restoration of artworks after the disastrous flood in Florence.) There in the dining room of the great hotel by the Arno I heard someone at the next table pronounce the name of Aubrey Bradshaw-Tucker. The people of that table were alternately speaking English, German, and Italian. I listened carefully but was unable to grasp precisely the subject of the conversation. Yet I heard once again the articulation of that name. The party left the dining room without my making out their identity, though I assumed, correctly I think, that they too were involved somehow in the restoration of the Uffizi.

The next time I heard the man's name spoken was on a shuttle between New York City and Washington. A garrulous old lady sitting beside me on that short flight insisted on knowing where I was "from." When I told her I was from Charlottesville, she said knowingly that my accent didn't sound like "old Charlottesville," and she speculated that I must teach at the University there. (She "knew people" there and had often been a visitor with some of the high-toned people.) I confirmed that all she said was so and confessed that I was originally from Tennessee. "Ah, Tennessee!" she exclaimed. "Nashville I'll bet it is!" Then she proceeded to tell me about a wonderfully attractive man from Nashville— "so he claimed." She had made his acquaintance aboard a South American cruise ship, and he had flirted with her "most scandalously." His name was Mr. Bradshaw-Tucker—"hyphenated no less!" she said. And then she laughed her merry laugh again. Suddenly I could see just how attractive she herself had once been, and I could understand how delightful it would have been to have found oneself on the South American cruise with her.

She said that Mr. Bradshaw-Tucker had the most beautiful Vandyke beard she had seen on any man. She liked beards on men, she said, and when she had told him so, he replied, with a twinkle in his bewitching brown eyes, that he only wore the beard to conceal "a very weak chin." Then she went on to say that Mr. Bradshaw-Tucker had deceived her wickedly and that *she* had clearly meant nothing to *him*. Only on the last day of the cruise did she discover that Mr. Bradshaw-Tucker was traveling in the company of another woman, a rich woman older than herself who during the voyage had kept mostly to their stateroom. I tried to reassure her —facetiously I suppose—that all Tennesseans were not such rascals, and I told her that my mother's maiden name had been Tucker and that she had had a cousin named Bradshaw. At this, that lady blushed to the roots of her snow-white hair. She made no further effort at conversation and managed not to hear any further questions that it now struck me to ask. I felt she was berating herself for having once again talked too much to a stranger. When she got off the plane she hurried away with the crowd without my learning so much as her name. And it was then that the fantasy first occurred to me that the country bumpkin, the outside cousin, had not disappeared into the countryside of Upper East Tennessee but had been interred with his erstwhile protector, the late Senator Tucker, and the new Aubrey had been released to make his own way, to take on a new persona and perhaps in that persona to take revenge upon the world.

At a party in Charlottesville some two years after that ride on the shuttle, I obtained a really conclusive piece of evidence that Mr. Bradshaw-Tucker and our cousin Aubrey Bradshaw were indeed one and the same. This occurred slightly over a year before my son Braxton would identify Aubrey as living on the same dead-end street with himself. The gathering that I refer to a year or so earlier was at a men's smoker—so called in old-fashioned academic circles—given one afternoon in honor of a visiting lecturer, a man who was being considered for an appointment at the University. Though I was on the selection committee, I felt reasonably certain that he would not accept such an appointment as we would be able to offer him. He was too celebrated, too "international" an expert in his field, to be willing to settle down in Charlottesville, Virginia. But he was our guest lecturer of the day, and we wished to please him. We happened on the subject of the old days of railways and what a delight traveling had been then. It turned out that our lecturer was a veritable collector of stories about trains. And, of course, wishing to please him, we all brought forward our stories on the subject. Perhaps I, more than the others, insisted on being heard and was soon running through my own repertoire. Yet I think everyone present would have acknowledged that our guest more or less urged me on.

When at length I proceeded to tell our lecturer about Grandfather's funeral train, I was careful to speak only of the comic aspects of the journey. In fact, I told him only about how my two uncles ended by getting very drunk and so altogether out of control that they finally, first one and awhile later the other, had to be turned over to the constabulary in the first two county seats where the train stopped after passing over the Tennessee state border.

Indeed, I had hardly sketched in my account of those two incidents when our guest lecturer burst out at me, exclaiming, "What a strange coincidence this is!" He bent forward and placed his well-manicured hands on my arm. But he was not even looking at me as he spoke. "This is a true story that I have heard before!" he said, bending toward me. "How very strange! How I do love such stories and most of all how I love to have them turn up in such dissimilar circumstances. I first heard of that train journey," he continued, "from a man by the name of Colonel A. N. Bradshaw-Tucker, who was himself present on that funeral train and who was, moreover, a relative of this dead Senator whom you referred to— up in the baggage car." (Obviously our guest lecturer had not bothered to catch my own name and my connection with the Senator, though I had already spent a day and a half in his company, squiring him about the University, introducing him to senior professors, deans, and one Vice-president. Clearly he did not recall that I had identified the dead Senator as my grandfather.) Presently he continued: "He was a very odd sort of person, this Colonel Bradshaw-Tucker, who told me his version of the same story. He was a very urbane and distinguished-seeming person. He was more like someone you might meet in Europe. One could not have guessed that his clothes even were American. He had a handsome beard, very beautifully trimmed. Altogether he was wonderfully well groomed in the old-fashioned way. He and I met in the house of a very wealthy lady in Bristol, Rhode Island. I never knew exactly what that relationship was— his and the Rhode Island lady's—but I gathered from little things he let drop that he saw himself as a great ladies' man. Anyway, he loved to talk about women—ever so confidentially. Perhaps he had a lot of money. He wished one, at any rate, to think so. Or perhaps he was the sort of man who lives off women. But the thing that interested me the most about that funeral train which he had been aboard," our guest lecturer continued, "was the presence there of the dead Senator's three young married daughters. I remember his holding up his forefinger and thumb like this and saying, 'Those young ladies, they were absolutely delicious.' He was like some very cultivated gourmet describing a variety of his favorite dishes! He made great distinctions and differentiations with regard to the young ladies' three kinds of beauty. He referred to them as innocent young matrons all properly married and perfectly protected, of course, but knowing nothing of the world. 'Genuine provincials!' he said. 'And absolutely delicious!' "

Suddenly I felt deeply offended and wished to hear no more from our lecturer and no more of Colonel Bradshaw-Tucker's view of my mother and my aunts. It was undoubtedly Cousin Aubrey that the lecturer had known, but the picture of this latter-day Colonel Bradshaw-Tucker he had painted was so far from what I had received from my mother and my aunts that I felt a kind of electric shock pass through me. When presently our talk was interrupted, I moved away from our guest lecturer and soon took my leave from the smoker. I was afraid that some faculty colleague there present might mention to him that my mother's name had been Tucker and that, like the Colonel, I too originally hailed from Tennessee. . . . I hardly need add here that the lecturer did not receive the nomination of the selection committee, and that though I continued to read his distinguished scholarly works I never saw him in person again.

From that day forward I had been sure, of course, that the man I kept hearing about was my mother's cousin. For a certain period after that I was less sure than formerly that I still wished to come face-to-face with Cousin Aubrey. Yet curiosity about his incredible transformation caused my interest in his whereabouts and his ultimate fate to persist. If the long-ago journey on the Senator's funeral train changed all our lives in some degree and if the significance of those changes was what I longed to understand, then a meeting with Colonel Bradshaw-Tucker—surely the most altered of us all—might facilitate my understanding. Only to look upon the man's countenance might solve mysteries about myself. Very soon after that, Aubrey's resurfacing in my life was destined to come one inch closer.

In Charlottesville there are many people, especially among the University faculty, who subscribe to the *Washington Post* as their morning newspaper. But since my wife is a native of a small town in Southside Virginia we have always read the *Richmond-Times Dispatch* for our morning paper and purchased the *New York Times* at the newsstand on the Corner. And that is how I happened to miss—or very nearly miss—seeing the newspaper picture of Colonel Bradshaw-Tucker. I first beheld his visage not in a paper that was delivered to my doorstep, and not in one for sale at the newsstand at the Corner, but in a fragment of newsprint wrapped around a vegetable that my wife, Melissa, brought from the market. It was from an issue of the *Washington Post* that was at least three weeks old. Even as the paper crossed my line of vision on its way to the trash can, I received an impression of the erect figure and the slightly out-of-focus face that was in the background of the photograph reproduced thereon. I quickly fished it out and spread it on the enamel-topped kitchen table. It purported to be a picture of one of those Washington hostesses whose entertainments one generally avoids unless one is seeking office or has some other self-interested purpose that requires one's presence there. The caption under the picture gave the famously rich hostess's name, describing her as one of Washington's most celebrated socialites. She was apparently so rich and so celebrated that it seemed worthwhile to mention her slightly out-of-focus escort in the background, one Colonel A. N. Bradshaw-Tucker. At last I had a blurred but indubitable image of the man that Aubrey Tucker Bradshaw had become. Though his beard was white, it seemed to me an absolute facsimile of the streaked gray beard my grandfather had worn in pictures taken not long before his death. Even though the image of his face was blurred, the dark eyes looked out piercingly toward the camera, just as the Senator's had always done in his campaign pictures, those which Mother had kept locked away in her leather-bound scrapbook and produced periodically for my admiration and edification. And I again had the eerie feeling that indeed it had been the old Cousin Aubrey whose end had come that September day in 1916 and that it was his body that had been substituted for the dead Senator's in the elaborately brass-trimmed coffin that was handed so clumsily into the boxcar of the special funeral train.

THE ACTUAL, very aged Cousin Aubrey, whose acquaintance Brax had made by chance at a nearby intersection of streets, was living in a large apartment complex up the street from Brax's rather shabby flat. They had struck up a conversation over what was merely the inordinate length of time it took a Washington traffic light to change from red to green. They had been aware of each other among pedestrians on several occasions before effecting their mutual introductions, however, when passing each other on their little dead-end street. It was easy to imagine that they should do so. Braxton Longfort was a great strapping blond fellow and was no doubt wearing the Left Bank blue beret which he sometimes affects. (It is really quite striking the way he gets himself up.) And the figure that Cousin Aubrey must cut nowadays on a Washington street corner—according to Brax's account, that is, and as I would presently be prepared to encounter him—is no less than striking.

Allegedly the old man was accustomed to going about in a

sort of Prince Albert garment, which nobody else has appeared in since my grandfather's day and that really had been an anachronism even then. But when one night Brax passed him on the street corner and came face-to-face with him, as I would ostensibly be doing soon, it wouldn't have struck anyone as being the least bit strange. It would seem, rather, that Cousin Aubrey was the norm and that all the world is somehow out of kilter. Yes, as I myself could vouch for under somewhat altered circumstances, the personality of the present-day Aubrey Tucker Bradshaw would inevitably strike one as being just that charming and—how should I put it—just that powerful. I believe that over the telephone from Washington to Charlottesville Brax managed to conceal from me the totality of his experience with the old man. In the first place, it seemed so unlikely that there could be a meeting between these two particular people in view of the fact that Brax had always expressed such antipathy and disdain for my obsessive search. Moreover, he had recently seemed determined that there should be some estrangement between the two of us—between himself and me. And yet I felt sure that I had noticed some softening in his apparent animosity toward me, and I recalled how my mother was fond of saying when I was growing up that one of the first signs of maturity is forgiveness of one's parents' faults and stupidities. It even occurred to me that Brax had managed to arrange this meeting with this old cousin of ours in order to heal what might have been thought wounds we had inflicted on each other. I soon learned the error of this reasoning! He did not try to hide his mixed feelings about it or the compulsion he felt about drawing us together since Cousin Aubrey's life seemed to be nearing its end.

And then he gave a more complete account of the meeting between them. The two of them, so he told me, had stood beside each other a good many times at the very same street intersection. And the older man's mode of dressing could not fail to take his attention. The strangest turnabout, though, in Brax's behavior—in my eyes, at least, and to my ears—was his description of a kind of experience he had hardly acknowledged at any earlier time of his life. It was because, though an artist, Brax had always been a matter-of-fact and practical person, not given to seeing ghosts or anything of that kind. But before they had even exchanged any words that morning, before the old man so much as cast a glance in his direction, Brax had an eerie feeling suddenly, even before the old man spoke or looked in his direction, that words were going to be passed between them. He, Brax, had a strange and powerful awareness of *my own* presence—something that was the strangest part of all, to my mind. And he even had a sense of guilt, which touched me most deeply, a strong impulse to get in touch with me by telephone. All of this before he had any notion of who the old man was or what possible connection there could be. Before Cousin Aubrey spoke, Brax acknowledged that they had exchanged glances and nods on previous mornings. As soon as Aubrey said his first words it registered on Brax's fine ear that there was the suggestion of a Tennessee accent, which was familiar to him, that came no doubt from my own speech. The both of them drew back to the curb for a minute instead of crossing when the traffic light turned green—in order to facilitate their exchanges. Other pedestrians passed on but not, I would guess, without giving a look backward at the contrasting appearance of these particularly striking figures who seemed to be for no reason stepping backward. Brax, of course, had never before seen Aubrey or seen a picture of him or had any thorough description of him. When Aubrey spoke the garbled version of his assumed name Brax was much taken aback, but when Brax gave his own the old man was obviously equally stunned and not altogether pleased. By mutual consent they repaired to a little coffee shop on the avenue and there each revealed his complete identity. Neither of them at first seemed to take much pleasure in these exchanges. At the end of this session they shook hands formally and provided each other with their addresses and telephone numbers. Meanwhile Brax wrestled with the idea of whether or not he should or should not be in touch with me about this encounter. Finally Brax added almost as an afterthought to me and in the manner of a parenthetical expression that before going to have coffee together Aubrey had seemed to look at him with a sort of mordant hatred. It was only when Brax had indicated what manner of life he was living—his artist life—that Aubrey had agreed to join him for a cup of coffee. Even at this remark about "mordant hatred" I laughed rather awkwardly, I suppose. I did not doubt that the fact that Brax had identified himself as my son would bring the image of the little boy on that funeral train to mind.

IT WOULD HAVE seemed unthinkable to him that that little boy on the train, the spoiled darling of his two aunts and his mother, could possibly be the father of the unconventional-seeming young man in the beret who had dedicated his life to art. Aubrey and Brax met several times for coffee after that day. I was never told which of them telephoned the other to make the engagement. It didn't matter, because the two of them were so clearly certain of what the other's life had become. It was only after Aubrey was sent to the hospital that Brax made his call to me and summoned me to the old fellow's bedside.

WHEN BRAX and I had first arrived at his own place of lodging, having driven there from the Union Station in the rather patched-together old car, he was able to point up the street to the apartment house where Aubrey had until recently been living. Somehow it was only then, as I looked up at that ugly, angular building over there and as I peered into the darkened windows that Brax indicated with the long index finger of his left hand, that it swept over me who the retreating figure in all my dreams had been. I confess that even to the most unsophisticated neo-Freudian this might easily and immediately have been apparent. But perhaps its very obvious quality had blinded me. Any such analysis is always blinding to oneself, I suppose. Or perhaps my unwillingness to see the obvious restrained me until this moment when simply not seeing it was no longer possible for me, no matter how much I desired not to do so. At any rate I could barely contain myself until I should come face-to-face with the man.

By that time, of course, Cousin Aubrey was hospitalized, and so it was to the hospital that I was taken to see him. There he greeted me at the door to his room attired in a long silk dressing gown with a tassel sash and navy-blue satin lapels, all of which seemed itself something out of an earlier and more elegant era. As he stood before me he was a little peaked, but he was up and about and properly groomed and his white mustachios were indeed a thing of beauty. He invited us into his room where chairs had been brought for us, and he began at once urging me to call on him at his apartment the next day, as though his removal was a certainty. It was altogether impossible to recognize him as the scowling, disapproving stranger that had so often turned up at our family gatherings or as the frightened, unhappy, and somewhat rattled misfit that I so clearly remembered from the funeral train.

At the hospital it was at once apparent that the nurses

adored him. They brought us crackers and cheese and pâté
and three wineglasses upside down on a tray. Then one of
them went directly to Aubrey's locker and brought forth a
bottle of Calvados brandy. It was difficult to see him through
the despairing eyes that Brax had revealed to us on the phone
the day before. According to Aubrey he had entered the hospital because there were "several matters of health that needed
looking into." Later he confessed to me: "Of first importance
was the question of a gallstone. But that's endemic with our
family, I believe," he said. "In most cases nowadays they
don't put you under the knife for that, so I'm told." As he
spoke all I could think of was that my grandfather, the Senator, had died "under the knife" during a gallstone operation
more than fifty years before. It was Aubrey's warm cordiality
and even elegance of diction that I was most unprepared for.
It had never been like this on the chance meetings we had had
in the past. Each time that Brax and I would go to see him in
the days that followed, my astonishment in this respect would
be renewed. But it was more positive than that. I was drawn
to him as to all people of great vitality and personal charm.
He seemed so genuinely interested in everything about me
that I was willing to reveal! And I was reminded of nothing
and nobody so much as the great wealth of descriptive anecdotes about my grandfather, with which my mother and
aunts had filled my head over the years. In one moment I was
remembering the light in the eyes of that certain old lady, a
complete stranger to me, whom I met on that flight from New
York and who it turned out later was actually speaking of
Cousin Aubrey himself. I believed that the change described
in the old man was genuine and permanent, but I did not fail
to want to know when and how the change had been effected.
One of the great charms of such people is the ability to show
interest in yourself and in themselves. He told his stories

about the great funeral train ride, which included much that my mother and aunts had not been able to provide. But he also listened to *my* stories. (When Brax was present at these moments I could not but feel the pain he must be experiencing —that, this elegant old gentleman here should take such a delight in *my* stories.) Even on our first meeting Cousin Aubrey began to speak of my mother. He asked me very directly what she had ever told me about him, and in a flash I knew I could never tell him of the revelation she had made during her last days about the brief love affair she and he had known. But each time I would see him during that fortnight I would return to my bed in Brax's studio and go over scenes my mother had described to me and wonder at the almost incredible transformation of that young man into this very old man.

WHEN WE WERE alone together in his apartment during this period, Brax and I actually found it difficult to make conversation. In the evening we sometimes sat together reading our books or watching TV. We would speculate sometimes on Cousin Aubrey's "condition" or upon the length of time he would remain in the hospital. It appeared that his ailments were so numerous and so varied, that as the old fellow himself said, "There's no use in opening discussions on that can of worms." But one day he or one of the nurses would speak of his being discharged the next day, or again it would be suggested that it would be a "long pull." The doctors, as if by previous instruction from the patient, would not talk with us at all. One day Braxton had to go on a longish errand in downtown Washington, and I went to the hospital alone to sit with the old man for a while. Presently, after we had settled ourselves in his room, he said to me, seemingly without any very pointed reference, "You have so exactly turned out just as I had thought you would do."

Somewhat taken aback, I replied at once, "And, you, sir, have turned out so very differently from any way I might have expected." In reply he laughed heartily for a moment and gave way to a fit of coughing. I hurriedly went to his bedside, intending, I suppose, to do something like pat him on the back. But he silently shook his head, indicating that the spell would soon be over, which it was. With me still standing close by, he closed his eyes, and I think he blushed to just the slightest extent.

With his eyes still closed, he said, "If I'm not mistaken you've spent most of your days as a college professor." Since his eyes remained closed I continued to look him full in the face. I was able to look upon the pure whiteness of his Vandyke beard and mustaches—and observe the heavy head of snow-white hair. The facial skin about his eyes and cheeks and on his broad forehead was almost entirely without wrinkles. It was the face of old country men that I had often seen in the Tennessee countryside when I was growing up. It made me feel that he had not a care in the world and had never had one. And to some degree it was as though he were wearing a mask. Presently he opened his eyes and said again, "If I'm not mistaken, you have spent most of your days as a college professor."

Still leaning over him and now looking into his clear, wide-open brown eyes, I said (quoting an old family saying I thought he might recognize), "I plead guilty to your soft impeachment, but I don't believe there's any disgrace in that."

Again he closed his eyes, saying, "No disgrace certainly. Honor and glory, rather." He wore a half-suppressed grin on his lips. "No disgrace, but certainly it is a safe harbor you selected."

"I think, rather, it selected me," I said. I went back to my chair now and waited for him to say more. I was eager to see where our exchanges might go from there.

With his eyes now open he sat up in bed, adjusting the pillows behind him. He looked over at me and said, "I remember you as a small boy with your mother—and even earlier with your father. But more especially with your mother. And sometimes with your aunts. You seemed always such a well-protected child. And, you see, that is something I knew nothing about. It was totally foreign to my experience."

I was not prepared for this direct encounter, though it was the very thing I might have wished for. "Why, I was always given to understand that you had the protection of the old Senator himself."

"Ah, yes," he said, now directing his eyes at the ceiling above him, "but after he was gone, what else was there for me? I was left on my own, and I had determined to become the very opposite number from the boy I had been. You would hardly believe it, but I gazed into the looking glass one morning and observed that the weakest point in my physiognomy was my chin. And from that day I would never again shave around my mouth and chin. Moreover, I had insufficient education for any career I could think of. And so I merely pretended to have the kind of education I might have had and wished I had had. I had learned from the lickings I got at Mr. Webb's school, and so I pretended to possess all the knowledge in the world, pretended to be as sophisticated a human being as I could imagine. I managed to make myself seem something I was not. And I learned to appeal to women especially in a way I had never before done. Though I was bookish by nature, and possessed a smattering of knowledge —with a minimum of Greek and Latin learning—I managed to be all that I might have wished to become."

Then suddenly he stopped, as though he had caught himself pouring out the words he had never intended to speak to anyone. He closed his eyes and gave signs of dropping off to sleep. I sat with him for a while yet, and when he woke, he woke as if from a deep dream. I felt that for a little while just now he had actually forgotten himself and the role he intended to play. But I was so touched by what he had revealed of himself—inadvertently or not, I wasn't sure—that I resolved to do whatever I could to comfort the old man. But there was not much I could find to say. Whenever he talked to me again about matters in the family, either he pretended to be or actually was confused about such things. He would say, "Now, let's see. You had three aunts, or was it four?" And then would follow up with something irrelevant.

A few days afterward I made a brief trip home to Charlottesville. In Brax's car on the way to the Union Station my son and I had exchanges that amounted to more than anything we had had to say to each other during the whole of that visit. He told me he suspected there was difficulty about Cousin Aubrey's paying his bills at the hospital and for the first time made clear why it was we were never allowed to visit the hospital after three in the afternoon. It seems there were several old ladies who always came to see Cousin Aubrey in the late afternoon, and he clearly feared our visits would overlap. We were in the midst of heavy afternoon traffic when Brax told me this. And in a fit of inordinately loud laughter along with noisy slapping of his right thigh, he almost lost control of the car. I reached over and put my hand on the steering wheel to steady him. But this he so resented that he shook my hand away and regained control of the vehicle.

He let me get out at the entrance to the station, without seeing me to the train. I was aware of his lingering vexation with me as he pulled away in a burst of speed. It was as if it was some expression of his relief—at how glad he was to be rid of me. On the train I reflected that it had been Brax who had asked me to come to Washington and that he must have wanted more than just my sympathy, for the crisis over the old man didn't seem to warrant any more than that. He had indicated more to me.

I resolved then that when I got home I would tell Melissa that I wanted to do something about Cousin Aubrey's hospital bill and perhaps even bring him to our house if he had nowhere else to go. Two hours later when I arrived by taxi from the railway depot in Charlottesville Melissa was waiting behind the glass side door of the house. I felt somehow that I had never been so glad to see her. It was as if I were returning home after a long journey. I threw my arms about her and kissed her and then led her into the living room, where we sat close together on the couch like a pair of lovers. After our first greeting she said, "Tell me about it. You have never stayed away so long on a jaunt to Washington." I had been gone for nearly two weeks, and she knew that on my various research projects I could never bear to linger so long.

"How did you happen to be expecting me just now?" I asked her.

"I was on the telephone with Brax about an hour ago, and he told me you were on your way."

"You called Brax?" I said.

"No. He called me. He sounded upset, and he said you were upset too. But how did you find Cousin Aubrey's condition?"

"I think all three of us are upset," I said. Then I said, "I think I may want to bring him home with us for a while after he is discharged from the hospital."

"But what is he like? Was he at all what you expected?"

"Not quite, I think," I answered. "His mind seems to wander at times. He is a very old man, of course. And sometimes I suspect he's putting me on." Presently Melissa bestirred herself to do something about dinner. But I held her close to me. I didn't want to be alone with my strange thoughts just yet.

"But tell me what he is like," she insisted.

"How can I tell you? Well, he is a very polished old gentleman. Or he dresses like one. I suspect the doctors all think he's rich as Croesus. They won't let him leave, and I think the nurses are all soft on him. They think he's beautiful. And he is so after a fashion."

"He must be ninety if he's a day."

"Of course he is at least that," I agreed.

I stayed in the house for the next three days, not going anywhere, not answering the phone. Occasionally I did hear the sound of the phone, and each time of course I thought it might be Brax with some news about Cousin Aubrey. I remained up in my studio most of the time, where I had no phone, and Melissa didn't call me and never once told me about whoever it was that had called. Sometimes I would pretend to poke away at something on my easel or would glance into a book for a while. I came down for meals, of course, and our talk was about everything *except* Brax and Cousin Aubrey. Once when we were at the table I said, "There's no news about Cousin Aubrey, is there?"

Melissa said, "No, no news about him." In retrospect it seems clear to me that she meant there was no news about him, but that there was some other news that she preferred not to give unless I pressed for it. I suppose I should have known from the long silence that followed that there was word of another kind from Brax, but I didn't allow myself to speculate about that. It was in the late spring of the year, and out the window of my attic studio I could see the apple trees in our side yard were in the last vestiges of their full bloom. But the jonquils had already ceased their prodigious blooming underneath the branches of the fruit trees. More than once I saw Melissa on her knees out there thinning the luxuriant growth of the perennials where they were crowding themselves out. I would see her glance up in the direction of my window to see if I were watching her down there. On two occasions especially when I could hear a phone ringing off in the house I saw her glance up toward me and knew that she must hear the insistent ringing. Clearly she was wondering if I would go and answer it. But I didn't. Normally the sound of the phone could set any of us in motion. But not so now. And at lunch or dinner there would be no mention of the unanswered phone calls.

On the third night I was unusually late in coming to bed. As I slipped under the sheet beside Melissa, she stirred. Half-asleep, I must suppose, she presently said, "Have you solved any problems?"

Before I could ask her what she meant, she'd dozed off to sleep again or pretended to have done so. But I put my hand on hers and asked what exactly did she mean. As she had always done she left me alone with any problem to solve it for myself. But I could be sure that she understood the confusion that was in my mind just now. And now she asked, "Are you intending to ask Cousin Aubrey to stay with us for a time?"

"Do you think you would mind if I did?" I asked.

She cleared her throat as if she had not spoken for a long time. "You know very well that I have always left important decisions to you." I acknowledged the truth of this. In every aspect of our life together she had declined to make any significant decisions in all things but one perhaps. But always, whether or not she had listened, I had shared any decision or experience with her—everything except the ever-vanishing figure of my dreams and nightmares. I had never known how to explain that part of my experience. *That* had always seemed too cowardly a business for me to go into—that nightmare figure always in retreat before me. How could I be so crass as to bring this fearful, faceless figure to the surface of our rational life? It was not so much that it didn't matter, but that it mattered too much to me to attempt to explain any finite moment. The possibility that that faceless figure was somehow my own self only made it the more unthinkable and unmentionable a matter for me. But I wasn't really sure what my own confusion was. Perhaps Melissa had got it all wrong and was in this moment only adding to my confusion. I was sure now it was more complicated than she could imagine.

I reminded myself that I had merely come home for a few days of reflection and I woke the next morning with a certain urgency. I *had* to be on the morning train. When I went out through the side yard to the taxi, which I had ordered, the world seemed completely changed. There had been a heavy fall of rain the night before and some wind. All the blossoms were gone from the apple trees. They were like a sheet lying on the grass below. All the indecision and confusion I had felt seemed of a mistaken variety. Momentarily I turned and headed back to the side door, and there I saw Melissa with her hands held up to her face, as if she were weeping. I don't know why, but I could not look back and face her that way. I waved to her and blew her a kiss, but it was all for appearance' sake, was not really for her benefit but for that of the taxi driver rather than any communication to Melissa. I climbed into the taxi and rolled away without once looking back. I felt that she knew something about my future that I didn't know, but I could not face it with her.

All the way to the Charlottesville depot I kept seeing her tearful face before me as it must actually have appeared behind the hands held up to conceal her tears. At first I was unwilling to know why I was so bent upon not seeing her tears. But even aboard the train to Washington I continued to deny their reality. They spoke out to me like uttered words, but still I could not hear them. Only as I was stepping off the train into Washington's Union Station did I understand they were tears of sympathy—sympathy for me, pouring out to me. To my real consternation, as I was stepping down to the platform in Washington, there was Brax and his Russian girl-friend, Masha, waiting to greet me. Brax seized me with a great bear hug, which was a most unusual kind of greeting from him. This hug of his was of a prolonged nature and consisted of holding my two hands close to my side as he enveloped me. "But how did you know I was coming today and on which train?" I asked. He seemed embarrassed by the question, and he cast his eyes down for a second.

"I talked to Mother an hour ago," he said. As he said this I could fairly hear the phone ringing in the house back in Charlottesville. But now, of course, Melissa would have answered it. We walked along the platform and into the station. I felt Brax keeping his eyes fixed lovingly on me. And Masha, shifting my piece of luggage to her left hand, took hold of my arm and leaned rather heavily on it, looking with unaccustomed tenderness up into my eyes. Presently, myself hardly understanding what I meant, I said, "I have a strange feeling that something has happened to Cousin Aubrey." Addressing myself to both of them I said, "I have Melissa's consent to bring him home to stay with us for a while."

WE WERE ALL three silent until we had done the business of getting ourselves into Brax's car. Once inside the car and without even fitting the key into the ignition, Brax turned his face toward me over his shoulder and said, "You're right. There has been some activity." He and Masha were both smiling at me with a certain sympathetic glint in their eyes.

"Prepare yourself for it," Brax began and Masha supplied: "Cousin Aubrey's going to be married to that elderly Mrs. Fisher."

And I replied in all good nature, not comprehending the significance or insignificance of what I was saying, "But don't you see I've arrived here just in time to save him from such a fate as that." And then I said, "Are these plans of long duration, do you suppose?"

"Not a bit of it," said Brax.

Still smiling I said, "But I come prepared to take care of all his hospital and doctors' expenses—to make him free of all such expenses." I suppose there were thoughts that could not be spoken by Brax and Masha. At any rate I got them to take me directly to the hospital. I suppose I thought that every moment might count. With some reluctance, as I could see so very clearly, Brax let me out at the Georgetown Hospital entrance and proceeded to his studio, taking along my single piece of luggage. It was agreed that I would join them there later. In retrospect I can see clearly that they were not satisfied with the course of action I had taken or had in mind. By the way Brax lingered holding my hand firmly in his grasp as we parted, I felt both his dissatisfaction and his sympathy.

It was just three o'clock when I entered the hospital room. The late-afternoon calls from the old ladies had not begun. As formerly, Cousin Aubrey was attired in his elaborate dressing gown. I was struck by the certainty of the changes that had taken place during the four-day interval of my absence. He looked noticeably thinner. To me it seemed just too unlikely that a man so sick as he clearly was today was preparing to be married. He receded in the usual hospital armchair with plastic upholstery on the back and seat. He sat very erect indeed for a man of his age and in his condition, and as I approached he gave me an old-fashioned military salute. Clasping his right hand between my two hands I said, "I understand you're to be congratulated. Can that be so?"

"Exactly, exactly so," he said. His face was serious and he indicated another chair for me to occupy.

"But I came prepared to take care of your hospital expenses and to take you home with me for a rest. That would be the best plan. You could even be married from our house in Charlottesville."

Suddenly he rose from the chair and went to the window as if he had heard an alarming sound out there. And now I had the outrageous feeling that if the window had not been protected by glass and wire screening he might have thrown himself out. I rose and went to him just to protect him from his own thoughts. I commenced describing for him the safe haven I had come to offer. I said we would only have members of the immediate family present at the wedding. I mentioned I would bring Susan from her goat farm and my two sons and daughters-in-law from their shop in New York City. I must confess that when he turned to me I expected some expression of gratitude. Instead what I recognized was the old fiery expression of the Cousin Aubrey I remembered from my childhood.

"Please forgive me," he said arrogantly, "but I cannot accept your generous hospitality. It would not be in keeping with my mode of life. It would ill suit my long-cherished anonymity. I do not wish to be drawn into such family ties. It may seem unsuitable to you, but the lady I am marrying is going to take care of all my indebtedness. I may not have long to live. Undoubtedly, I should say I have a very short time." I felt my face reddened by my overwrought feelings and was not able to interrupt his flow of words. "I see you are blushing," he said, "and I am sorry to embarrass you with the facts of my life. I'm sorry to be forced by you to plan this marriage in order to protect myself from your interference—from your insistence upon my identity. As for this lady, she knows I cannot last long, and she will not allow me any form of identity but the one she offers. Why is it you people are so invariably alike?" he continued. "So predictable in every circumstance of life? Why are you unwilling to accept original thought or behavior of any kind? And why are you everlastingly unwilling to allow others to deviate from your behavior and instead to draw them into your patterns—into your net? It is apparent in the youngest of you, the little boy child one meets on a train." And presently he seemed to be speaking more to himself than to me: "Ah, why didn't they leave me alone with those mountain people? Compromise, always compromise. That's their rule of life."

I felt that there was ample justification for much that he said. I tried to interrupt him to tell him so, but he was so exercised, so intent upon the subject by then, that he could not stop and he *would* have me hear him out.

"My life may be one big fabrication and lie. I'm sure it seems so to you." Again I tried to interrupt him, but there was no stopping him and I wanted to hear all he was going to say.

"I acknowledge that my life is all one big fabrication and lie. I have heard sometimes how our paths have crossed since you came to Virginia. Or nearly crossed, time and again. As long as your mother and your aunts lived, I think I could not resist turning up in the shadow of their existence now and again. But for the most part I managed only to get there in time for the funerals."

I did interrupt him now. "Exclusively on these occasions, I think," said I.

"Naturally you would think so," he said. "But there were other times of no significance that I traveled great distances to be in their shadows."

I wished to tell him that I had noticed that at my mother's

funeral he didn't appear. But I now understood that he had been too old for such a journey. "The women I have consorted with in my lowly way were modeled on those three women in one way or another. But of course you remember me only on board the famous funeral train and during the times of those funerals. Those women I have consorted with have each of them in their own way reminded me of one of your aunts or of your own mother. To that extent those three sisters have influenced my whole life. And don't imagine I was not as aware of you on many other occasions, not just as the little boy on the funeral train, as the adolescent at later funerals, as the young man present at the time when your grandfather's remains were so foolishly removed from Knoxville to Elizabeth City."

"I only got a glimpse of you," I told him, "in the rearview mirror of my car on that occasion."

"You were by then the young man I would have predicted you would have become."

"But I thank God I was not really that."

"You were part of the world you were brought into and playing always the role I would have predicted for you." Even as he spoke, I heard the soft rapping at the door of the hospital room. I turned about, and there stood one of those anonymous Washington old ladies. Taking up my hat, I then took leave of Cousin Aubrey, and giving a polite little nod to the lady to whom he was now making absurd bows, I passed out into the corridor. When I had gone from the room I was no doubt represented by my cousin to be some tradesman who had been dispensing some business with him—some indebtedness to him which she would eventually be required to take care of.

Then some forty-five minutes later I arrived on foot at Braxton's place. I found no one there, but the key had been left faithfully under the mat. Upon entering I saw my lone piece of luggage, which Brax had set just inside the entrance door. Quickly I perceived that things were in considerable disarray. Many books were already in packing cases. Most disturbingly, none of Brax's own paintings hung on the walls of the principal rooms. Rather they leaned, some of them half-crated, against the empty bookshelves. The strange fact is, however, that I was instantly struck by the high and altogether original quality of his work. The progress, the advances, he had made since leaving home were almost beyond belief to my very practiced and critical eye. I reminded myself that I did, whatever else I did and didn't know, know what was good in this medium. The truth was, since moving into this place of his, he had kept almost all of his current work under lock and key in the skylighted studio room beyond his actual living quarters, and whatever meager portion of his current paintings he did allow himself to hang on the walls of the front rooms of his place I had scrupulously avoided making any mention of or even once being caught casting a glance in their direction. I knew from old that with Brax all work was work in progress. And I knew that with a young man of his temperament, criticism or praise from a father—or from any other man—would not be welcome until the painting had been placed in a public gallery for exhibition. I can say therefore that I had scarcely until now had an opportunity to give more than a passing glance to Brax's recent efforts. Gone were the old abstractions, gone the expressionist imitations, gone the neorealism, only the true lines, the true colors of life observed, were now displayed. I was so overwhelmed by what I saw that for an hour I gave myself over to sorting out the more than a dozen pictures I found there, in my excitement tearing wrappings off canvases that had already been sealed for shipment of some sort.

But at last, as if I had come to my senses rather, I began hurriedly resealing some canvases. At one point I even took up a stray hammer that I found lying on an empty bookshelf and restored a piece of crating I had forced open. Somehow I felt myself panic-stricken by the whole incident of discovery and uncovering, and the more so by the undeniable evidence I exposed of Brax's intention to move out of this place and away. Was it a well-kept secret that I had stumbled on by chance? Or did it represent a carefully laid plan on Brax's part? Was it his way of telling me something that he could not find words for? Had he left the apartment empty so that I might discover it for myself? It had to be something more than an ordinary move to another part of the city. Else it would not require so much packing up of possessions. And presently I observed the addresses stenciled on three of the packages. One to be delivered to the Guggenheim Museum, and two being sent to the Museum of Modern Art. This overwhelming discovery and all that it implied supported my new recognition of the maturity of Brax's work. It was, of course, beyond anything I had ever attempted, and I began to understand that it would forever set us apart.

Since Brax had not spoken to me of any possible move, even I did not want to give him the impression of spying or anticipating what he had in mind for a future or the wonderful recognition he was about to receive. On an impulse I decided that I might hurry back to Charlottesville this very day. I turned and, picking up my little suitcase, withdrew from his apartment. In the street below I hailed a cab and was able to make the late-afternoon train. I had a book with me inside my single piece of luggage, but aboard the train it did not occur to me to take out the book and read. When the conductor called out the first stop at Manassas I stirred almost as from a dream and had to remind myself what journey I was making.

As if trying to return myself to the real world, my lips actually formed the phrases, "First Manassas and Second Manassas." And when the conductor asked for my ticket I considered making a joke, asking him if it were First Manassas or Second Manassas we were approaching. I made no such bad joke of course. But for some time my thoughts about my grandfather's funeral train vied with my thoughts of the Gallant Pelham and the abandoned railway stop at Brandy Station. In the midst of these half-waking reveries I suddenly got to my feet. I seized my bag and my hat with the intention of jumping off the train and somehow returning to Washington. A sudden vision of Brax's studio apartment in such disarray awaked me to some possibility that I had not faced before. At first it struck me that violence had been done him there— done him and perhaps Masha. Presently the unlikeliness of such an idea, any such literal interpretation of events, returned me to my seat. Then I did dig out my book and made a pretense of reading. And now it came to me that the disarray in his apartment and the shipment of his canvases could only mean that he was going to abandon us all and begin with the other life that was inevitable for him. I could imagine that there had been a mutual confession between him and his old cousin and that I had been the subject of their exchanges. It seems almost that I rode the rest of the way to Charlottesville without moving a muscle of my face or body.

AFTER I LEFT the apartment I had been consoled temporarily by the thought that Brax was after all only moving off to New York. The addresses on the wrapped canvases were very explicit in their meaning. Those addresses stuck in my mind so very vividly that for a time it seemed I could recall something else. This son of mine was going to the old familiar

Greenwich Village where I had once been such a failure. He was going to take up residence there as such a figure in the world as I had never been. During the rest of the trip I was sitting so rigid and upright that I imagined the other passengers were looking at me as though I were going into a trance. And actually it was very nearly that. I understood to some degree from that moment that Brax was not merely moving off to receive new honors at a new address. Perhaps his life henceforth would be as different from mine as Cousin Aubrey's. I felt that I might have been standing there on the street corner where they had had their first encounter, dressed in no less than striped trousers and winged collar. It came over me once and for all that the difference between us could not be a quantitative but a qualitative difference. And in that sense he would be as far removed from us as from my mother. We—his mother and I—would keep in touch with him, we would know where he was; but our division would be a matter of a different kind. And there would be mysteries that I had not penetrated. Why had he been so tender with me in Washington? Why had he been so secretive if he had only been going to Greenwich Village to live in a loft? I shook my head as if in some kind of fog rather than in the brightly lit railway car. And why had Melissa been so mysterious with me and so emotional about his removal from Washington and his rising star? I could not help thinking that *her* secretiveness was of the same kind in relation to her writing. I began even then to understand it all had to do with sparing *my* feelings.

IN CHARLOTTESVILLE it was already dark and there was a mist of rain when I stepped off the train at the depot, and I had some difficulty in finding a taxi. As I hurried up the metal steps to the street level, I was speculating on what kind of story I could concoct to explain to Melissa my returning so soon. But what I was not prepared for when the taxi pulled into our driveway was to find Melissa not holding her hands up to her face as before but staring straight ahead at me. In the peculiar light there at the side door she looked like nothing so much as the preview I had had of her suggested by the white-haired old lady at the Kenyon guest house. And she was staring at me with the same wonder and concern. I knew at once by how she stood there that she had received another telephone call from Brax. It occurred to me in that moment that Brax and Melissa, and the other three children for that matter, had ever been conspiring to spare me from my own sense of disappointment—my abnegation of the role of artist in favor of that of a mere art critic. It was what I myself had taught them to observe and sympathize with. I could now understand without being actually or literally *told* that Brax had received that distinction which would put him in some sphere beyond ourselves. It was what Brax himself imagined even. And I began to suspect then that even Cousin Aubrey had been told and had consented to see me only out of respect and concern for Brax.

"Has he told you all about things?" Melissa said.

"He didn't have to tell me. I knew without his telling me," I said.

Now she suddenly signaled for the departing taxi to halt. "You must go back to Washington to see Brax off," she said. Standing still in the drizzle of rain I motioned for the taxi to go on without me. "I'm glad you were not able to stop him," she said. At first I thought she was talking about the taxi driver, and then I thought she might be talking about Cousin Aubrey and his forthcoming marriage. "He's still in the hospital and is going to be married to one of his old-lady girlfriends," I said, knowing very well that it was Brax she had in mind. I could not be sure whether it was Brax's going away or my own feelings she was aware of. Her teeth were chattering so in her head by this time that I could not tell what it was she was trying to say. It was as though she were having a chill. Then she went quite rigid. It was as if she had just got hold of herself and was in charge of the situation. She pulled away from me quite suddenly, and before I could restrain her she ran from me into the house. Inside the house I dropped my hand luggage and put my arm around her to keep her from saying anything more until she had composed herself. Once again she commenced to grind her teeth together and I heard her say through clenched teeth and with a certain exaggeration, "It's you I'm thinking of, my darling, not your cousin, for God's sake!" After this confusing exchange between us I led her into the living room where I got her to lie down on that same couch where my mother had lain, and though she scoffed at me for it I placed a lap rug over her. She lay there quietly for some time, and then I watched a single tear roll down her face, but there was no heaving of sobs or any other indication of emotion. I poured her a little glass of brandy, but she would not accept it. For a time she continued to lie on the couch as if to indulge me. "We will still be in touch with him," she said, for my own comfort and consolation, "though it will be different." I saw now that she had understood better than I all along. To myself I reflected that no matter how far away Brax went or whether our separation was quantitative or qualitative, we should not try to stop him. Like those men I had heard about even before he was born, he was plunging into the terra incognita from which no man willingly returns. Belatedly but firmly I resolved in that moment that no one should ever search out anyone else in any way at all who has set out on that journey. It is one of the inalienable rights that people have—those that have the need of it or the strength for it. The rest of us have the ordinary tedium of life to deal with—to contend with. That is all.

SINCE THAT DAY when I first came back from Washington, Melissa and I have spent a long quiet summer together. Much of the time I have been at my desk in my attic study, winding up my book on the English Pre-Raphaelites. Melissa has kept in touch with our other children and our two daughters-in-law. During the course of the summer they have come for their usual "protracted visits." Life goes on as if there had been no interruption in our pattern of existence. Meanwhile, Melissa seems to have given up her writing altogether, and I tell her, without feeling any real confidence, only to be patient, that it will all come back to her at last. And she says, "I know it will, I know it will." All summer we have sat here together, she and I—with me talking and talking, trying to understand what it is that has happened in our life. I continue my efforts to reassure both of us about Brax and his complete dedication to his work, his will to find himself in his own terra incognita. Sometimes I hear myself saying, "He knows that we sense what his own capabilities are and the breadth of his vision, all of which sets him so apart from us." And I say, "In a way that makes for our principal difficulty. It is because we know we have essentially the same values, that he does know *how* we know. He knows in some immeasurable way how wide his separation from us must be. And knowing, as know he does, yet he is everything we could wish him to be. He fears that if we confront this hard truth of ours concerning our own limitations, it will be deeply and permanently wounding to us." I grasp what Melissa must have grasped at some earlier time—that the District of Columbia was never far enough away for Brax, that instead he is bound by his nature to go the full course. But watching Melissa's face as I talk on and on during the summer I see it is not the face of the frightened old lady with the white hair that I saw long ago at Gambier, the face that I anticipated seeing on Melissa in our old age. About her mouth and on her forehead there are some few wrinkles to be detected, but on her rich, chestnut-brown head of hair there is not one white hair to suggest her age. She is no commonplace old lady. Her strength and wisdom are as apparent in her gray-blue eyes as they must have been when I could not see those qualities there, as they must have been when I did not read them correctly.

It is late summer now, and I can only assume that my cousin Aubrey Bradshaw is dead. By now Braxton Longfort has adjusted to the new circumstances of his life. We hear from his two older brothers that he frequently drops by to see them in their New York shops. And they have themselves become brokers for his work, which is in demand everywhere nowadays and which recognition we view with great pride and satisfaction. Since my retirement I think I have come to terms with the way my life has gone, though I do not know whether it is more a result of my own nature or of the circumstances in which I found myself. And I cannot be altogether sure what determined the way Brax's has gone. How can one be certain? In any case, when nowadays I hear the phone ring or when I observe Melissa stepping out onto the side porch to fetch the mail, I don't look up from my book or cast a glance over the newspaper to see if there is anything for me. Certain thoughts may occur to me sometimes, but I've taught myself better than to voice them—not even questions about Cousin Aubrey Bradshaw and whether his course was perhaps the better one.

A NOTE ABOUT THE AUTHOR

Peter Taylor was born in Tennessee in 1917. He is the author of eight books of stories, including *The Collected Stories of Peter Taylor*, *A Long Fourth*, *In the Miro District and Other Stories*, *The Old Forest and Other Stories* (which won the PEN/Faulkner Award for Fiction in 1985), and *The Oracle at Stoneleigh Court*; two novels, including *A Summons to Memphis* (which won the Pulitzer Prize for fiction in 1987); and three books of plays. Mr. Taylor has taught at Harvard University, the University of North Carolina, and Kenyon College, from which he graduated in 1940. In 1967, he became Commonwealth Professor of English at the University of Virginia. He lives with his wife, the poet Eleanor Ross Taylor, in Charlottesville, Virginia, Tennessee, and Florida.